"A heroine to die for... *Dead Girls Are Easy* will both thrill and chill you."
Teresa Medeiros,
New York Times bestselling author

'I LIKE TO PLAY WITH MY LOVERS, AND SOMETIMES I PLAY ROUGH.'

I gave him a wicked grin. "I doubt you know what you'd be getting yourself into."

He watched as I slid out of the car. I leaned back in before closing the door. "As for your heart—you can keep it. It's not the part of your anatomy I'm interested in."

The look on Dr. Handsome's face was priceless. It wouldn't do for him to form any impressions about me that weren't true—I wasn't the kind of girl he'd take home to his mama, and I didn't want to be.

I was having too much fun being young and single, and if I enjoyed being a little on the wild side, I wasn't going to hide it.

By Terri Garey

DEAD GIRLS ARE EASY

TERRI GAREY

DEAD GIRLS ARE EASY

AVON

An Imprint of HarperCollinsPublishers

AVON BOOKS
An Imprint of HarperCollins*Publishers*
10 East 53rd Street
New York, New York 10022–5299

Copyright © 2007 by Terri Garey
ISBN: 978-0-06-113615-3
ISBN-10: 0-06-113615-8
www.avonromance.com

First Avon Books paperback printing: September 2007

Avon Trademark Reg. U.S. Pat. Off. and in Other Countries, Marca Registrada, Hecho en U.S.A.
HarperCollins® is a registered trademark of HarperCollins Publishers.

Printed in the U.S.A.

10 9 8 7 6 5 4 3 2

For Bob, who believed from the beginning,
for Sheila-Rae, who believed when I didn't,
and for my mother, Louise,
who believed in ghosts,
and believed in me.

ACKNOWLEDGMENTS

Huge thanks to Erika, my wonderful editor, for helping me make this book the best it could be; to Annelise for her calm confidence and business savvy; and to Christina for her contagious enthusiasm and steady support. May the roads rise up to meet them, and the wind always be at their backs.

Whoever said, "Dead men tell no tales," obviously wasn't listening very hard.

Unfortunately for me, I've always had a very good ear.

And dead men *love* to talk. A lot.

But dead women are the worst.

My name is Nicki Styx, and I'm a dead chick magnet. A psychic magnet, if you will. One near death experience, and my life was changed forever. Now restless spirits seem to sense a kindred one in me, and they all want to tell me their stories.

Believe me, those stories aren't always as fascinating as you might think. When a girl who's been murdered by her boyfriend wants to whine about how misunderstood the jerk is, I'll take my coffee to go, please.

CHAPTER 1

"She's coding. Give me another round of epi, stat."

"Doctor—"

"Keep bagging her, nurse. I'm not letting her go yet. Charge it to 360."

Had I left the TV on? I'd never cared much for medical dramas. Too much intensity, too much crying, too many doctors undergoing personal crises of faith—I'd rather believe they were professionals who knew what they were doing and leave it at that.

The body on the table jerked at least a foot in the air when the paddles touched its chest. A hand flopped to the side, revealing red fingernails and a silver thumb ring. A woman.

A high-pitched whining from one of the machines was getting on my nerves, but I had to give the director credit. The urgency on the faces of the people clustered around the gurney looked pretty real.

"Again." That doc just wasn't gonna give up, was he? Maybe he was hoping for a daytime Emmy—wasn't that what they gave for bad soap operas? The heartburn that made me lie down on the couch was finally gone, but it seemed too much trouble to look for the remote, so I just watched.

The camera angle shifted so that now I was above the action, looking down from a high corner of the room. There was a blond nurse standing at the head of the table, squeezing a bulb-like thing over the patient's face.

The body flopped again at another jolt of electricity while I winced in sympathy. She wasn't a car battery, for goodness sake.

"Check her pupils." The nurse holding the bulb stepped back while another one leaned in with a little flashlight and pried the woman's eyelid open with a thumb.

"No reaction, Doctor. Nothing on the EKG, either."

The guy holding the paddles let his shoulders slump, while the two nurses gave each other significant glances. It was then I got a good look at the woman on the bed. Dark hair, cropped short like a boy's, with a telltale streak of pink.

She was me.

No sooner had the realization hit when a pulling sensation jerked me up and out of the deathbed scene. Suddenly I was in a dark tunnel, rushing along like I was on the subway, only there were no seats, no drunks, and no rhythmic rattle of rails. There was just me, and a light that grew steadily brighter the faster I went.

I was weightless, and somehow a *part* of the light, becoming more so the closer I got. It radiated and shimmered like coiled lightning, pulsing white with a golden center, and it drew me like a lodestone. I couldn't wait to see what lay beyond it.

Silence gave way to music, but it wasn't like any I'd ever heard before. It seemed to be coming from the light itself, yet it was all around—true music of the soul. There were others there, though I couldn't see them clearly, bright shapes pulsing and flowing.

My forward progress slowed, then stopped. I heard a voice.

"It's not your time, Nicki."

"I'm dreaming, right?"

"You've awakened unto Life, but the dream is not yet over."

I can't explain what perfect sense that statement

made, any more than I could explain how so many things that had troubled me in the past suddenly made sense. Like why my mother gave me up for adoption before the cord that bound us had even been cut, or why really bad things happen to really good people. For a few precious moments I actually saw the fabled "grand design" stretched out before me like an infinite spiderweb. I barely had time to grasp it before it was snatched away.

"Go back, Nicki, but don't forget—do unto others as you would have them do unto you."

My body felt strange, heavy. It was an effort to open my eyes, and when I did, I wished I hadn't. The glare of a fluorescent bar surrounded by stained ceiling tiles was not the light I longed for.

"Hey." I felt a hand touch my hair. Evan's face came into view, a very uncharacteristic look of concern in his blue eyes. "How you feeling, girlie?" he asked.

My chest felt like there was an elephant sitting on it and my mouth was dry as sand, but I managed to croak out a reply.

"Like shit."

That brought back the lopsided grin I knew so well, and made me feel a little better. My best friend since childhood, Evan wasn't the type to play nursemaid unless there was a handsome guy around who wanted to play doctor. We'd shared backyards, homework, and confidences while we were growing up, so it had come as no big surprise in junior high when we shared a crush on the same football player.

"What happened?" Talking was an effort.

"You faked a heart attack and almost gave me one in the process." Evan's joking still carried overtones of worry. "Good thing I decided to come check on you when you didn't answer the phone. I knew you didn't have a date, and I couldn't believe you'd go out for Chinese without me."

I licked dry lips, not entirely sure I was awake. "A heart attack?"

"Mitral valve prolapse."

I slid my eyes toward the unfamiliar voice. There was a dark-haired man at the foot of the bed, studying my chart. He wore green surgical scrubs and the typical stethoscope around the neck, and when he glanced up, I recognized him. He was the soap opera guy who tried so hard to save the woman on the gurney.

Me.

"A small heart defect, normally benign, but in your case nearly fatal."

He moved to stand across the bed from Evan. "We thought we'd lost you, Miss . . ." He consulted the chart again. ". . . Styx, is it?" He grinned. "I guess you didn't have the right change for the ferryman."

Evan looked at him blankly, but I managed a weak grin. Anybody who understood Greek mythology couldn't be all bad. I'd always found it so ironic that the wholesome, middle-American parents who'd chosen to raise me had the same last name as the dark river that divided the world of the living from the world of the dead. And yet they'd found my teenage goth period troubling—I considered that fact weird in itself.

"I'm Dr. Bascombe." He lowered the chart and looked at me critically. "I was the attending E.R. physician when you were brought in last night. You have a weak valve in your heart, usually genetic, which may cause an occasional erratic heartbeat or a racing pulse—what we call a 'heart murmur.' Does this type of thing run in your family?"

"I have no idea." That answer would have to do. I was too tired to explain.

The doc frowned and took my wrist between his fingers.

"What about drugs? Did you take any recently?"

I opened my mouth, but Evan got there first.

"Nicki doesn't do drugs." He sniffed, as though highly offended. "I already told you that. Why don't you check your 'tox screens' or whatever they are and move on?"

Dr. Bascombe cocked an eyebrow at Evan but didn't seem to take any offense.

"Had any dental work done recently?"

"Yesterday. Just a cleaning."

"Ah." He hooked his stethoscope in his ears and put the other end to my chest, listening intently.

Up close he was kinda cute, even if he did smell like hand soap. I closed my eyes, taking my observation as further evidence that my heart wasn't quite ready to give up the ghost.

"You're doing very well, Ms. Styx, and I'm pleased to say it looks like there was no lasting damage."

I opened my eyes, relieved but not really surprised.

After all—it wasn't my time.

"We'll need to do further tests, of course, and keep you for a few days just to make sure, but I think you'll do fine."

While he was talking, an older woman came into the room and stood quietly by the door, as though waiting for him. She was wearing a loud floral print blouse over black stretch pants.

"That's it?" Evan sounded outraged. "A twenty-eight-year-old healthy person has a bad heart and you're not gonna fix it? What? Is there a problem with her insurance?" His voice was rising, taking on that histrionic note I knew so well. "If she was an old bat on Medicare you'd be falling all over her to give her a heart transplant, for God's sake!"

To my surprise, the woman by the door was nodding in total agreement.

Dr. Bascombe sighed. "There's no need for such drastic measures here. I'd planned to discuss this with the *patient* when she was feeling better, but MVP is hardly a death sentence." He looked down, addressing himself to me and effectively ignoring Evan. "You need to be aware of it, of course—watch your stress levels, take antibiotics before any dental work or surgery, avoid drugs and limit alcohol—that type of thing—but there's no reason you can't live to be an old bat on Medicare yourself."

He was smiling at me, apparently unconcerned about offending the old bat who stood by the door. "Surgery might be needed in extreme cases, but you're not one of them."

"Could it happen again?" My voice still sounded pretty wimpy—I hated that.

His smile faded slightly. "I can't promise that it won't. But something tells me you're a fighter." He took my cold hand in his warm one and squeezed my fingers. "So fight."

What a great idea. One I'd attend to as soon as I could keep my eyes open.

When I woke up again, Evan and the doc were gone, but the old lady was still there. She was sitting in the chair beside my bed, plump fingers crossed over her plump stomach, patiently watching me sleep.

"How are you feeling, dear?"

The woman's voice was almost as brassy as her outfit. The garish purple flowers on her blouse clashed with her hair—an unfortunate shade of orange, faded and thinning.

"I'm okay." I felt better. Tired and thirsty, but better.

Stiff from lying in the same position so long, I made an effort to hoist myself up. She didn't make any move to help, though her fingers twitched as if she considered it. Rings glittered on both hands, outshone only by the polished length of her fake nails.

"You've slept the day away, dear. Good thing I had nothing better to do."

The drapes on the window were closed, but I took her word it was evening. The quality of light in the room had changed, and the noises from the corridor were quieter now, more muted.

"Do I know you?" I'd never seen the woman before, but she acted like we were old friends. "I'm sorry, but I've had a pretty bad day. Things are still fuzzy."

She waved a hand, dismissing my words. "*Ech.* Don't tell me about a bad day—you should have

the kind of bad day I've had." Then she laughed.
"Oh, wait—you did."

There was an edge to her laughter that raised the
hair on my arms. I glanced around for the nurse's
call button. There was always one handy in the
soap operas, wasn't there?

"Don't bother calling anyone." She reached up
and patted her hair in what seemed a habitual gesture. "They can't see me." A charm bracelet tinkled
on her chubby wrist.

More and more convinced I was entertaining an
escapee from another wing of the hospital, I found
the call button on the bed rail and pushed it.

The woman shrugged. "Suit yourself, dear."

I eyed her warily while I waited, saying nothing.
Who knew what would set the fruitcake off? She
didn't say anything, either, examining her nails as
though completely unconcerned.

"Sleeping Beauty wakes." A black nurse, plump
and smiling, bustled into the room holding a tiny
cup. "Just in time for meds." She put the cup down
on the bedside table and picked up a plastic pitcher
sitting there. "How you feeling, honey? How about
some water?"

"Nurse, I think this lady is confused."

The nurse's eyebrows went up. "This lady?" She
shook her head, chuckling. "Would 'this lady' like
a drink?" She poured water into a foam cup and

offered it to me, never once glancing over at the woman in the chair.

I shot a horrified glance at the old lady, and she shrugged again, as if to say, *I told you so*.

"You don't see her?" My voice came out as a squeak. "You don't see the lady in the chair?"

The nurse's smile became fixed. She followed the direction of my gaze, then looked back to me.

"Honey," she said decisively, "you were right the first time. The lady *is* confused." She picked up the little cup of meds, rattling the pills. "They ain't nobody here but you and me. Now you take your medicine like a good girl, then lay back and close your eyes. I'll get you a dinner tray and be back in five minutes. We'll get some food in your belly and get you comfortable. You'll be better tomorrow."

In a daze, I did as she asked, and she bustled from the room a moment later, a cheerful, professional smile firmly in place.

"Irene Goldblatt." The woman in the chair spoke as though we'd never been interrupted. "The name is Irene Goldblatt."

"Nicki Styx." I answered automatically, still dazed. This whole experience had such a sense of the surreal about it that talking to an invisible woman seemed to fit right in.

"I need you to do me a favor, Nicki." Irene

leaned forward, serious now. "I need you to go tell my Morty that I didn't mean what I said about his matzo balls."

I giggled. This was one weird dream.

"His matzo balls?" I giggled again, unable to help myself.

She rolled her eyes at me, obviously impatient. "Yeah. His matzo balls. You go tell him that they weren't dry at all. I just said that because they were better than mine. It wasn't his fault."

A hiccup of laughter escaped me. Irene frowned, so I tried to contain myself.

"What wasn't his fault?"

Irene looked at me like I was an idiot.

"That I choked to death on them, of course."

I'd never been so glad to see morning come. Long before light crept in around the hospital room drapes, I heard the building stir to life. The squeak of shoes and the rattle of stretchers, murmured voices and ringing phones—all were a relief after the night I'd had.

Irene finally left me alone, but not until she'd told me her life story and made me promise to help her. *As if I'd had any choice.* Who wants a Jewish grandmother with a grudge popping up any time she feels like it? Irene made it politely clear she was willing to be, as she put it, a "nudnik" about the whole thing. I understood only that she'd make my pathetic little *goyishe* life a living hell unless I talked to her Morty. Her funeral was the day after tomorrow, and we would both be attending.

Pretty creepy stuff. Either that or I'd suffered brain damage during the heart attack and was hallucinating about a little old lady with a Yiddish accent. Needless to say, I hadn't slept much.

"Miss Styx?" A swath of light spilled from the corridor as the door swung open. Dr. Bascombe saw I was awake and said, "Good morning. Early rounds. Can I turn on the light?"

"Sure." The fluorescent lighting flickered, then flared to life as I rolled onto my back, shading my eyes against the glare. "Could you adjust the bed so I can sit up?"

A low hum and creak of machinery brought me upright. "How's that?" he asked.

"Great," I mumbled, raking both hands through my hair. I knew from experience that dark spikes would be sticking up everywhere anyway, so I might as well make it look like it was intended as a fashion statement.

"How are you this morning?" Dr. Bascombe picked up my chart and flipped through it. "Any chest pain during the night? Twinges? Weird feelings of any kind?"

I almost laughed, thinking of the weirdness of

the last twenty-four hours. Those weird feelings weren't the kind Dr. Bascombe was asking about, so I wasn't going to mention them. I wasn't quite ready to admit I was crazy. Yet.

"My chest feels tender, but only on the outside," I admitted. "My ribs are sore, but I feel pretty good—almost normal, in fact." Here I couldn't resist a smile, but he thought I was just being friendly.

"You're anything but normal, Nicki." He returned my smile, and for a moment there was something in his eyes that was very undoctorly. Then he blinked, and the health-care professional was back. "You died, and came back to life." Dr. Bascombe lowered the clipboard, holding it flat against him. "Anything you can tell me about the experience?"

Wary now, I hedged. "What do you mean?"

He shrugged, and sat down on the foot of my bed, clipboard on his lap. "Many people have odd hallucinations and sensations during a near death experience that they recall in vivid detail afterward. Some even claim to remember their own death."

"They do?" I couldn't keep the hopeful note from my voice.

"It's not uncommon to be confused after a traumatic event." His voice was carefully neutral, raising my first inkling of suspicion. "If you'd like to talk about it, I'd love to hear it."

"What did the night nurse write on my chart?" I could see the notes but couldn't read them. Somehow I didn't need to.

He paused, but had the grace not to deny it. "She noted you were talking to yourself for quite some time. Your vital signs are normal and your appetite's good—so let's talk about what's going on inside your head."

"Sorry, Doc, but I don't let anybody inside my head without an expensive dinner and a bottle or two of wine," I snipped, feeling like I'd been tattled on. "Are you a shrink, too?"

He rose, giving me a rueful grin. "Nope. But I'll take you up on that expensive dinner after you've been discharged. You'll have to go easy on the wine, though—doctor's orders."

"That's not what I meant." Did he think I'd been asking him out? Or had he been asking me out? My brain was fuzzy.

Dr. Bascombe went back to reading my chart, taking his time with it. There was something different about him today. He was wearing jeans, for one thing, stethoscope dangling against a faded blue sweatshirt instead of hospital scrubs. I sneaked a glance at his hand. No ring.

"Do you always start work this early?" I liked the way his dark hair curled against his neck. He needed a trim, but the shaggy length suited him.

"Depends on the shift," he answered absently. "But I wanted to come in early today." He glanced at me as though about to say more, then stopped as though he'd said too much.

"Can you sit all the way up? I'd like to listen to your heart and lungs."

His manner was nothing but professional as he slipped my hospital gown from my shoulders and touched that cold stethoscope to my back and between my breasts. He was gentlemanly enough not to mention my nipple ring or the tiny tattoo of a broken heart, but then again, he'd seen them before.

"Sounds good." This time he didn't smell like hand soap. He was close enough for me to pick up his natural scent, warm and male. "I'd like to keep you one more day for observation, and assuming all goes well, release you in the morning." He stepped back, recording his comments on the chart. The polite smile was the same one I'm sure he gave all his patients.

"And if I did have some kind of weird near death experience?" What the hell. "Hallucinations, even. Could it be brain damage or something?"

Dr. Bascombe's gaze turned sharp. Green eyes, disconcertingly direct. "All your neurological scans are clear, but we can rerun them if you like."

I shook my head, already regretting my big mouth.

"It really might help to talk about it, Nicki." He smiled, eyes crinkling. "I'm bound by doctor-patient confidentiality. I can't repeat anything you tell me unless you authorize it. As a doctor, I'm probably going to tell you it was all the result of chemicals flooding your brain, but as a person who's seen far too much death—I'm fascinated. I've been considering writing a paper about NDEs for years, but E.R. doctors don't have a lot of time for follow-up research."

He seemed sincere, and he *was* kinda cute—did I mention that? Not my typical tortured poet type, but obviously open-minded. It made it a helluva lot easier to spill my guts. I told him how I'd seen myself on the gurney, seen him apply the paddles to my chest and how the nurses had worked frantically to save me. By the time I got to the part about the tunnel and the light, I couldn't stop myself if I tried. I told him about the music, remembering again—with both awe and regret—the beauty of the sound and the incredible sense of total understanding. Then I told him about the voice.

"The voice said it wasn't my time. I had to go back. Then I woke up here, in this bed." I watched him nervously, certain I was talking myself into another wing of the hospital—where one jacket size fits all, if you know what I mean. "That's when I met Irene."

"Irene?"

"Irene Goldblatt."

Dr. Bascombe frowned. He'd been nodding thoughtfully as I told my tale, but now he went still.

"Irene's dead. Says she died yesterday—right here in this hospital. Choked to death on a matzo ball. She wants me to go tell her husband it wasn't his fault." I waited for the good doctor to call the guys in the white coats to take me away, but he didn't move. "How's that for a hallucination?"

"Epinephrine is a strong stimulant. It can spark vivid dreams." His face was thoughtful, all trace of humor gone. "Logic impels me to point out that you might have overheard someone talking about Mrs. Goldblatt while you were in the emergency room. Just because you had a dream about her doesn't mean she's actually talking to you."

"Who does he think he is, Dr. Spock from *Star Trek*?" Irene walked in, orthopedic shoes squeaking. Dr. Bascombe never turned his head or gave any indication he'd heard her speak. "'Logic impels me'?—*ech.*"

"So there really was an Irene Goldblatt who died yesterday?" I wanted my facts straight.

Dr. Bascombe looked vaguely uncomfortable. "Yes. Foreign matter aspirated into the lungs."

"Which means?"

He sighed. "She choked on her food. By the time the paramedics got to her, she'd been too long without oxygen. It was too late."

Irene gave me a satisfied smile, plopping herself down in the visitor's chair beside my bed.

"Nicki? Are you all right?"

Dr. Bascombe was eyeing me warily, no doubt wondering why I was staring at an empty chair.

"I'm great, Doc." I gave him the most insincere smile I could muster, taking my cue from the medical profession. "Just great."

"So where's your friend?" Irene had the decency to wait until Dr. Bascombe left to start talking again.

"My friend?"

"You know, the nice *faigelah* boy who was here yesterday. My friend Ruthie has a grandson he should meet." She settled herself comfortably, as though planning to stay awhile.

"Irene." I began carefully, feeling the need to take control of the situation. "I told you last night I'd help you. You don't have to babysit me. I gave you my word I'd be at the funeral, and I will."

She lifted her hands and shrugged, fake nails gleaming. "It's not like you've got a crowd of relatives down here taking care of you, is it? What else have I got to do, dear? Who else have I got to talk to?" Irene sniffed and patted her hair. "I thought it'd be nice to have a chat over your morning coffee, just like me and Morty used to do."

I fell back on the pillow and closed my eyes.

"So what's your friend's name and where is he?"

I was drained. Why fight it? "Evan. His name is Evan. I imagine he's on the way to open the store right now."

"He's a sales clerk? Ruthie's grandson is in retail, too. I should give you his number."

"Evan's not a sales clerk. He's my business partner. We own the store."

"You own a store?" Irene sounded dutifully impressed. "At such a young age?"

I kept talking with my eyes closed, hoping she'd go away. "A vintage clothing store called Handbags and Gladrags. I bought my half with the life insurance money my parents left me. They died in a car accident six years ago."

Irene made sympathetic clucking noises. "Poor dear."

There was silence for a moment, and I began to hope she'd leave me in peace. Death has a way of rendering people awkward—it's a definite conversation killer once the dutiful condolences are over.

But personal boundaries don't seem to matter if you're already dead.

"My Morty was a big believer in life insurance. Good man, my Morty—good provider, too.

I was the planner, the brains behind the throne, you know? I planned every detail of the funeral in advance—men are hopeless about that kind of thing."

"Irene—"

I opened my eyes and looked at her, and she looked at me. It was on the tip of my tongue to say something inexcusably rude when I remembered the voice.

Do unto others, Nicki, as you would have them do unto you.

A sigh escaped me. I pushed the bedcovers aside and started working my way out of bed, feeling wobbly.

"Let me go use the john and splash some water on my face."

There was no rule that said I had to be gracious, was there?

"Then you can tell me all about your funeral."

CHAPTER 2

"*Ech*—can you believe that woman? As if my Morty would ever be interested in a skinny *kvetcher* like Gladys Finch."

Irene and I stood in the shade of a large oak, watching as a simple pine coffin was lowered into the ground. "My Morty" was a chubby, balding man in his sixties who stood at the edge of the grave and wept openly, round cheeks wet with tears. Clinging to his arm, murmuring comfort, was a thin woman who couldn't look more like her name if cliché were the rule.

There were no flowers, no songs. The turnout was decent, though, for at least thirty people were gathered to lay Irene Goldblatt to rest. All the mourners wore black, of course, stark figures outlined against the gray tombstones. They listened in respectful silence to a reading of Psalms, standing still as clothed statues ruffled by the breeze.

"She's had her eye on my Morty for years," Irene said. "Owns the condo next door." Another sniff and pat to her hair. "But he's tasted her cooking—she'll never have my Morty."

The Rodeph Shalom Cemetery was a peaceful place, a huge mosaic of green grass, stone and marble. The serenity invited you to stay and visit, to linger on shaded benches and listen to the silence.

"Don't you want him to be happy again?"

Irene gave me a look. "Of course I do, dear. That's why you're here, remember? I don't want my Morty to live with guilt on his conscience. But I know my husband—he'd never be happy with a woman who can't cook and constantly whines about how her kids never come visit." She threw up her hands. "Why should they come visit? So they can get stomachaches?"

Irene's gossiping seemed out of place given the solemnity of the occasion, and besides—I didn't care. This sweet little Jewish grandmother had been driving me crazy for two days, and I wanted my life back. "*Shhhh*. You dragged me all the way out here to see this. I wanna hear the rabbi."

He'd lowered the Psalms and was reciting something from memory, eyes closed and face lifted to the sun. I didn't understand the language, but the cadence of the words was beautiful.

"Kaddish." Irene murmured. "A mourner's prayer."

We listened together in silence. Morty's sobs, muted during the prayer, became sniffles as the rabbi finished his prayer and stepped back, away from the grave. Then the sniffles stopped, leaving only the rustle of wind in the trees, soft as a sigh of farewell.

Morty bent and scooped up a handful of dirt, tossing it into the yawning hole. One by one others came forward and did the same, touching Morty sympathetically on the shoulder or murmuring a word in his ear as they filed past. They moved in knots and clusters down the hill toward their parked cars, leaving Morty to stand, obviously grief-stricken, by the grave. Gladys tried to draw him away, but he shook his head. Whatever he said to the woman sent her trailing reluctantly after the others. He then stood alone, staring woodenly down at the coffin, as two men with shovels moved in to cover it forever.

"He doesn't want to let you go." I turned to Irene, expecting to see her cheeks wet with tears. Instead, I found her serene and smiling, eyes alight in a way I hadn't noticed before.

"We'll be together again soon enough," she said,

as though there were no doubt. "I'll be waiting for him."

Remembering the Light, it all seemed so clear, and so simple. I knew why Irene wasn't sad. I swallowed hard, suddenly wondering who would be waiting for me when my time came.

"What do you want me to say to Morty?" The memory of the Light beckoned, drawing me as well as Irene. For the first time, I felt Irene's impatience as though it were my own.

"You tell him that 'the rain in Spain falls mainly on the plain.'"

"What?" Peaceful visions of everlasting understanding splintered.

"You heard me, dear. He'll understand." Irene wasn't looking at me. She was watching her Morty. "Then you do this."

To my astonishment, Irene recited in a singsong voice, curtsying midway, "Schlemeil, schlemozzle, Hahsenfeffer Incorporated."

"You want me to sing the theme song from *Laverne and Shirley*?" I'd watched enough weekend reruns to recognize it. What she was asking was just too much. "He'll think I'm a lunatic!"

She reached out to pat my hand, but stopped short. I wouldn't have felt it anyway. I'd already learned that Irene could be seen and heard, but she had little or no influence on the physical world.

"Don't worry, dear. It's our little code. Just do it."

"Oh, jeez," I muttered.

"And by the way . . ." She smiled with such sweetness my heart clenched. ". . . thank you." Irene faded, but I knew she was still there. I knew it as surely as I knew my own name.

Taking a deep breath, I stepped from the shadows and marched toward Morty.

He didn't notice me at first. The rhythmic sound of shoveling—*scrape, plop, scrape, plop*—had a hypnotic quality. Morty was crying again, silently this time, while the two men doing the shoveling stoically ignored him. I'm sure it wasn't the first time they'd filled in a grave while family watched.

"Nice day, huh?" *Oh, my God. Great opener there, Nicki.*

Morty barely glanced at me before he went back to watching the hole fill with dirt. He didn't answer, mopping at his face with a crumpled tissue.

"What I mean is, at least it's not raining. You know, like in Spain."

"Miss, I don't know who you are, but I'm burying my wife." Irene's Morty had a voice like gravel, no doubt hoarse from weeping. His plump face crumpled, then steadied. "I don't have any money, and I'd appreciate it if you moved along."

He thought I was a either a hooker or a vagrant! That's what dressing funky could get you—totally typecast. Either my heavy mascara and dark red lipstick branded me a vamp, or my waifish build and vintage clothes labeled me a beggar. Which was it? Desperate to get Irene's message over with, I blurted, "The rain in Spain falls mainly on the plain."

Morty's eyes widened.

Now he thought I was a lunatic hooker/bum. Great.

"Mr. Goldblatt, your wife wants you to know that your matzo balls weren't dry and that it wasn't your fault she choked on one." Morty's mouth fell open. "And she said you'd understand if I did this—'Schlemeil, schlemozzle, Hahsenfeffer Incorporated.'"

The rhythm of the shovels ceased as all three men gaped, but I didn't care. It was done, it was over, and I was free.

"I'm sorry about your wife." I started backing up, away from the grave.

"Irene?" Morty teared up again, the hope in his voice painful to hear. It was hard to watch a grown man cry. "You've talked to my Irene?" He took a step toward me.

I really didn't wanna get into the whole story—I'd already acted like a lunatic, and I didn't need to reinforce that impression by giving him the details. The two men covering Irene's grave muttered to each other, eyeing me suspiciously. I'd done what

Irene asked, hadn't I? Turning, I glanced toward the spot I'd last seen her.

She was there, purple flowered blouse and brassy hair, gazing at her Morty with so much love on her face it made my heart twist. She was surrounded by light, an aura of brilliance.

Then she turned, still smiling, and took a single step away from us, into the Light. A quick flash, and both Irene and the Light were gone, as though a diamond sparkled and a door closed.

I gasped, feeling a rush of remembrance, and a tiny twinge of envy. Irene was going to like where she was going. But now she was gone, and there was nothing left but the quiet gray and green of Rodeph Shalom, each headstone and bench in sharper focus than before.

"Is she here?" Morty grabbed my arm, still crying. "Where is she?"

"She's gone. She's in a better place." I was happy for Irene and sorry for Morty, but I needed to get out of there. This was *way* too heavy for me.

"How do you know that? Tell me what happened. I have to talk to her . . . can I talk to her?"

I pulled away, taking a few steps backward. No way was I even gonna go there. I was a business owner, not a psychic.

"That's all I can tell you, Mister . . . um, sir. Bye-bye."

Then I turned and ran like hell, ignoring Morty's delayed shout. "Miss . . . miss . . . come back . . ."

I ran all the way to my car. I'd parked it at the base of the hill outside the cemetery where the shade was thickest, far enough away that no one could easily read the license number, but not so far that I couldn't reach it pretty quick.

I thought I was home free when I grabbed the door handle—until someone called my name.

"Nicki!"

"Dr. Bascombe?" I couldn't believe the timing. "What are you doing here?"

He was wearing a black suit. Dolce and Gabbana, unless I missed my guess. The tie was a blue patterned silk, crisply knotted. He looked well-tailored and well-off, and so unlike the two previous times we'd met that it was no wonder I hadn't recognized him among the mourners. Just showed how eager I was to be rid of Irene that I could miss a hunk like that, even if corporate boy toy wasn't my usual taste.

"Call me Joe." He smiled, and my heart did that annoying flip thing it does. At least now I knew why—*not true love, just a heart defect*. "Irene Goldblatt's obituary was in the paper. I came to pay my respects." He hesitated. "But I was really looking for you."

My radar went up. "As my doctor or . . ." I let the

question dangle, very curious to hear the answer. A quick glance at the mirrored surface of my car window confirmed I was looking pretty good—hardly the weak, pale creature he'd known in the hospital. I'd just run down a hill and was barely out of breath. My heart was as reliably unreliable as ever, so why was Dr. Handsome looking for me?

"Research, actually." I blinked at my reflection, not expecting that one. "I'm going to write that paper on near death experiences, and I wondered whether you'd consider being my first test subject."

"Your what?" The words "test" and "subject" were not in my vocabulary. "I really don't like the sound of that."

So much for my delusions of vanity—Mr. Cute Doctor was there to do a sanity check.

"You should see your face." Joe grinned, looking truly amused. "I didn't mean it the way it sounded. I was just hoping you'd agree to an interview so I could record your experience. Your impressions, your feelings." He leaned against my car and kept talking. "How it's changed you."

I still didn't like the sound of this, and I liked even less that he'd hit on the one thing that was bothering me. For the experience *had* changed me, and I wasn't sure I wanted to be changed.

"No thanks, Doc." I unlocked the car door and

opened it, forcing him to step back a pace. "I've already forgotten most of it, and I'm the same old Nicki Styx I was before. No life-changing revelations here."

"Oh, really?" The skeptical tone of his voice was unmistakable. I turned, hand on the door.

"I suppose the old Nicki Styx was in the habit of approaching grieving widowers and singing the theme from a seventies sitcom?"

I was mortified. He'd seen me make a fool of myself. "*Laverne and Shirley,*" I said icily. "And it's none of your business what my habits are. I do a lovely rendition of *Gilligan's Island*, too—but I save that one for bar mitzvahs."

Joe burst out laughing, unimpressed with my sarcasm. He had a great laugh, rich and full. It made it hard to hold onto my annoyance, especially when his eyes invited me to laugh with him.

"Be quiet," I hissed, glancing back at the cemetery, toward the headstones. "You're laughing loud enough to—" I tried hard to keep a straight face. "—wake the dead."

He laughed even harder, and this time I joined in, the ridiculousness of the situation covering any awkwardness.

"Miss . . . miss . . . are you here?"

Morty's voice floated down the hill. In a sudden panic, I slid into my car and pulled the door shut.

"I'm sorry," I said over my shoulder to Joe, "but I gotta go."

A single click came from the ignition, but the car didn't start. I twisted the key the other way and tried again, but it wasn't happening.

"Dammit!"

"We can take my car. It's right around the corner."

I shot Joe a look.

"How about it?" He obviously wasn't the type of guy to waste an opportunity. "I get you out of here and you jump-start my long-delayed paper on near death experiences. It's a fair trade, isn't it?"

"Sounds like blackmail to me."

"I'll throw in a cup of coffee," he added cheerfully.

"Hello? Is anyone there?"

There was a thrashing in the bushes, as though a wild animal sought to free itself from a trap. The cemetery gate was several yards away, but it appeared as though a determined Morty was about to find it.

Desperate, I jumped from the car and snatched Joe by the arm. "Which way?"

He grabbed my hand and pulled me down the street. When we reached the corner, he pointed his keys toward a black BMW parked by the curb and unlocked it with a discreet *beep*. I reluctantly let go of his big, warm hand and dove into the passenger side, breathing deep of the leather interior.

More black. My favorite.

A minute later we were two blocks away, leaving Morty Goldblatt and Rodeph Shalom Cemetery far behind.

"Things were getting a little sticky back there." I stopped glancing over my shoulder and relaxed into the seat, giving Joe a grin. "That's the second time you've saved my life."

"Not true." His face was somber. "I declared you dead. Then you took in a deep breath and let it out," he smiled and shook his head, "and then another one." For a moment his gaze slipped inward, as though he was thinking of something else. "You're a miracle."

"Gee, Doc—maybe you can take that into account when you send me the bill, *hm*? My insurance premiums are killing me."

"Joe, remember? And you should see the cost of malpractice insurance." He kept his voice light, shooting glances at me as he drove. "But enough boring doctor talk. You already know about me, but I don't know much about you. What do you do? International fashion model, perhaps?"

Before I could respond, he added, "That's a great outfit, by the way."

I'd dressed for comfort today in gray pinstriped

pants and low-heeled boots, teamed with a white silk T-shirt and an oversized jacket. It gave me the boyishly feminine look that was one of my favorites.

"Are you flirting with me, Joe?" I'd always found directness gave me an advantage. Most guys didn't know how to handle it.

"What if I am?"

He guided the car into a parking space in front of a local coffee shop, then turned it off, giving me his full attention.

The moment stretched while I met his eyes, considering. No question—he was a good-looking man. But he was also part of a world I avoided, the world of responsibility and conformity, of country club politics and starched shirts.

"We have to lay some ground rules," I said. "The first one being that if you flirt with me you might get hurt, and you have to be okay with that."

Joe unbuckled his seat belt, smiling. "Are you trying to tell me you'll break my heart?"

I looked at him very seriously. "No. I'm trying to tell you that I like to play with my lovers, and sometimes I play rough." I gave him a wicked grin, going from nice to naughty in a split-second. "I doubt you know what you'd be getting yourself into, boy toy."

He watched as I slid out of the car. I leaned back in before closing the door. "As for your heart—you can keep it. It's not the part of your anatomy I'm interested in."

The look on Dr. Handsome's face was priceless, no matter how fleeting. It wouldn't do for him to form any impressions about me that weren't true—I wasn't the kind of girl he'd take home to his mama, and I didn't wanna be. I was having too much fun being young and single, and if I enjoyed being a little on the wild side, I wasn't going to hide it.

"Did you just call me 'boy toy'?" His head popped up on the other side of the car pretty quickly. He shut the door and walked toward me.

I grinned, waiting for him to catch up.

"Surely I'm not the first."

He looked vaguely pleased, but cautious, uncertain whether to take my remarks seriously. "You're a very interesting woman, Nicki. Quite a dichotomy."

We'd reached the door of the coffee shop. He held it open, and I flapped a hand at him as I passed. "Don't try to impress me with those big words, Doc. There's nothing contradictory about me—what you see is what you get."

"I hope so," I heard him murmur. "And the name is Joe."

"Then what happened?"

Evan was checking out the new dresses I'd

brought him after an afternoon of thrift store shopping. He'd laid them all on the bed and was eyeing them keenly, but I knew he was just as interested in hearing about my coffee date as he was in examining sequins and stitching. "Did you scare him away with your 'ball-buster' routine, or was the good doctor ready to bend over and cough?"

I laughed. I couldn't help it. Evan knew me so well.

"Don't be crude." He shot me a wicked sideways glance, knowing he was outrageous. "He bought me coffee, broke out a tape recorder and started asking me questions about what happened in the hospital." I picked up a red-beaded evening gown. "What do you think of this one? Nineteen forties, maybe?"

Evan shook his head. "Fifties. It needs relining, but once I've replaced some of those beads and had it cleaned, it'll be a show stopper. We'll put it on Jayne, and stand her in the front window." One of Evan's artist friends had turned our bland, anonymous store mannequins into glamorous replicas of early film stars. It didn't hurt the shop's funky reputation to have our restored vintage gowns displayed by Jayne Mansfield, Jean Harlowe, or Audrey Hepburn.

"We talked for about an hour—he asked a bunch of questions about my parents, where I grew up, stuff like that. I guess he had to rule out my being some kind of weirdo."

"What was he doing at the funeral, anyway?" Evan was checking the hem on a tea-length peach chiffon but stopped, rolling his eyes at the stupidity of his own question. "What am I saying? He couldn't resist the devilish Nicki Styx any more than the rest of the male population of Atlanta—*that's* what he was doing there."

I reached out and pinched Evan's perfect behind before he could swing it out of reach. "You're just jealous, sweetie. I saw you eyeing him while you were hovering over me in the hospital. Maybe you could join a survivor support group and meet somebody that way. You know, the 'Gay Men and the Women Who Love Them but Don't Have the Grace to Die' group."

That earned me a sniff. "I am not jealous, and don't joke about dying like that." Evan dropped the gown he was holding and walked out of the room, heading toward the kitchen. "Now I have to pour myself a glass of wine to steady my nerves."

I trailed after him, absently admiring his apartment, as I'd done so many times before. The art deco furniture was all authentic, down to the black lacquer coffee table and white leather sofa. A gorgeous glass skyscraper cabinet was filled with handpicked pieces of Lalique, while framed vintage prints added splashes of color to the walls. It was spotless, and about as far from my messy, hodge-podge place as you could get.

"Here you go." Evan poured two glasses of char-donnay and offered me one. I almost took it, then shook my head.

"I need to cut back—doctor's orders."

An arched eyebrow from Evan spoke volumes. "You're taking orders now? My, my. That's not like you—you must like the guy more than you're saying. When are you seeing him again?"

I shrugged, settling myself on a red and black bar stool.

"I dunno. He was a perfect gentleman, after all," here I flashed him a grin, "and I'm not really into gentlemen."

Evan took another sip of wine, and a different tack. "What about your car? Did you have it towed?"

"No. It was the funniest thing—Joe took me back there to see if it would start, and after he fiddled around under the hood for a minute, it started right up."

"*Hmm.*" Evan's grunt sounded noncommittal, but I knew better.

"What?"

"Your gentleman doctor knows his way around cars, huh?"

"I guess so."

"Kinda funny he just happened to be there when it wouldn't start. Had it been giving you trouble?"

I shook my head, suspicion growing.

"Can't be too much harder to connect a battery cable or an ignition wire than it is to disconnect one, can it?" Evan gave me a bland look across the kitchen counter, wineglass dangling from his fingers.

"Well, I'll be damned," I murmured. "Looks like Joe Bascombe has a naughty side after all."

"I don't know if I like this, Nick." Evan started pacing, his standard method of dealing with worry. "Things are getting weirder and weirder. You almost died, you've been hallucinating, and now your doctor is following you around?"

"I am not hallucinating," I snapped. "And if I was, I'm not anymore." Irene Goldblatt was gone, that much I was sure of. I couldn't argue about the weirdness, but I was grateful I hadn't told Evan just *how* weird things had gotten. No need for him to worry his pretty little head about me unnecessarily. "The good doctor has made it clear he wants help with his paper, and if he wants more than that he'll have to work for it."

"Then why are you helping him at all?"

I was ready with a snappy comeback about manly bulges, but I didn't say it. Instead, I told Evan the truth.

"Because something happened to me that I don't understand." I reached across the counter and caught his hand in mine, both for its familiar comfort and to stop his pacing. "It was—" I searched for the word. "—incredible. Not just what I saw, but what I felt, what I heard . . . what I *knew*."

His face softened, worry lines easing. I'd already told him about the near death experience—more than once—but I hadn't told him everything. It seemed obvious to me that I'd returned from my trip to the Light with a passenger, but the first time I'd mentioned Irene, Evan was ready to call in the shrinks. So I'd shut up about my promise to a dead woman, only telling him I was attending her funeral out of morbid curiosity. But Evan was my best friend, and I wanted him to understand that something profoundly life-changing had happened to me, even if I didn't fully understand all the implications yet.

"Okay," he murmured, squeezing my fingers. "But you keep me informed, you hear? I wanna know immediately if you start seeing more dead people or if this doctor guy gets too pushy." Evan's expression went from worried to playful. He glanced over his shoulder toward the hallway, keeping his voice lowered. "Butch has a leather biker's outfit he wears to fetish night at The Olympiad—I'm sure he'd use it to scare away Dr. Goodbody if I asked him nicely."

"Butch?" My eyebrows rose along with my curiosity. "There's someone here?"

Evan waved a negligent hand. "Oh, don't worry . . . he's in the shower. And besides, he's a love—body like a tank and the mind of a flower child. He wouldn't hurt a fly, but most people don't know that."

Evan's taste had always run to the extreme end of the spectrum. Manly men who made him feel like a girly girl seemed to be the norm.

"No thanks." I got up from the bar stool, ready to head home. "But you enjoy."

My house seemed emptier than usual, and I didn't like the feeling. Strange, because I'd always enjoyed solitude. Now the quiet seemed too loud, the living room too big, the pile of mail by the door too much trouble to sort through.

I tossed my keys on the coffee table and set my bag beside them before flopping down on the couch. Closing my eyes, I saw again in my mind the stone sentinels and shaded benches of Rodeph Shalom Cemetery. The silence there had been peaceful, but the silence here was just . . . empty.

"Crap."

Depression had never been a problem for me, even after my parents died. They'd loved each other dearly, loved me even more, and when they died together on a rainy stretch of road, I'd taken comfort from those things. And Evan, of course. It was hard to be sad around Evan.

But Evan wasn't there, and neither was anyone else.

"Double crap."

Why now? Was I really so changed by my own brush with death? If anything, I should have been relieved to know that life goes on after the body gives out. Instead, I was bothered by a nagging sense that I was missing something in the here-and-now.

I was lonely. And being lonely sucked.

Irene had "her Morty." Evan had Butch, even if his leather-clad flower child was only one bloom in a long daisy chain of lovers. I'd had my own smaller string of blossoming relationships, each plucked and dropped without any care for what happened when they fell. I'd even taken pleasure in grinding a few under the stiletto heels of my favorite boots.

There'd only been one guy who'd ever meant anything to me: Erik Mitchell, from my senior year in high school. I thought we'd be together forever, but the only souvenir I had of that relationship was a broken heart tattoo and an aversion to cute little cheerleaders named Cindy.

"Oh, my God." I sat up, shoving my hair back with my fingers. "You're pathetic, woman. Enough of the cry-baby routine, already."

My eye fell on my purse, a great find at a garage sale earlier in the year. Genuine Rosenfeld, black velvet with a cameo clasp. And inside—inside might just be the cure for momentary melancholy. I snatched it up and rummaged around until I found the square of white I was looking for.

Then I picked up the phone and dialed, a wicked little smile already lifting my lips and my spirits.

"Joe? It's Nicki. Are you busy tonight?"

CHAPTER 3

The Vortex is a well-known hangout down in the Atlanta neighborhood of Little Five Points. Evan and I were regulars, and I was thrilled to find out that an all-girl band called The Cherries was headlining. The happy hour crowd was gone, and the place was hopping with night owls just like me—mostly women, girls who just wanted to have fun. The beat of the music was deep and hypnotic, loud enough to feel, but in a good way.

"Come here often?" I'd heard that cheesy pickup line far too many times to have any patience with it, but when I turned to sneer, there was Joe, drinks in both hands and a plucky grin on his face.

I didn't have the heart to tell him how out of place he looked in his button-down dress shirt. But at least he had on well-worn jeans, nicely faded, particularly in the crotch area. I made myself a note to send him for more drinks soon, just so I could watch him walk away.

"All the time." I took the fancy pink drink from his hand—Cosmopolitan, I think, though I had no way of knowing—and patted the seat beside me. "Saved you a seat."

Joe sat down and put his own pink drink on the table, eyeing both it and our surroundings with a bit of trepidation.

Taking pity on him, I leaned over to ask, "You don't really drink that stuff, do you?"

"Only for medicinal purposes." He picked it up and took a sip, grimacing. "Good thing I'm not sick."

I laughed, glad to see his expression relax a bit. "Then why'd you order them?"

He shrugged, then met my eye. "I was trying to impress you with my knowledge of what hip young women drink. My sister Julie told me it was these"—he waved a hand at the pink froth—"or apple martinis. Next time I'll try the martini."

"Ah. *Sex in the City* fan, right?"

He put his head in his hands for a moment. "Oh, boy. The blind leading the blind—is it that obvious?"

"Oh, it's obvious." I pushed my beer toward him, willing to share. "But it's kinda cute you went to your sister for advice."

He grinned, taking a healthy swig before pushing it back toward me. "Then I'll take what I can get."

He'd left me wide open on that one. The music was pulsing, the lead singer belting out a song about bad habits, the lighting dim. I leaned in closer so he could hear me without having to raise my voice.

"*You're* kinda cute, too."

"Just how many beers have you had?"

"Are you asking as my doctor?"

He shook his head. "I'm not your doctor anymore, Nicki."

"Too bad. I've got a nurse's outfit I wore to a Halloween party once, and I was thinking we could play Hide the Stethoscope."

He laughed, eyeing me appreciatively. "You like to shock people, don't you?"

I shrugged, grinning. "Is it that obvious?"

"Oh, it's obvious. But it's kinda cute."

Now I was the one to laugh, appreciating the way he'd picked up on the turnaround of our earlier remarks. I took another sip of beer, then pressed him a little harder.

"Well? Whaddya think?"

"What do I *think*? Sorry, but I don't let anybody

inside my head without an expensive dinner and a bottle or two of wine."

The wicked glint in his eye sparked a memory of me saying the exact same thing to him while I was in the hospital.

I drew back, smiling. I liked a man who could hold his own. "Why do I get the feeling you're avoiding the issue?"

He was watching the band now instead of me, his gaze sliding over the bass player and moving on to the drummer, a redhead with wild orange streaks in her curls.

"Is there an issue?"

I gave a melodramatic sigh, toying with my now nearly empty bottle. "You don't know what you're missing."

He stood, leaning in until his lips brushed my ear.

"Considering I've already seen you naked, I know exactly what I'm missing." Did I imagine the heat in that husky whisper? "But I wouldn't want you to think I was easy."

He pulled back, and damned if I didn't sway toward him.

"I'll go get us a couple more from the bar."

I sighed again, quietly this time, but I had my consolation prize. Those jeans looked every bit as good from the rear.

***

After two beers, some great music, and lots of cheerful vibes, the band had finished their set. They took their cheers and jeers and left the stage, leaving a momentary lull in the action until the laughter and conversation started to pick up.

"How about we go somewhere for a late night coffee?" Joe said. "I'll even kick in for a Danish if you can find us one."

"Big spender, huh?" Damned if Joe wasn't getting better-looking as the evening went on. Blue was a nice color for button-down shirts, though I'd put him in something darker. Eggplant or plum maybe, richer shades to set off his dark hair. He looked boyish and smart, like the wholesome guys all the good girls had crushes on in high school. Not geeky enough to be a nerd, not nerdy enough to be a geek.

Those girls should have spoken up when they had the chance. I, for one, was happy to take him down the street to Moonbeans, the Little Five Points equivalent of Starbucks.

"Interesting neighborhood."

It was nearly midnight, but Little Five Points nightlife was just getting started. Reggae music spilled from the open doorway of Hey Mon's, warring with the screech of punk rock across the street at The Crypt. Winos leaned against the psychedelic murals on the buildings, shaking down passing preppy couples for spare change.

"You've never been down here before?"

Joe shook his head, taking it all in.

"'Little Five' is an Atlanta institution. Old hippies come here to die, like an elephant's graveyard." I was joking, of course, at least about the dying part. "It's part time-capsule, part brave new world." A guy with spiked hair and a nose ring walked by with a girl in "glam gear"—bright pink eyelashes matching the lacquered beehive wig—proving my point.

"I haven't had much time to explore since I moved here three years ago," Joe said. "I had my residency to worry about, then work took over."

"You should see it in the daytime. Major tourist trap and local hangout all in one, but it has real character, too. That's why I opened my place here—lots of traffic and plenty of open-minded people."

"Your place?"

I stopped on the sidewalk, weighing my options. Coffee and Danish or a deeper glimpse into my personal life? I gave him a grin. "Next block over. Wanna see?"

"That depends." He gave me a wicked grin in return. "It's not an S&M dungeon, is it?"

My whoop of laughter caused heads to turn,

but I didn't care. "You wish." I reached out and slapped him playfully on that cute behind. He barely flinched, grinning even more broadly. "It's a perfectly acceptable vintage clothing store. Instruments of torture not allowed."

He gave a skeptical snort. "Uh-huh."

"Why, Joe" —I leaned in and took him by the arm— "that sounds like a challenge."

The wail of a siren cut off his reply. A fire truck rounded a corner and pushed its way down the street, lights flashing and horn blowing as pedestrians scattered. Little Five Points was a rabbit warren, narrow streets and sharp corners. The driver of the truck had to do some maneuvering to make the next turn. The noise was ear-splitting, but that wasn't what brought the hair up on the back of my neck.

"That road's a dead end. They're heading toward my shop."

I took off at a run as the rear of the truck disappeared around the corner. Dodging people already headed the same way, it took me longer than I'd like to make it to the end of the block, and by the time I got there the EMTs were already huddled over someone on the ground across the street. A knot of people blocked the front steps of Indigo, a Jamaican grocery. The local cops were holding off curious onlookers and breaking out the crime scene tape.

"I'll go see if I can help the paramedics." Joe edged past me as I came to a halt in front of Evan's gorgeously decorated display window. Indigo was owned by my friend Caprice and her boyfriend, Mojo. They closed at ten, and I was glad to see the lights were off and the front door was shut. At least it didn't appear to be a robbery.

"Doesn't look too good, does it?"

"Caprice! Where'd you come from, girl? What's going on?" I craned my neck, watching Joe as he talked his way past the cops and over to the EMTs. One of them shook his head at Joe, then stood up and started talking to him. The other paramedic, a woman with a short ponytail, flipped a sheet over the body on the ground.

A cold chill went down my spine. Somebody had done that to me not too long ago.

Caprice didn't answer. Like me and everyone else, she was watching the drama taking place with morbid fascination. The rhythmic red flash from the top of the fire truck caught the side of her face and the beads woven into her dreadlocks, turning them various shades of pink and crimson, casting a garish tint over the tropical print of her blouse.

A man's shout came from the other side of one of the police cars, followed by what looked like a struggle.

"I didn't do it! I didn't do nothin', I said! This

ain't right!" Cops swarmed like ants over a guy who obviously wasn't taking their directions too well. "This ain't right!" Within a few seconds, the guy was on the ground and handcuffed, then hauled to his feet and hustled toward the open door of a cruiser. I saw his face.

"Mo! Caprice, it's Mojo! What the hell is going on?"

But Caprice was gone, and in her place was a red-faced frat boy. His beer breath was way too close to my face, and I elbowed him away. The crowd was getting bigger.

Joe was walking back across the street, working his way toward me. He shook his head as he got close.

"Too late," he murmured in my ear. Taking my arm, he pulled me back into the doorway of the shop, obviously not wanting to broadcast his news to the avid crowd. "But at least they got the guy who did it."

"Did what? To who?" I was so upset I didn't wait for his answer. "I know that guy—he owns the grocery store—Mo wouldn't hurt a fly."

"Well, somebody did." Joe looked uncomfortable. "Did you . . . did you know his girlfriend?"

"Of course I know his girlfriend—I was just talking to her. Her name's Caprice."

Joe was looking at me strangely, and then it

dawned on me that he'd used the past tense. Nausea churned, bringing a bitter taste to the back of my throat. "She was just here," I added weakly.

Then I threw up all over his shoes.

"Stop fussing over me."

I fished for my keys, glad to be home, and glad for the umpteenth time my dad had put the front porch light on a timer when I was a kid.

"I'm a doctor. It's what I do." Joe kept his tone matter-of-fact. "Now be a good girl and let me help you into bed."

I groaned, more embarrassed than anything. "Why didn't you say that a couple of hours ago, huh? Then none of this would have happened."

"I don't know about that. Even great sex won't fix too much beer on an empty stomach."

I flashed him a look, because I'd only had two beers. "That wasn't it."

Joe gave me a rueful glance and looked down at his shoes. "I beg to differ. These sneakers could easily be arrested for drunk driving."

I couldn't help but smile just a little. "Oh, well. At least you admit it would've been great."

At least I wasn't the only one who'd been thinking about sex.

Only I wasn't thinking about it now.

"I didn't get sick because I drank too much. It

was something else." I unlocked the door, flipped a light switch and stepped inside, making way for him to follow. My hands were still shaking.

"Home, sweet home."

The place was a hodgepodge, slightly messy but—I liked to think—charming in its messiness. It was the same house I'd grown up in, but it was mine now, and my parents would have wanted it that way. Out was the floral wallpaper and beige carpet, in were hardwood floors and rose-colored walls. Crisp white trim at the baseboards and ceiling was Evan's touch. My sofa, a well-worn velvet I'd found at a garage sale, had fashion magazines and swatches of fabric scattered over the burgundy cushions. The coffee table had more of the same, plus a lipstick-stained cup and a half-eaten bagel. I was particularly attached to the artwork above the couch—a charcoal sketch of a reclining nude, feminine back and buttocks drawn in broad, sweeping strokes.

"Can I get you something?" I wrinkled my nose as I took in Joe's stained shoes and splattered jeans. "A bed pan, maybe?"

Joe grinned. "Nothing. I just wanted to make sure you got home safe." He hesitated. "You seem a little shaky."

Bravado fled and tears welled. I tossed my purse on the couch and slumped down beside it, covering my face with one hand. "I just can't believe it. Are you sure the cops said her name was Caprice Dumaine?" My black eyeliner was smeared. I swiped at it with a knuckle, making it worse. "What did she look like?"

He took a seat on the couch next to me. "Mid-thirties, black, slightly plump. Beads in her hair—wearing jeans and one of those tropical shirts you'd find at the beach resorts. Green and blue, I think."

I closed my eyes and moaned. That was Caprice.

Joe moved in closer, sliding an arm around me. My shoulder found a home against his rib cage.

"Caprice was my friend." My voice was muffled against his chest. "I've known her for six years, ever since Evan and I opened the shop." And I was sure I'd seen her, spoken to her, there on the sidewalk. Tonight. "She's really dead?" I'd almost hoped for a bad dream instead, one that could still be made right. "I have to call Evan."

"I'm sorry, Nicki." For just a second Joe rested a cheek on the top of my head.

I pulled away and looked at him. "How'd she die?"

He hesitated. "Broken neck. Looked like she'd taken a blow to the head, too—but that could have happened in the fall. They won't know for sure until after the—" The look of horror on my face stopped him mid-sentence.

"Autopsy," I finished. "Oh, man." I buried my face in my hands.

Joe settled deeper into the sofa and pulled me against him. I came willingly, trying to get *that* image out of my head. We sat in silence for a few minutes. I knew he was just offering comfort, but he smelled like cherries and chocolate, a melt-in-your-mouth scent that made me all too aware of him as a man.

"There's something else, Joe."

"What's that?" he asked.

"I think something's happened to me since I was in the hospital." I sat up, hand on his thigh. I knew a little distance might be a good thing, but I couldn't bring myself to budge any further. "Maybe you can help me figure it out."

His thigh muscle flexed, warm and strong through his jeans.

"Ever since the near death experience, I've been seeing things."

"You're having more hallucinations? Why didn't you tell me?" Joe's medical training kicked in as he straightened, moving up on the couch, and dislodging my hand in the process. "Headaches?" He touched my chin and looked in my eyes. "Blurred vision? Flashes of light?"

I shook my head, pulling my chin from his grasp.

"People who died." I kept looking him in the eye. "Two of them now."

He didn't want me to see how skeptical he was, but I knew. He'd already tried to explain Irene Goldblatt away through the power of suggestion and post-traumatic stress, but this . . .

"You saw your friend Caprice tonight—after she died?"

I nodded. "I didn't know she was dead at the time."

"Nicki, do you realize what you're saying?" Joe took my hand, voice gentle. "It's not possible. You can't see the dead, or talk to them."

"Explain that to them, would you?" He was being so sweet to me, I couldn't get mad. The guy had a right to be skeptical. Besides, his hand was warm, his fingers strong.

"What happened? Tell me."

"It was Caprice. I know it was. She was standing right next to me while you were talking to the paramedics." I wanted Joe to believe me, but for now it was enough that he still held my hand.

He hesitated, and suddenly I wanted to kick myself. *What was I doing?* Trying to convince the cutest guy I'd dated in months that I was crazy? Here

I was going on about ghosts when there were better things we could be doing—throwing myself a pity party wasn't at all how I'd hoped to end the evening.

Joe stared into my eyes, a faint crease of worry between his brows, then stood. "I'm ordering some tests tomorrow." The doctor side of him was obviously used to giving orders.

Problem was, I didn't tend to take them very well.

I looked up at him, knowing my mascara was smeared and my hair was a mess.

God, he was sexy.

"You don't believe me."

"It could be a lingering reaction to medication. I just want to make sure you're okay. You've got a bad heart valve, remember?"

I smiled a little at that, cocking my head to one side.

"There you go with the doctor stuff again." It was sweet, really, except we were way past the usual doctor-patient thing. I might have a heart defect, but I wasn't blind. "Tell me, Dr. B, do you get a stiffie for all your heart patients?"

I reached out and cupped him there, and for a moment time stood still.

"Don't." He ground out the one word, stepping back even though he didn't seem to want to.

"Why not?" I murmured, a wicked gleam in my eye. I left my hand where it was, inches from his straining zipper.

"I'm married."

CHAPTER 4

"Married."

Why was I so shocked? Great-looking guy, successful career . . . I snatched my hand away from Joe's pants and jumped to my feet. "Get the hell out."

"Wait, Nicki—it's not like that."

I was halfway to the door, snapping at him over my shoulder, "Then what's it like, huh? What wifey doesn't know won't hurt her, or wifey doesn't care if you cheat as long as you use protection?" Now my blood was boiling. "Either way, I'm not interested. I'm no home wrecker, and I don't do sloppy seconds."

He actually looked offended at that. As if *he* had some right to be offended. I flung the door open and stood there, squeezing the doorknob as hard as I could, the way I'd like to be squeezing his balls. "Get out."

"There's no need for this."

That reasonable "doctor-speak" infuriated me even more. My heart was pounding, and for that reason alone I struggled to get control of my temper. Wouldn't do to have another heart attack, particularly in front of Dr. Dolittle.

"A lot of guys wouldn't even have bothered to tell you the truth." Joe flushed—embarrassment or anger, I wasn't certain. "Or waited until after they'd screwed your brains out." He took a step closer, eyes intent. "It's not like I didn't want to, you know."

The heat in my cheeks wasn't just the result of outrage. I'd wanted him—and unfortunately for me, I still did. I'd come on to him pretty strong, but he'd held me off all evening. At least now I knew why.

Time to regroup.

I bit my lip, letting reason take over. If he hadn't stopped me, we'd be naked on the couch by now, with me none the wiser.

"It's been a long day, Joe." *Had it ever.* "I think you'd better go."

He sighed, running a hand through his hair. Damn if he didn't look good when he wasn't all calm, cool, and collected. His hair looked better mussed, doctorly decorum gone. There was a damp smear of mascara and tears on his chest.

"Nicki, I—"

All my anger drained away, leaving me exhausted. "It's okay. Just go." I held the door open a little wider. I wanted nothing more than to sleep, and forget about hospitals and doctors and death and sex and married men. "I'm tired."

He walked past me and out the door, pausing on the threshold. "I'm still ordering those tests."

I shook my head. "I'm done with tests, Doc. Have a nice life." Then I shut the door in his face, ignoring the concern etched on his features.

Let his wife take the tests.

"Nicki." He was still there, still on the other side of the door. I leaned against it, not answering.

"I'm sorry."

His footsteps moved away, down the stairs, and then there was silence.

"So am I," I murmured. "So am I."

I woke in the night with a bad feeling. Thankfully, it was only cramps.

Time for the monthly routine again, right on schedule. I never minded, though—not really. What most women used as an excuse to be bitchy and eat chocolate, I saw as an affirmation that women were special. Men might provide some of the ingredients but they couldn't deliver a miracle—unless you counted remembering to put the toilet seat down after they'd used it.

Besides, who really needs an excuse to be bitchy or eat chocolate?

Not bothering with any lights, I got out of bed and went to the bathroom, taking care of things quickly. One of the advantages of living alone is that things are always where you left them. Finding your way in the dark becomes second nature. On the way back to bed I stopped and adjusted the thermostat a few degrees. The house was chilly.

"You did right to kick his ass out."

I knew that voice. I squeezed my eyes shut and leaned against the wall, telling myself not to listen.

"Can't trust a man any farther than you can see him. Granny Julep done told me that when I was a little girl, and she was right."

How many times had I listened to tales of Granny Julep and her all-knowing advice? I stifled a hysterical giggle, afraid it would turn into a scream. Wonder if Granny Julep had any words of wisdom when it came to the dead?

"No reason to be afraid, Nicki. And I know you can hear me."

I forced myself to open my eyes. The bedroom was dark, but I could still make out an even darker silhouette over by the window.

"Caprice? Is that really you?"

The familiar click of beads as Caprice nodded her head convinced me. "You know it is. I need your help." The silhouette moved, and I reached for the light switch.

"Don't. Leave the light off."

"You're freaking me out here, Caprice."

She gave the throaty chuckle that was her trademark. "I'm sorry, girlfriend, but it's better this way. I done been to the morgue and seen myself—don't nobody else need to."

Goose bumps rose on my arms. Having Irene show up in my hospital room had been bizarre, but this was downright creepy. Reminding myself that Caprice was a friend, I edged back into bed and sat against the pillows, drawing the covers up to my chin. It seemed colder than ever in the room.

"What happened?" I kept my voice low, as if someone were listening. Hell, for all I knew, maybe someone was. Maybe the dead were all around, all the time.

A heavy sigh came as Caprice moved to the darkest corner of the room. "That damn Mojo. He got himself a woman, and I found out about it."

The Mo I knew was the most easygoing, laid-back

guy in Little Five Points. Stoned on weed most of the time, never a harsh word for anybody. Caprice had been crazy about him. I still had a hard time believing he could have killed her.

"He met up with her at the shop after we closed—left me at home and said he'd forgotten to close up the register, but I knew something was up. That man might forget his own name sometimes, but he never forgets to close up the register. I waited a few minutes, then drove down there on my own."

"You caught him with somebody else?"

"Hell, yeah, I caught him!" The anger in Caprice's voice made me nervous, and I pulled the bedspread closer to my chin. "I caught him with that skinny piece of trash who supplies us with that damn organic soap! Organic, my ass—like I don't know she cooks that stuff up on her stove with bottled spices!"

Caprice had always had a temper. I kept quiet and let her finish the story on her own.

"I told them to get the hell out, and told Mojo to clear out of our house, too—that we was done. I thought it was all over until that bitch sucker-punched me while we was coming down the stairs."

"*She* hit you? Not Mo?"

A disgusted snort answered me. "Mo ain't got the

balls to squash a bug. Me and her got into it right and proper, and I almost had the skinny bitch until she shoved me backward. Then bam—" Caprice smacked her hands together, making me jump. "— out went the lights. Next thing I know, I'm looking down on myself laying on the ground, blood on my face and the bitch nowhere to be found. Mo was crying and moanin' into the phone, calling the ambulance."

"He's been arrested, Caprice. They think he killed you."

"What the hell you think I'm doing here? You need to get him out."

"Me?" The word came out as a squeak.

"Who else? It's not like I can go down there and tell 'em myself, is it? If I could do something, I'da done it before now."

"But—"

"No buts, girlfriend. Mojo may have done me wrong, but I ain't gonna stand by and watch him take the fall for that skinny-ass 'ho of his. You go down there and tell them the truth."

"Caprice, I can't just walk into the police station and tell them dead people are talking to me." I tried to make myself sound reasonable, but I was starting to feel panicky. "They'll put me in the cell right next to Mo until they can find a padded one—they're not gonna believe me."

There was silence, and I didn't like the sound of it.

"You're gonna have to find a way to make them believe you." Caprice said this as though the request had been turned into an ultimatum.

Stalling, I asked the question I'd never gotten around to asking Irene Goldblatt. "Why didn't you go into the Light, Caprice? What are you still doing here?"

The beads in her hair rattled again, the familiar sound now raising the hair on my arms. "What light? I didn't see no light except for the street lamps and the fire truck. And I already told you what I'm doing here."

The shop bell jingled as Evan swept in, obviously surprised to see me there so early. He was almost always the first one in.

"What's with the police tape in front of Indigo's?" He didn't wait for an answer. "And can you believe somebody puked all over our doorstep?"

I gave him a weak smile. "Sorry."

He took a good look at my face and both eyebrows went up.

"What's the matter, Nick? You look like hell." He locked the door behind him before coming over to the counter.

"Gee, thanks." I slid off the register stool. "Bad

night. Come in the back and I'll tell you about it." I caught Evan's quick glance toward the front door and knew his compulsive need for cleanliness warred with his curiosity. "That can wait—it'll come right off with the hose."

A half hour later I'd told him everything. The Vortex, the fire truck, Caprice's murder, and why I threw up. Joe's marital status and my late night conversation with a dead woman, my disappointment over Joe and my fears about Caprice.

"Joe thinks I need more tests, but tests won't help. Caprice isn't going to leave me alone unless I find a way to get Mojo out of jail." I looked at him, begging him to believe me. "I mean, I feel sorry for her—and I'm really sorry she's dead, but she's angry, and kinda scary." I waited, absolutely exhausted and in dire need of advice.

"Oh my God, Nicki." Evan broke his own rule of "no makeup on the couture" and enfolded me in a big hug. I blinked back tears, grateful as always for his acceptance and understanding. Except when he was being a drama queen, Evan was the best.

"Why can't you just be normal like everybody else?"

"Oh, and I suppose you're a great example of 'normal'?"

Evan gave his best insulted sniff, hugging me even tighter.

"Heaven forbid." He took me by the shoulders and held me away, searching my face. "You look exhausted. Now you lay down right here on the office couch and get some sleep. I'll cover you up and shut the door." He fussed like a mother hen, tucking me up as though I were an invalid. "Don't you worry about a thing. I'll take care of everything today. We'll talk about what to do about Caprice when you're rested."

"You believe me? You don't think I'm crazy?" I don't know why, but it meant a lot to me to hear it.

Evan cocked his head, smoothing the hair back from my face. "I think you're one crazy chick." He gave me that lopsided grin. "Of course I believe you."

The image on the store's security camera was almost as fuzzy as my tired brain, but I recognized the man who'd just come in and started browsing the men's section.

The look on Evan's face went from politely interested to hostile in two seconds, the time it took Joe Bascombe to turn around.

Yeah, Evan. You deal with him. Send him back to his wife with a bug in his ear and a pissed-off drama queen on his ass.

Too bad there was no sound. We'd never invested

in microphones, just cameras. I adjusted the pillow beneath my head, getting comfortable while I watched.

Whatever Joe said to Evan earned him a suspicious stare.

Evan crossed slender arms and thrust out a hip, delivering a no doubt scathing retort.

Joe didn't flinch, saying something else.

An eloquent shrug from Evan.

Joe kept talking, undaunted.

Evan dropped the affronted pose and turned, walking back toward the counter. He tossed words over his shoulder, straightening clothes on the racks automatically as he passed.

Poor Joe would have to work a little harder than that.

He frowned, then said something else, taking a step forward.

Evan flared. Hands on hips, radiating offense. Slim black trousers and a boldly patterned shirt in gold and white made him look like an outraged runway model. High drama now, accompanied by a flamboyant sweep of the hand.

Take that, Dr. Zhivago.

I turned off the security monitor and closed my eyes, confident that Evan had my back. Joe Bascombe would have to find other girls to tempt.

* * *

"What the hell do you mean, 'Joe bought the Valentino?'" The smug look on Evan's face made me want to slap him. "You're on a first name basis now?" I sat up, still groggy. Daytime naps had never agreed with me. "What time is it?"

"Almost three-thirty," he answered, handing me a cup of hot tea. Green chai, I think, heavily sweetened and steaming with fragrance.

"You know I can't resist a fashion challenge, Nick. The poor thing needed my help." Evan lifted his shoulders in a fatalistic shrug, taking a sip from his own mug. "What's a girl to do?"

I glared at him, instantly suspicious. "What's going on here? I told you he's married." But I couldn't resist asking, "Was he looking for me?"

Evan took a seat in the office chair, crossing those long legs as elegantly as only he could. "As a matter of fact, he was looking for me."

Could he *be* any more smug?

"For you." I waited, but nothing more was forthcoming. "You telling me he swings both ways now?"

"Oh, honey," he flapped a hand, "don't be ridiculous. It was obvious from the moment I saw him he's straight as an arrow." A melodramatic sigh. "More's the pity, particularly after I saw him in that Valentino. It fit him perfectly. But no, he just wanted me to convince you to get those tests done.

Says you can do them on an outpatient basis and you'll never have to go near him to do it." He took another sip of tea and added nonchalantly, "I think he's really worried about you."

A tiny spark of pleasure flickered, but I quashed it. "Sounds more like he's worried about a malpractice suit in case of brain damage."

"Don't be so cynical, Miss Thing."

My eyebrows went sky high at that. "Me? What did you put in this tea, anyway?"

Evan smiled, unperturbed. "Maybe I'm just a believer in true love."

"Since when?"

A leather clad foot, polished to a high shine, swung back and forth. "Since I saw Manny Vittoro naked in the shower back in high school gym class." He sighed. "He's still the love of my life."

I snorted. "Slut."

"Whore," he answered sweetly.

Order restored, we drank our tea in companionable silence.

"So I think you should have the tests."

"So I'm not gonna have the tests."

More silence, broken only by an occasional slurp.

"So I think you should give Joe another chance."

"So I'm not gonna give Joe another chance."

Evan's chair creaked as he leaned back. "So what *are* you gonna do?"

I sighed. "I guess I'm gonna have to go down to the police station."

The chair *thunked* as it came forward again. "You've got to be kidding me."

"Do I look like I'm kidding?" I put down my mug and stood up, stretching the kinks from my neck. "I don't *want* to. But I don't want Caprice haunting me the rest of my days, either. And besides, Mojo shouldn't be there. He didn't kill her. It's not right."

"What are you gonna say? They'll think you're nuts."

"I'll think of something."

"I'm coming with you."

I gave Evan a smile. "I was counting on that, but a cute guy like you might drive those inmates crazy. I've seen that cable show about prison life—*Oz*, or whatever it's called."

Evan gave a delicious little shiver. "Ooooh, now I *have* to go."

We closed the shop early, flipping the sign in the window and locking the door behind us. I stood on the sidewalk and looked across the street at Indigo's, where scraps of yellow crime scene tape flapped from the front steps. Somebody had hosed down the sidewalk, leaving no sign of blood. The place just looked empty and forlorn, like it was wondering where all the life had gone. Business was usually pretty steady, whether weekday or weekend, some of it, I was sure, from a little harmless dealing of weed in the back room. The colorful wind socks Caprice liked to hang from the front porch were still there, twirling in the breeze.

"Hard to believe she's gone." Evan had come up beside me, echoing my thoughts. "She was quite a character."

An involuntary shudder rippled through me. Automatically, I said, "Somebody just walked across my grave."

"Don't say that!" Evan spoke sharply, frowning. "You know I don't like that kind of stuff."

I took his hand and patted him like a child. "Okay, okay. It's just an old expression. Let's go."

The drive took forever, as usual. Atlanta traffic was a nightmare, particularly after four o'clock in the afternoon, and we had to drive north past downtown to get to the jail. We finally crawled into a parking space about an hour later.

Fulton County Jail looked every bit as uninviting as it sounded, at least twelve stories of ugly brick surrounded by barbed wire. I'd used the drive time to think about what to say, but I was still clueless. The best I could come up with was to see if they'd let me in to see Mo and hope for the best.

The lady cop behind the counter at the visitor's station had other ideas.

"You're not on the list."

"What list?"

She gave me a bored look, having obviously been through this too many times to count. "The visitation list for Maurice Brown. He's got three people on here, and you ain't one of 'em."

I turned to Evan. "What now?"

He ignored me.

"Didn't I see you on *Cops* last week?" he said. The woman behind the desk fixed him with a baleful stare. "Listen, Officer—" He leaned over to read her badge. "—Ashante, is it? Doesn't that mean 'African queen'?" No softening in her expression that I could see, but Evan persevered. "Anyway, we're friends of his. He just got here late last night—probably didn't expect to see us today. Isn't there something you could do? Love the hair, by the way."

Since I happened to know Evan thought cornrows were a crime against nature, I kept my mouth shut.

"Only way to bypass the list is if the watch commander approves it," she answered grudgingly.

"Oh, goody." Evan clapped his hands together like a gay homecoming queen. "Could we see him, please?"

She curled her lip in a cynical excuse for a smile. "Sure." Heaving her ample bottom up off the chair, she added, "This oughta be fun." She moved to pick up a red phone hanging from the wall behind her and muttered something into the receiver, glancing over her shoulder as she listened to the other person's reply. The smirk on her face got bigger. When she hung up the phone, she gestured toward the blue plastic chairs that lined the room. "Sergeant Stone will be right out. Take a seat."

"Sergeant Stone?" I murmured the name under my breath as we gingerly did as she asked. The chairs were old and streaked with unidentifiable stains. "That doesn't sound too promising."

Evan patted me on the knee. "Not to worry—I've gotten us this far, haven't I? Let me do the talking."

I was happy to, especially when a buzzer sounded, releasing the lock on the metal door that led inside the jail. It opened, and a man stood there who would have intimidated the bravest of the brave.

Easily six foot something, coal black skin and bulging muscles that distorted his uniform in every conceivable way. Heavy black belt loaded with a radio, nightstick, handcuffs, and, of course, a big ol' gun on one hip. Next to me, I heard Evan's gasp, and thought we were done for.

Oddly enough, Sergeant Stone took one look at us and went dead still for several seconds. Then, without missing a beat, he glanced at the lady cop behind the counter.

"Let 'em in." Even his voice sounded like gravel.

Then he turned around and faced the metal door, waiting until she'd buzzed him back inside the bowels of the place.

Officer Ashante looked as shocked as I felt. I turned to Evan and whispered, "What was that all about?"

Evan smoothed a strand of blond hair behind an ear, shooting me a coy look beneath his lashes.

"Don't ask, don't tell," was all he said.

"Oh, jeez."

"Here's your visitor's pass." Officer Ashante slapped two yellow pieces of paper down on the counter with ill grace, along with a two bright orange keys. "Sign the book and put your valuables in the locker over there. You're subject to search, and can and will be charged if any contraband is found."

Evan didn't budge. "I'll wait here, Nicki. I've had enough excitement for one day. You go ahead. Tell Mojo I'm pulling for him."

"Gee, thanks."

I picked up the yellow visitor's pass, peeled off the backing and stuck it to my shirt, signed the book, then put my purse in the locker, tossing Evan the key. The lady cop heaved herself up again and gave me a cursory pat-down while I dared Evan with my eyes not to giggle. Then she buzzed me in, and I entered a world I hoped never to enter again.

It was a big room, industrial and echoing. Somebody had obviously made an attempt at some point to make it friendlier by painting it a pale shade of blue, but the blue had faded to gray and the fluorescent lighting gave it a harsh look. There were tables scattered around, most filled with men in orange jumpsuits visiting with wives or girlfriends. It smelled like sweat and disinfectant. I was led to a long table at the far end of the room with a Plexiglas screen down the middle and little dividers between the chairs that gave an illusion of privacy. A single door was on the other side on the Plexiglas.

I sat down and waited, trying not to listen to the guy in a blue suit at the far end—obviously an attorney—argue with his client about hearsay evidence, or something like that. I stared at the round metal grille cut into the Plexiglas in front of me and tried to think about lying on a beach somewhere with a tropical drink, far away from this noisy, depressing place.

After a few minutes the door opened, and there was Mojo, handcuffed and orange-clad. He looked sullen and red-eyed, dreadlocks drooping. The deputy escorting him waited until he took a seat, then removed the handcuffs and left the area. I heard the snick of the electronic bolt as the door closed behind him.

"Hey, Mo." I kept my voice low.

"What are you doing here, Nicki?" Mo didn't look too happy to see me. "If you came to talk about Caprice—" He hesitated, swallowing hard. "If you came to talk about Caprice, I ain't allowed to. Lawyer says don't talk to nobody." He looked away, blinking rapidly as he leaned back in the chair.

"I know you didn't kill her, Mojo." I'd already decided on the direct approach. "I'm here to help you."

Mo looked back at me and shook his head. "How you gonna help me, little girl? You wasn't even there. You don't know nothin' about it."

I leaned in closer, speaking as close to the grille as I could. "I know because Caprice told me."

That brought him upright, but slowly. He eyed me warily, obviously wondering what I was talking about.

"I know this is gonna sound crazy. I know you're probably not gonna believe me any more than anybody else will, but it's true. I saw Caprice last night, Mo. Twice. After she . . . after she died."

The skeptical look I was expecting was there. "You saw Caprice?"

"It's true. The first time was on the street, right

after it happened. I'd been to the Vortex and followed the fire truck because I was worried about
the shop. She was right there, standing next to
me."

Mojo was listening, saying nothing.

"Then she came to my house in the middle of
the night." I'd swear he paled, his dark skin going
a sickly ash color. "She told me about the other
woman, and what happened on the stairs. She
wants me to get you out."

There was silence while Mo stared me down. I
met his eye, not looking away. When he spoke, his
voice was low and urgent.

"You got to get rid of her, Nicki. You got to get
rid of her now."

That was the last thing I expected to hear. I sat
back, temporarily at a loss for words.

Mo leaned in, glancing around uneasily. "You
don't know what you messing with here, girl. That
thing ain't Caprice—it's a duppy. You need to go to
a mambo and get rid of it, quick."

I felt like I was in the middle of a bad movie and
the actors had just started speaking in code.

"What are you talking about? She wants me to
help you."

He stood up, signaling toward the camera mount-
ed near a corner of the ceiling. Then he leaned in
one more time, putting his mouth close to the grille.

"Don't come here no more. It can't reach me here
. . . it's too far, but I ain't taking no chances."

It?

The door behind Mojo opened and a deputy
stood there, waiting. Mo turned and walked away
without another word. I watched in stunned silence
as the handcuffs were put back on his wrists, then
the deputy took him by the arm and led him away.
He didn't look back, and the door closed behind
him with a snick of finality.

CHAPTER 5

What the hell was a "duppy"? Or a "mambo"?

Evan had been no help, as he thought one was a fish and the other some kind of dance step. We'd discussed it over egg drop soup and lemon chicken at our favorite Chinese place, to no avail.

So I did what any twenty-first century girl would do, and turned to the Internet. After Evan dropped me off in Little Five Points to pick up my car, I drove home and poured myself a glass of wine. Then I turned on my laptop and settled myself in the middle of the bed to do some serious searching.

My first pass on *duppy* turned up little except

the title of a famous Bob Marley song, "Duppy Conqueror," which at least told me I was going in the right direction. *Mambo* did indeed appear to be some kind of dance, which threw me off again. I went back to Bob Marley, did a lot of skimming, finally hit pay dirt.

"A duppy is an 'evil spirit' that once inhabited a human's body." A definite chill went down my spine as I said the words aloud. I read further. "According to Jamaican folklore, all people have a dark piece of the soul that in life is restrained by the will. In death, that restraint can be ignored."

Well, wasn't that just lovely? I suddenly remembered all those religious candles and handmade charms Caprice had always claimed were for the tourists. Maybe there'd been more going on in the back room of Indigo than a little ganja dealing.

Almost afraid of what I might find, I typed *Jamaican voodoo* into the search engine and kept digging. Within minutes I'd discovered that a mambo was a voodoo priestess, the female equivalent of a "houngan"—a voodoo priest.

"Oh, shit."

Nagging little Jewish ladies were one thing, but evil spirits and voodoo were another. This was seriously creepy stuff.

A call to Evan was in order, but as I reached for the phone I noticed the answering machine light was blinking, and hit PLAY MESSAGES instead.

"Nicki, it's Joe Bascombe. I know you don't want to see me, but I'd like a chance to explain. Please call me back." A pause, then, "I'm worried about you." Another pause. "I'd like to see you." Dead air. "Please." Then the click as he hung up.

He must have gotten my phone number from hospital records, or else Evan had given it to him. After the soap opera sympathy routine Evan had given me this afternoon, I wouldn't put it past him.

I'd really liked Joe and would've enjoyed loosening him up. He had kind eyes—and a great butt. But I don't do "married."

Dialing Evan's number, I put aside thoughts of my nonexistent love life and focused on my more immediate problem.

"Hello?" Evan's voice had a lilt that told me he was expecting a caller other than me.

"It's voodoo, Evan. Mojo was talking about voodoo."

He made an exasperated noise. "You don't believe in that stuff, do you?"

"I don't know. I didn't believe in ghosts, either—until I started seeing them. According to what Mo said, I need to go see a voodoo priestess to get rid of an evil spirit."

"Sounds like Mo's been smokin' something besides weed, Nick. This is crazy."

Morosely, I answered, "Yeah, I know." I hesitated, then added. "Maybe *I'm* crazy."

"If you're crazy then I'm a choirboy in the Mormon Tabernacle Choir," he snapped. "Now put the computer away and go to bed. Too much surfing on the Internet can make you believe anything—remember when I had a sinus infection and convinced myself it was brain cancer?"

I ignored his logic and asked, "Will you go with me?"

"Nicki, you know I love you, but the only black magic I'm interested in is six-foot-three and works at the county jail. And even I'm not fool enough to go back for seconds. Go to bed. We'll figure something else out tomorrow."

Sensing I wasn't going to get anywhere tonight as far as Evan was concerned, I gave in. "Okay. Nighty-night. Don't let the bedbugs bite."

Evan hung up after his traditional response. "Bite this."

Having had a phobia about bugs since childhood, he always hated it when I did that. Which meant I did it all the time.

I took his advice, though, and turned off the laptop. Then I got ready for bed and settled in early, hoping to catch up on lost sleep.

As soon as I turned out the light, she was there.

I smelled her first—that mixture of tropical fruits

and coconut that always reminded me of piña coladas. Caprice applied body lotion to her caramel-colored skin every day, saying it reminded her of home.

"Caprice?"

My eyes hadn't adjusted yet, so I saw nothing but darkness. I reached for the bedside lamp.

"Leave it off, girl. I like it better this way."

I swallowed hard, willing my voice not to quiver. "I don't. I don't like any of this, Caprice. I think you should go away and leave me alone."

A heavy sigh. "No can do, bebe. You the only one who can help me—help my man, that is. Can't nobody else help me no more."

"I tried to help Mo, Caprice. He won't even talk to me." I was afraid to tell her why. "He told me not to come back."

Silence.

I ventured a question. "Why don't you want me to turn on the light?"

"Day for you, night for me," she answered cryptically. "Go see that skinny 'ho, Felicia. Tell her you'll go to DFCS about them kids of hers and get 'em taken away if she don't tell the truth."

This was getting worse and worse. "You want me to blackmail somebody by threatening to have her kids taken away? I'm not gonna do that, Caprice."

This time the silence sounded ominous.

"Don't make me mad, Nicki." Caprice's whisper came from right beside my ear. "You was my friend once. Be my friend now."

I jumped out of bed so fast I nearly tripped on my way to the light switch, and flipped it up, flooding the room with brightness. I turned around, afraid of what I might see.

There was no one there.

High fever, abdominal pain, delirium, sudden onset.

That's all the information I could get from the emergency room nurse after rushing down there at three in the morning. Evan's friend Butch had called a half hour earlier, telling me Evan was sick and asking me to meet him at the hospital. Thank God Evan always listed me as his next of kin or the old battle-ax nurse behind the counter wouldn't even have told me that much.

I left her at the main desk, pushing her papers with a sour expression on her face, and went into the waiting area. Sure enough, sitting in a chair that looked far too small for him was a worried-looking behemoth in jeans and a leather jacket, shaved head gleaming under the harsh fluorescent lights.

"Butch?" The giant stood, nodding. "I'm Nicki. What's wrong with Evan? What happened?"

He rubbed the top of his bald head as though it helped him think. "I don't know—it all happened so fast."

I sat in the empty chair next to him, and he sank back down. "I was asleep. He woke me up, thrashing and screaming. At first I just thought he was having a bad dream."

Joe strode through the double doors marked NO VISITORS PAST THIS POINT and into the waiting room, looking harried and professional in his blue scrubs, stethoscope looped around his neck. Just my luck. Of *course* he'd be on call tonight, of all nights. He glanced at me briefly, but focused on Butch.

"You the guy who brought in Evan Owenby?"

Butch shot up from his seat. "Is he all right? What's the matter with him?"

"We're not sure yet, Mister . . .?"

"Carson. Butch Carson."

"I need to ask you a few questions, Mr. Carson, if you don't mind. It might help me find out what's wrong with Evan."

Exactly what I wanted to know, so I kept quiet and let the two of them talk.

"Sure, sure. Anything you need."

Joe gestured toward the chairs before taking a seat. Goliath sat down as well, looking more worried than ever.

"Can you tell me what you were doing just before Evan got sick?"

The guy actually blushed, a dull red flush spreading from his cheeks to where his hairline would have been. "Well, we were sleeping, actually." He seemed to take courage from Joe's carefully neutral expression. "We'd been out earlier, had a few drinks, and then, well"—he gestured vaguely—"you know. Anyway, Evan was fine all night, just fine. Until he woke up screaming." Butch looked bewildered. "One minute we were sound asleep, then he was screaming. When I tried to calm him down, I felt how hot his skin was, then he started moaning about his stomach hurting. I turned on the light, and he was just out of it, man—you know what I mean?"

Joe answered carefully. "I'm not sure I do."

"His eyes were rolling around like he was crazy . . . he kept saying 'day for you, night for me,' or something like that."

My blood ran cold. *It couldn't be.*

"He curled up in a ball, and every time I got near him he'd scream, until I finally convinced him it was okay. Then I just picked him up and put him in the car and brought him here."

"Any drugs, Mr. Carson? Anything at all other than alcohol?"

Butch shook his head vehemently. "Evan doesn't

do drugs, Doc, and neither do I. Just a few drinks, not even that many. He was fine when we went to sleep."

Joe sat back.

"Thanks, Mr. Carson. I'll let you know as soon as I have an idea of what's going on." The big man nodded, gnawing at his lower lip.

"I wanna see him." Those were my first and only words to Joe.

Joe shook his head. "I gave him a sedative. He's sleeping."

"Take me to him or I'll go looking for him myself," I threatened.

He tried to stare me down, but gave in pretty easy. "You would, wouldn't you?" He sighed, then stood up. "C'mon, then."

I followed him through the double doors.

The familiar smells of fear and sickness stalked the corridors and permeated the air. All the cleaning fluid in the world wouldn't get rid of them. It suddenly struck me that I'd been here myself less than a week ago, unconscious and totally oblivious to all this activity. The place was an antiseptic beehive, people in scrubs moving in and out of curtained cubicles, all moving fast and looking like they knew what they were doing.

I could hear moaning behind a curtain. Joe moved it aside slightly, then stuck his head in and spoke to whoever was there. "My guess is indigestion, Mr. Martinez, but we'll run some tests to make sure. Enchiladas with hot sauce is hardly the best choice for a midnight snack. The nurse will give you an esophageal cocktail and see if that helps. If it doesn't, we'll set you up for cardiac tests with Dr. Quinn."

A nurse came up and handed Joe a chart. "Lab work on 3B, Dr. Bascombe."

"Thanks, Nadine—nobody can bully those guys in the lab like you can." Joe scanned the chart and signed it quickly. "Hematuria . . . probably a kidney infection. Tell Ms. Thompson I'll be in to explain the results in five minutes." He passed the chart to the nurse and kept walking, me trying to stay out of the way and keep up at the same time. The medical personnel behind the scenes in the emergency room obviously worked harder than the nurse who manned the front desk.

"I take it you're still mad at me," Joe said, pausing outside a door at the end of a short corridor.

I gave him a fake smile, in no mood to debate the issue.

"I'm not mad. I'd have to give a damn to be mad."

He acknowledged the jab with the slight lift of an eyebrow, but evidently decided not to go there.

"Evan's in here," he said instead. He pushed

open the door and held it for me. "I'll tell the nurse you can stay."

Evan looked awful. He was pale, hair damp with sweat. His eyes were closed, one hand clutching at his stomach even in sleep.

I sat beside him and held his hand, knowing he'd do the same for me. Evan was rarely sick, the occasional flu or maybe a hangover. This time I didn't know what was wrong, and I sure as hell didn't know how to fix it. Chicken soup and Bloody Marys were no good to me now. It was a helpless feeling, and I didn't like feeling helpless.

Around seven in the morning he opened his eyes and looked at me blankly.

"How ya doin', superstud?" I made myself smile, reaching to smooth the hair from his forehead.

He flinched, and I drew back my hand, shocked. Then recognition set in, and to my horror, tears filled those big blue eyes.

"Don't let her touch me, Nicki. Make her go away."

He sounded so pitiful I almost started crying myself. I reached out again and touched his hair, still holding his hand tightly in my own.

"*Shh,* sweetie . . . *shh.* It's okay. Everything's okay. You're sick, that's all."

"If she touches me, I'll die. She said I would."

A chair creaked from the other side of the bed as Butch leaned in and took Evan's other hand. "It's okay, baby. Butchie's here. Nobody's gonna hurt you. You're not gonna die."

Evan closed his eyes, tears seeping from beneath closed lids. Butch looked at me helplessly.

"Oh my God, Nicki." Evan gave a low moan. "How can you stand to look at her?"

When Butch told me on the phone that Evan was sick and talking crazy, I'd put it down to a high fever or something. But as I could feel for myself, the fever was gone. His skin was cool beneath my fingers.

"Evan, you're sick. You had a bad dream. Go back to sleep and we'll stay with you, okay?"

He shook his head back and forth on the pillow. "It wasn't a dream." The three of us sat in awkward silence for a few moments, then Evan gave an audible sniff and opened his eyes. "For heaven's sake, somebody hand me a tissue."

Butch jumped on the assignment, while I raised the head of the bed so Evan was nearly sitting. He wiped his eyes and nose, then gave Butch a sweet smile.

"You've been here all night?"

Butch nodded, a worried look on his face.

Evan patted those big, hairy knuckles and said, "You're such a love. Go home and get some sleep. Nicki will stay with me."

When Butch looked uncertain, he added, "You know you need your beauty sleep. You have to work the door tonight at the club. I'll be fine, I promise."

"You'll call me later?"

"I will. Now go on, you big brute. There's only room for one baby here, and I'm it."

Obviously reluctant, Butch did as he was told. He asked me directly, "You'll call me right away if he gets any worse?"

His devotion was touching. I found myself happy for Evan and slightly envious at the same time. "I promise."

As soon as the door closed behind him, Evan took a final swipe at his nose. His hands were shaking. Then he took a deep breath and looked me in the eye.

"It was no bad dream. It was Caprice."

"Evan, I—"

"Wipe that skeptical look off your face and listen to me. I believed you, didn't I?"

That shut me up.

"She was right there, standing beside the bed. I even smelled that awful pineapple-y lotion she uses." The hair on the back of my neck prickled, and there was a faint buzzing in my ears. "I was petrified . . . I couldn't move . . . like I was paralyzed or something. She said she was there to give you a message." The tissue Evan was holding rapidly became a twisted, soggy mess. I handed him another without thinking.

"She said it was a lesson on friendship, or something like that." He shook his head, looking scared. "She said, 'You tell Nicki, "Day for you, night for me," and if she don't help me she'll be sorry.' Then she leaned in—" Evan squeezed his eyes shut, voice quavering. "—and she blew her breath right in my face. It was so hot . . . I could feel it . . . and it smelled awful. Like death."

I was speechless. I took hold of Evan's hand and squeezed it, whether seeking comfort or giving it, I couldn't say. A threat, and a warning. Caprice was free to roam in and out of my life, while I—and those I loved—were asleep and helpless.

Evan opened his eyes, terrified at the memory of what happened to him. "Then I got this sharp pain in my stomach, like somebody'd stabbed me with a knife. I screamed, and Butch woke up, and she was gone. The next thing I know, I was here."

"You . . . you saw her?"

"You know I always sleep with a night-light by the bed. I couldn't see her perfectly, but I saw enough. Oh God, Nicki—it was horrible! Why didn't you tell me how bad she looked?"

The buzzing in my ears got stronger.

"What did she look like?"

If Evan found the question strange, he didn't show it. He was obviously just anxious to get the whole experience off his chest.

"The side of her face was covered in blood. Her head looked lopsided, like it had caved in on itself, you know?" He held the tissue to his mouth, as though he might vomit. "She kept looking at me sideways, the way a big, ugly bird might."

Broken neck. Looked like she'd taken a blow to the head, too. Joe's words came back to me, unbidden.

"When she smiled—" Evan swallowed, obviously fighting to keep his gorge down. "—even her teeth were stained with blood. It wasn't a nice smile, Nicki."

Oh my freaking God. What did I do now?

CHAPTER 6

"I need your help."

Joe looked up from paperwork as I pushed open the door to his office. It was pretty bland, just some file cabinets, a desk, and a couple of chairs—very impersonal.

"Hello to you, too. What's the problem?"

The detached tone was the same he'd use with any patient's family member, I'm sure.

I paused, hand on the doorknob. "It's about Evan."

"His condition was stable last time I checked, even if we're still not sure what the problem is.

We're running tests and I'm keeping him at least another day for observation."

"You're not gonna find out what's wrong with Evan through tests."

I came farther into his office, closing the door behind me. The thought of what I needed to do to keep Evan safe made me a little panicky, but Joe's steadiness could help.

Besides, he kinda owed me. I sneaked a peek at his ring finger. Still no ring.

Joe eyed me cautiously.

"Evan's going to be fine, Nicki. You don't need to worry. We'll take good care of him." He ventured a half smile. "In fact, my guess is he's enjoying all the attention."

I didn't smile back.

Joe sighed. "What's going on, Nicki? If you're still mad about the other night, I'm sorry, but what happened between us," he shot me a pointed glance, "or *didn't* happen—doesn't affect my ability to do my job. Evan's getting the best possible care."

"It's not that."

"Then what is it?"

I hoped humble pie tasted good, because I was about to eat some. "Listen, there's a lot of stuff going on, and I could really use a friend."

Joe sighed again, losing some of his stiffness.

"Sit down, Nicki. Tell me what's wrong."

I plopped down in one of his office chairs and shook my head, staring down at my lap.

"You're not gonna believe me," I murmured. I raised my head and looked at him, begging him to see the truth in my eyes. "It was Caprice. Caprice made Evan sick to make me do what she wants."

Joe's eyebrows went up.

"You see? I knew you wouldn't believe me." I crossed my arms, turning mulish. "Go ask Evan. Ask him what happened."

He answered carefully. "Nicki, Evan was in the grip of a high fever. He was delirious. It's highly unlikely he knew what was going on."

"He's not delirious now. His fever's gone, and so is the pain in his stomach." I said the words defiantly. "Besides, he's scared to death." I leaned forward, intent. "He saw her, Joe. Evan saw Caprice. She made Evan sick to teach me a lesson—to threaten me."

Mildly, Joe asked, "Why would she do that? I thought she was your friend."

My head of steam began to deflate. "Because she wants me to do something I don't wanna do." I looked away, biting my lip. "And because she's evil. She's not the Caprice I used to know. She's . . . she's something else."

Joe's chair creaked as he leaned back.

"Okay. Just for argument's sake, if you really believe this, then what's to be done? How can you fight a—" He waved a hand, uncertain which term to use. "—a ghost?"

I stared at him, trying to read his expression. He kept his face carefully neutral.

"You're just humoring me," I said flatly. "But I don't care. I know what I know."

He stared back, refusing to look away until I did.

I didn't, but I eventually give him an exasperated huff. "I need to go somewhere, and I'm afraid to go alone. Can you humor me long enough to go with me?"

"Depends on where it is."

Here we go.

"I need to find a voodoo priestess."

"You really like trying to shock people, don't you?"

I shot up from the chair. "Yes. Yes, I do. What gave it away, the pink in my hair or the fact I came to an asshole like you for help?" Almost to the door, I flipped him the finger and added, "I like to do this to people, too." A tight smile. "Some people, anyway."

"Dammit, Nicki—" He stood up, obviously annoyed. I expected him to ask me to leave his office. Instead, he said, "All right, all right. I'll help you."

I lowered my hand, watching him suspiciously.

"You will?"

"On two conditions."

"Ah, a catch. I should've known."

Joe spread his hands wide. "Hey, fair's fair. If you want me to go on some sort of a witch hunt, I think I'm entitled to something in return."

"Which is?"

He took a deep breath. "You let me make an appointment for you with a friend of mine, Ivy Jacobson."

"A friend of yours." I repeated the words, waiting for the punch line.

"She's a psychiatrist."

My eyes went wide. "A shrink?"

"She's had experience with situations like yours."

"'Situations like mine'?" I didn't care for the sound of that at all.

"Near death experiences, Nicki. Ivy's done a great deal of research on near death experiences. What would it hurt for you to talk to her, just once?"

I could see it now: "Here, Ms. Styx, take two Prozac and call me in the morning."

"It won't do any good." I tucked my hair behind my ears, crossed my arms. "And I'm not crazy."

"I don't think you're crazy." Joe kept his voice level. "You had a traumatic event . . . why not talk to her? Afraid you might learn something about yourself?"

He'd scored a hit, and he knew it. Green eyes stared at me in challenge.

"And what's the second condition?"

"I take you out to dinner tonight."

I shook my head. "Uh-uh. No way. You're married, remember?"

"You came in here saying you needed a friend. A friend of mine would give me a chance to explain."

Another direct hit.

He followed it up with, "Maybe I'm the one who needs someone to talk to, okay?"

I grinned, surprising us both. He'd played the sympathy card pretty well. "Oldest line in the book. Can't you do any better than that?"

He gave a mock sigh, willing to play along. "All right. I hate to eat in restaurants by myself because women won't leave me alone. They throw themselves at me. With you there, they wouldn't dare."

"That's better," I said.

Why had I run to Joe Bascombe for help?

My last customer of the day had just left, and I locked the door of Handbags and Gladrags behind her, glad to be alone.

I hadn't even thought about it. I just walked out of Evan's room, asked the first nurse I saw where Dr.

Bascombe might be, and went straight to his office.

Most of my friends were the same as Evan's, and hardly likely to accompany me to search down a voodoo priestess. But I hadn't even considered asking any of them. I'd run directly to Joe. The implications were troubling enough, but now I'd agreed to go out to dinner with him.

"You're an idiot, Nicki Styx," I said aloud.

It was early, just after five, but I'd done a good day's worth of business. At least two teenage girls were going to be wearing vintage evening gowns on prom night. Now I stood staring through the storefront window across the street at Indigo. The crime scene tape was gone.

As I watched, the front door opened and a man stepped out. I recognized one of Caprice's many cousins. Acting on impulse, I unlocked the front door and went outside.

"Jimmy! Wait up."

He'd already started down the sidewalk, but stopped when he heard me shout. He looked around and I waved, briefly checking for traffic before darting across the street. As I got closer I could see he looked tired and unhappy. His customary knit cap was flattened to his head instead of tilted at its usual jaunty angle.

"I'm really sorry about Caprice, Jimmy."

He nodded, saying nothing.

I tried again. "She was a good friend." Then I lied. "I'll miss her."

"Yeah, she liked you, too. Said you was real spunky."

I smiled, feeling awkward. What should I say next? *Know a good mambo who can get rid of her for me?*

"The funeral is tomorrow at two. She'd like it if you was there."

Another funeral. Great.

"Wouldn't miss it. Where's it gonna be?"

"Trinity Cemetery on Mills Road. Graveside service. Granny Julep won't have it no other way."

The top of my head tingled. "Granny Julep? I thought she was dead."

Jimmy smiled for the first time, teeth a startling white against the blackness of his skin. "Oh, she alive all right, though she must be near a hundred by now. She too ornery to die."

Must run in the family.

I bit my lip before I could say what I was thinking.

"What about Mojo?"

The smile disappeared from Jimmy's face like it'd never been.

"I hope he rots in hell."

Then he turned and walked away, and I didn't bother to call him back. What else could I say?

Evan Owenby was a dead man.

The second I opened my front door and saw Joe standing there in a dark red shirt, black tuxedo pants, and the famed Valentino jacket, I decided that if Caprice didn't finish Evan off, I would.

Joe looked good enough to eat, and I was suddenly starving.

"I hope you're hungry," he said, cheerful smile in place. He'd combed his hair back instead of parted to the side, and damned if the look didn't suit him.

"You have no idea."

His gaze took in my black beaded top, flouncy tiered skirt, and Lucchese cowgirl boots. "Wow."

"You look pretty 'wow' yourself, Joe. Evan knows his stuff."

Joe actually blushed. "You don't mind I went to the store?"

"Why should I mind? I happen to know that jacket cost a fortune." I grinned, slinging my purse over a shoulder. "My accountant thanks you."

We drove to a Thai place on Newbury Street I'd never been to before, me trying not to breathe too deeply of the great smell of leather upholstery combined with freshly shaved male, and Joe trying to watch the road and hold his own while we talked about the appeal of vintage clothing versus modern fashion.

As we pulled into the parking lot I said, "This is a surprising choice of restaurant. I took you for a meat and potatoes kind of guy."

Joe laughed. "I am. Never eaten Thai food in my life, but it's never too late to try new things, is it?"

"Only when you're dead," I quipped, and immediately regretted it. For a brief while I'd actually forgotten that I wasn't a normal girl out on a normal date. Not that I'd ever been "normal" per se, but now I was a freak of nature who talked to dead people.

Tactfully, Joe said nothing, getting out of the car and coming around to the passenger side to hold the door open for me. I made sure he got a nice flash of leg while I got out.

If I couldn't have him, I could at least make him suffer a little.

The restaurant was all clean lines and contemporary styling, lots of black lacquer and mirrors. Dim lighting and the tinkle of Asian music gave it a nice ambience, and the smells that drifted from the kitchen were heavenly.

"Two Thai beers," Joe told the waiter as soon as we were seated.

"Aren't you just Mr. Take Charge? What if I wanted something else?"

He grinned at me over the flickering candle. "Then I'll drink 'em both myself. I have a feeling I'm gonna need 'em."

"Better order two more, then. And tonight I promise they won't end up on your shoes."

He laughed while I picked up the menu and started browsing.

"Since you've never eaten Thai before, I'll tell you up front that spring rolls are a great appetizer. How far are you willing to go with your interest in new things?"

Joe leaned back, looking relaxed and happy. "I put myself in your hands."

I hid my smile behind the menu. Silly man had best watch what he said. I might be a freak of nature but I was still only human.

"I usually go for a chicken curry, but anything with peanut sauce is worth trying. Here's a beef dish served with either noodles or rice, smothered in some kind of special sauce."

"Smothering's not my thing."

Something in his voice made me glance up. His wide smile had faded to a more introspective one.

The waiter chose that moment to return with our beers, and I took the liberty of ordering appetizers and entrées for us both while he was there. After he'd bowed politely and taken the menus away, I took the direct approach.

"Tell me about your wife."

Joe looked at me. "I guess the small talk's over, huh?"

I didn't answer. The beer tasted good, slightly sweet and slightly sour.

He took a healthy swig of his own, then set it back on the table, rotating the glass slightly as he spoke.

"We met while I was in med school. She was with the Peace Corps, and I was eager to save the world one person at a time. Seemed like a match made in heaven." It would be hard to miss the irony in his voice. "We dated for a year, married when I started my residency." He fell silent.

"And?" No way was he gonna leave me hanging like that.

"Uh-uh." He took another sip of beer. "Your turn. You already know a lot more about me than I do about you. I talk, you talk. It's only fair."

I sighed, exasperated. "Not much to tell, Joe. My parents are dead, and I've never been married. Evan's pretty much all I've got."

"Tell me about your parents, then."

That was easy. The pain of their deaths had faded in the six years since the accident, leaving me with nothing but happy memories.

"Dan and Emily Styx. Best parents ever. Dad was a tie-dyed-in-the-wool ex-hippie who would've moved to Canada to avoid the draft if he hadn't already been too old to fight. I think he was always disappointed he couldn't do it." I smiled, remembering Dad ranting about the evils of war. "Mom adored him. They tried to have kids for years, never could, and adopted me when they were in their early forties."

Joe's gaze sharpened. "You're adopted?"

I nodded. "Spoiled only child of middle-aged parents. House in Ansley Park, private schools, all that stuff. Thank God they were open-minded enough to let me be myself in spite of it." I proved what a bad girl I was by putting both elbows on the table. "Your turn."

He didn't insult me by hesitating. He shrugged and picked up where he left off. "Kelly couldn't handle being a doctor's wife. When you're in residency, your life is at the hospital. You eat, sleep, and breathe it. You're on call for days at a time, exhausted when you're not, consumed with academic peer pressure and dealing with life and death situations on a daily basis. There's not much time for a personal life, much less a new marriage. She wanted to start a family, and I wasn't ready for kids. Our priorities were different."

Our friendly waiter made his way over with a plate of steaming spring rolls and put them on the table, refilling our ice water and taking Joe's order for two more beers. When he left, Joe said, "Your turn."

I helped myself to a roll first, taking my time.

"Mom and Dad were in a car accident when I was twenty-three. I took the insurance money they left me and went into partnership with Evan." I took another bite, swallowing before I added, "We were next-door neighbors when we were kids. He's always been my best friend." A sip of beer to wash it down. "Your turn."

Joe was enjoying the spring rolls, polishing off three in quick succession.

"She got more involved in the Peace Corps. Her assignments took her farther and farther away. Said she had to do something to fill her time. Then one day I got a letter saying that she'd met someone else and wasn't coming back. I haven't heard from her in almost four years."

Interesting—and somewhat fishy. "What about a divorce?"

He shrugged again. "Kinda hard to divorce someone when you can't serve the papers. Third world countries are hardly known for the reliability of their legal systems."

"You seem awfully okay with it." I eyed him over the table while he looked at me blandly.

"After a while it didn't seem to matter one way or another. It's not like I was in any hurry to repeat the same mistake, and I've had my career to keep me busy. My attorney says that if I don't hear from her within a certain time frame, I can have the marriage annulled based on abandonment. Until then, I'm still married."

"And when will that time frame be up?"

"Next year."

The delicious odor of curry met my nose as the waiter placed our dinners in front of us, but I seemed to have lost my appetite. Seems like Joe was free to sleep with anyone he chose—so why hadn't he chosen me when I'd all but unzipped his pants?

"Her name's Kelly?" There was something more here.

Joe took a forkful of his chicken curry, chewing it gingerly before he answered.

"Kelly Charon. Sound familiar?"

"Not at all. Should it?"

He smiled ruefully, as though at a private joke. "Charon was the name of the ferryman who carried lost souls over the river Styx."

"Oh . . . yeah . . . right." Not that it mattered. Feminine curiosity now had me firmly in its grip. "What did she look like?"

Joe put down his fork and dabbed at his forehead with his napkin. I wasn't sure if he was sweating from the curry or because the conversation was beginning to make him nervous. He put the napkin back in his lap and laid both hands on the table.

"She looked a lot like you, actually."

"Like me?"

I wasn't sure I cared for that little fact at all. I wasn't eager to be anybody's "replacement."

He nodded, eyeing me appraisingly. "No pink in the hair, of course."

"Of course," I said acidly. He ignored the comment.

"Kelly wore her hair long. And she was very serious, very politically minded. Didn't have your—" He waved a hand. "—joy of living, shall we say?"

"Oh, let's." This comparison was beginning to tick me off.

"But other than that, she looked enough like you to be your twin."

He paused and took a healthy swig, finishing off the first beer. The empty glass made a solid chunk as it connected with the table.

"In fact, I think she is."

CHAPTER 7

"What the hell are you talking about?"

A twin? That had to be the stupidest thing I'd ever heard. I was an original, and proud of it.

"I'm dead serious, Nicki." I winced at Joe's choice of words. "I thought it was coincidence at first—you looked like her, you're the same age. But it's more. You share some of the same physical traits—" He hesitated while my face flamed. He'd seen me naked in the hospital. "—and even some of the same mannerisms. You're adopted. So was she."

"You actually think I have a twin sister out there, and you're married to her?"

The very idea had something weirdly incestuous about it.

"Oh, and by the way, she disappeared, and you have no idea where she is?"

Who would have ever thought the wholesome Boy Scout routine actually hid a nutbag? The evening was not going well.

Joe looked at me helplessly. "I know it sounds crazy. The resemblance is so amazing I couldn't help but be intrigued. I just didn't know how to tell you."

"How about, 'Gee, Miss Styx, you remind me so much of someone I used to know. My wife, in fact. Do you have a sister?'"

He looked uncomfortable.

"Wait a minute." My heart tripped, reminding me not to lose my temper over this. "You tracked me down after I left the hospital. You lied to me about wanting to do a paper on near death experiences."

"That part's true. I do want to do a paper on NDEs. But it wasn't the only reason I followed you."

I wasn't sure whether to be furious or disappointed. Maybe a little of both. I thought the spark between us had been something more than somebody else's old flame. My ego might never survive.

"Yes, it crossed my mind that if you *were* somehow Kelly's sister, I might be able to find her and put this whole marriage thing behind me." He leaned in, the candle between us flickering. "But to be completely honest, the more I looked at you, the less I thought of Kelly."

His eyes met mine, and I heard something in his voice. Something unspoken that made me believe he was telling the truth. "That dimple in your cheek when you smile—that's all yours. The way you always tuck that pink streak of hair behind your ear—" He smiled suddenly, breaking off. "But I think you might be her sister. And I had to tell you before we went any further with our friendship."

Friendship.

Yeah, friendship. That's what we'd agreed to, wasn't it?

Besides, even unrequited lust couldn't completely erase those middle-class morals Dan and Emily Styx tried so hard to instill. I was pretty sure that sex with a possible brother-in-law was out of the question.

"You do realize how crazy this sounds, don't you?"

To Joe's credit, he didn't argue.

Stubbornly, I insisted, "I'd know if I had a twin sister."

"Not if your parents didn't know. What if they

weren't told? And even if they knew, why would they tell you? Adoption records are sealed—they'd have no way of finding her. Kelly grew up in foster care . . . she moved around a lot. She never mentioned the possibility of a twin sister, either, but that doesn't mean it doesn't exist."

Foster care? What an awful thought. "One final question, and then I'd like to drop this."

Joe waited, saying nothing. The smell of chicken curry would now forever remind me that variety could be overrated—the spice of life sometimes stunk. "Where was she born?"

"Right here in Atlanta."

"I think you need to take me home."

Joe slid his car next to the curb in front of my house and turned the engine off. All the way home we'd both been subdued, absorbed in our thoughts.

"Listen, I'm sorry for all this." He shifted to face me. "I never lied to you, not really. I still want to help you, and I still want to document all the aftereffects of your near death experience. I don't want it to end like this."

We stared at each other in the darkened car, blanketed by privacy and silence. There were all kinds of ethical questions at work here, and not all of them were about getting involved with patients.

Joe took the plunge. "I'm attracted to you, and

unless I'm way wrong, you're attracted to me."

Attracted wasn't the word. Why the hell was forbidden fruit always the sweetest?

"I'm not interested in being anybody's replacement."

His face was pale in the darkness, eyes inscrutable. "I'm not looking for a replacement, Nicki. You're you, and I'm me—and we just happened to meet. My marriage is over, has been for years. I had to tell you the truth before things went any further, in case . . ." Joe's voice trailed off.

I felt myself weakening, so I unfastened my seat belt and reached for the door.

Joe gave it one more shot.

"Can I come up?"

There it was, then. All laid out on the table.

And here I was, suddenly very sick of looking at the menu without being able to eat.

On impulse, I leaned toward him, trying hard not to think. His hand rested on the console between us, and I trapped it there with my body, feeling his arm tense. The dark cherry chocolate smell of his aftershave sent heat to pool between my legs.

I put my hand on his chest and he didn't move except to breathe. I let him feel my weight and wonder at my intentions. My eyes slid to his mouth as I answered his question with a question.

"If I kissed you right now"—my breath was

a mere inch from his lips—"would you think of her?"

Joe took his time answering, holding himself in check as I brushed my nose ever so gently with his.

"I don't know," he said.

"An honest answer." I was glad he hadn't said no. If he had, I would've never believed him, and I'd never get my kiss.

His honesty was rewarded with a brush of my lips against his cheek, followed by a whispered question in his ear.

"Would you like to find out?"

How I managed to hold on long enough to tease him I wasn't sure—if I didn't kiss him soon, I was going to incinerate.

"Yes," he breathed.

The single word slipped into my mouth and stole the oxygen from my brain.

I kissed him, long and deep, exploring the texture of his lips and the taste of his tongue. He let it happen, kissing me back, while I thought of nothing except how good it was. And when it was over and I pulled away, hand on his shoulder, it was all I could do not to kiss him again.

He was quiet, breathing fast.

In a voice that was only slightly unsteady, I murmured, "Who am I to you?"

"You're an incredibly sexy woman," his voice was husky with strain, "and one I can't stop thinking about."

I gave him a shaky grin. "I'm about to do something totally out of character, Joe." I reached for the purse between my knees. "I think it's called 'the right thing.'"

Then I got out of the car and went inside.

Holy shit.

What had I done?

I'd just heard I might have a twin sister, and instead of being thrilled at the possibility, I already knew I hated her.

She'd thrown Joe away, and I'd kissed him.

I unlocked the door to my house and flooded it with light. I was already shaken up, but there was still Caprice to deal with. I went from room to room until every bulb in the place was on, determined to stay up all night if I had to.

Then I called the hospital to check on Evan. Butch was there, treating his new boyfriend like a queen. I was glad. Right now Evan needed more TLC than I could give him.

"How's the big baby doing?"

"Never you mind about Butch," Evan drawled into the phone, "and I'm feeling much better, thank you." He sounded better. "I slept most of the afternoon, the pain in my stomach is gone—I'm ready to go home tomorrow."

Butch murmured a comment in the background, and Evan said, "I might stay a few nights in Peachtree City, even take some time off."

"Good idea. Whatever you need. Tomorrow's Sunday, anyway." I was relieved. Life in the Atlanta suburbs was probably boring as hell, but it was safer. He didn't need to be near me or the store right now.

"Your cute doctor was in to see me today." Evan couldn't keep the gleeful pleasure from his voice. "He told me you were having dinner together tonight."

"We did, and guess what?" I tried to keep my voice upbeat and cheery. "He told me that he thinks the woman he's married to is my twin sister." Silence. "He says she was adopted, too, and used to live in Atlanta. And oh, by the way, she disappeared four years ago and he has no way to contact her."

A strangled noise made it through the phone.

"He says her name is Kelly."

"Are you serious," Evan gasped, "or are you drunk?"

I laughed, *wishing* I was drunk, but those days were behind me. My fluttery ticker had enough to deal with.

"*He* was serious."

"Well, what did you do? What did you say?" Evan's voice was rising. The TV went silent. "Stop making me drag it out of you, woman, and tell me everything!"

"I asked him to bring me home—" I hesitated. "And then I kissed him."

More silence. Then Evan said with certainty, "You *do* like him."

Even though Evan was in high drama queen mode, and deservedly so, he knew me best.

"Yeah."

"But he thinks he's married to the twin sister you didn't know you had, and nobody knows where she is?"

"That's it."

"Holy shit."

"That's what I'm talking about."

There wasn't a lot more to say. I could picture Butch hovering in the background, and I'd given Evan enough to curl his toes, so I decided to let them get back to their domestic bliss.

"I'm okay, really. Weird stuff seems to be the norm these days," I joked. "Just had to tell you or I'd never get to sleep. Will you call me tomorrow when you're settled in with Butch? All right, nighty-night." I didn't have the heart to throw in any bugs tonight, and hung up feeling better.

A sister. I might have a sister. It was almost too much to wrap my mind around. While I'd been having tea parties with Evan and painting my bedroom purple, she'd been shuffled from house to house and family to family.

I wandered into the room that used to be Mom and Dad's. It was a guest room now, because I couldn't bear to sleep in the bed they used to share. I'd done some redecorating over the years . . . new bedspread and curtains, a new rug. The notches in the door frame were still there, though, a lasting reminder of the growth spurts of my childhood. I tried to imagine two sets of notches. Would a sister have left her mark on this house the way I had?

I frowned, both liking and not liking the thought. Bad enough she'd left her mark on Joe.

My lips still tingled from that kiss.

After a long, hot shower, some flannel pajamas, and a cup of Red Zinger tea, I'd stopped thinking about Joe's kiss and what—if anything—I was going to do about it. My love life was over anyway, as long as an evil spirit could go after those I cared about.

As for the possibility of a twin sister, the drama and the trauma of that little situation would have to wait.

I needed to learn more about duppies.

With the drone of TV to keep me company, I

spent some quality time with my new best friend, the Internet. A few eyestrained hours later I'd learned more than I ever wanted to know about "shadow catchers" and "soul stealers," and read a myriad of stories about Jamaican voodoo ceremonies and superstitions. It was a secretive and scary world. I'd hoped differently, but it seemed I had no choice but to seek the help of one of the Obeah people, the voodoo priests or priestesses.

"I hope I don't get hexed into wearing a Rasta cap and pedal pushers," I muttered, "or mugged in some dark alley."

At least now I had a valid reason to go to Caprice's funeral. Caprice wasn't dead to me, although I'd already ceased to think that what was left was really, *truly* Caprice, either. Granny Julep could help me, I was sure. I just had to find a way to speak to her alone.

"Nicki."

I couldn't see Caprice, but I could hear her whisper. I scanned the room, back of my neck prickling.

"I'm over here, Nicki." The whisper came from a corner of the hall, the only pocket of shadow in the house. "Come closer."

I didn't like her tone, and no way was I leaving that couch. Creeping around in the dark was not my thing.

I gathered my nerve and yelled at her just the way I wanted to—no matter how stupid that idea might be. "How could you do that to Evan, Caprice? He was your friend, too."

"Evan was never my friend." A low laugh came from the shadows. "He never had time for me. He was *your* candy-ass little friend. I just scared him some. I coulda done worse."

"That's not the way to get my help."

"Then what is?" I heard the sharp hiss of frustration in her words. "Get Mo out of jail, or you won't like what happens next."

There was something ugly there, hiding in the hall. It wasn't Caprice—it was something evil. Fear tripped down my spine.

I fought back panic. Running away would do no good—I had to get rid of it. "I'm working on Mojo's release," I lied. "I hired a lawyer for him."

Things got very quiet. What if it knew I was lying? I was terrified it might step from the corner.

"You have to give me time." I sat on my hands to keep them from shaking, but there wasn't a whole lot I could do about my voice. "You can't keep freaking me out at night and expecting miracles the next day. And you can't hurt or threaten Evan." I let her hear how determined I was about that. "That's it."

The sickly sweet smell of rotted fruit filled the

air— bruised bananas and sour pineapples, melons left too long in the sun. I heard her whisper, "Don't take too long." A sigh. "I'm tired."

Good. With any luck she'd eventually fade away. Right now I'd just like a break from having the shit scared out of me.

"I promised I'd help you, Caprice."

My laptop flew across the room, smashing against a framed print on the wall in an explosion of glass. I shrieked, watching as both print and computer fell to the floor in a jagged heap of broken shards and bent frames. The laptop screen gave a few frantic flickers before it died.

"Damn right you will."

I let Caprice's whispered pronouncement be the last word.

I huddled on the couch and stayed there, wide awake, the rest of the night. When dawn came, I gratefully stumbled to bed and slept, blinds wide open, until noon.

I needed the nap, because I still had a funeral to attend.

In the end, I didn't have to find a way to get Granny Julep alone. She came to me.

Trinity Cemetery was one of Georgia's oldest graveyards, a tangled garden of headstones on a sunny hillside. The sky overhead was a cloudless blue, and a clapboard church stood at the grave-yard entrance, the triple crosses on the steeple like beacons to the wandering or lost.

At least fifty people came to Caprice's funeral. Most black, some crying, some not. Almost all of them were holding a single white flower. The graveside service was simple, just a long prayer led by an elderly black minister, and then the flowers were tossed on the coffin as it was lowered by men holding onto heavy straps. There was silence as the straps were removed and the men stepped back from the grave and picked up shovels. A bird trilled from one of the steepled crosses, an ordinary event made awe-inspiring by circumstance. One woman started a hymn and everyone joined in. Other songs followed, the woman leading each chorus, and no one stopped singing—not even the men who shoveled dirt on the grave—until the last shovelful of dirt fell and the grave was covered, nearly ten minutes later. It was very spiritual, and very solemn.

I stood by a weathered headstone and listened, trying to reconcile this peaceful farewell for a good woman gone too soon against the evil thing I knew Caprice had become.

As people turned away, the service complete, I stayed, watching an old woman in white who stood by the grave. She was ancient and stooped, by far the oldest woman there. Her gray hair was braided tight and wound into a rope crown atop her head. She saw me staring, and stared right back. When an elderly black man tried to take her by the elbow, she shrugged him off. Then she made her slow way around the headstones and came directly to me.

"You a friend to Caprice?" Her face was seamed with wrinkles, made deeper as she squinted at me in the sunshine.

"Yes, I'm Nicki." I shook her knobby-fingered hand carefully, noticing a piece of brown string tied around her wrist. "I own the store across the street from Indigo."

"That's nice. Now tell Granny Julep what you want."

So much for subtlety.

"I need a mambo."

Granny Julep nodded knowingly. "The jumbies don't leave you alone, do they?"

I blinked. *Jumbies* was a Caribbean word for spirits. How could she know?

"You one of the four-eyed, yeah," she added decisively. "I see the flutters all around you."

"The four-eyed?" I hadn't worn glasses since Lasik surgery. My vintage Carrera shades were nothing but a fashion statement.

"They know you can hear them if they try hard enough." The old woman looked not at me but to the air, eyes measuring. "They hovering 'round you like bees to honey."

"Great." Just what I needed to hear.

"Don't worry, girl . . . you on hallowed ground. It makes them weak. No need to fear the ones that were put to rest good and proper."

On the bright side, it appeared I'd found my Obeah woman.

Granny Julep smiled. "You got to learn to tune them out, girl. They're drawn to your energy, but that don't mean you got to give it to them."

The old lady was either as crazy as I was or she knew what she was talking about. Either way, it was strangely comforting.

"What if they try to take it anyway?"

Her smile faded. "Is that why you here?"

I nodded. There was a stone bench in the grass a few steps away, and I brushed off a few twigs while I considered how to tell this frail old lady that her recently deceased granddaughter had become one of the walking dead. I offered Granny Julep a seat and she took it, settling her birdlike body with a grateful sigh.

Most of the mourners were gone now, only a few cars still at the church. An elderly black man waited patiently in the parking lot, leaning on a fender and smoking a cigarette.

"It's Caprice, Granny Julep. Caprice won't leave me alone. Her spirit's not quiet."

Her wrinkled face turned to marbled stone.

"Something bad's happened to her."

"Of course something bad happened to her," Granny Julep snapped. "She done been murdered by the man she loved—ain't no wonder her spirit's not quiet." She blinked back angry tears while I waited, silent. Then she dabbed her eyes and nodded her gray head. "I knew she was still here. I felt it. But we'll take care of Caprice during the nine-night." The old woman reached out to pat my hand in absent comfort. "She'll be home with Jesus by the time the last setup is over."

I'd read about the Jamaican custom of nine-night. Mourners hold get-togethers, called "setups," to remember the deceased. The ninth night after the burial is the big blowout farewell, when the dearly departed are finally sent on their way with extravagant good wishes and excruciating hangovers. The Caribbean way of putting spirits to rest was apparently by partying them to death.

I was thrilled to hear it, but I was afraid it wasn't enough.

"There's more, Granny. She's trying to make me

do something . . . something I can't do. She threatened to hurt my friend. She made him so sick he ended up in the hospital."

Granny Julep's look turned dark. I saw myself reflected in the muddy pools of her eyes, and suddenly wondered if Caprice had learned more than just jerk chicken recipes at her grandmother's knee. This old woman was hardly the wild-eyed voodoo priestess I'd envisioned, but she had a disturbing edge nonetheless.

"You don't know what you're talking about, girl." I was tempted to get the hell out of Trinity Cemetery as quick as I could, but I'd gone too far to turn back now. "Why would Caprice do somethin' like that?"

"She wants me to get Mojo out of jail."

"Now I know you're lyin'." Granny Julep struggled to lift herself off the stone bench. I would have helped her, but she waved me off, gaining her feet on her own. "That man killed her. They's at least three people who saw him do it. Why would Caprice want that cheatin', low-down *cochon gris* to go free?"

I didn't need a translator to tell me Mojo would get no sympathy here. Three actual eyewitnesses?

Lesson number one: Never agree to help a pissed-off ghost without checking the facts first.

Why *would* Caprice want her murderer to go free?

Granny Julep turned and started toward the parking lot, obviously dismissing me.

"She doesn't like the light," I blurted.

The old woman paused.

"She hides in the shadows and creeps around in the dark. She won't let me see her." I swallowed, hesitating. "There's a bad smell—like something rotten."

Granny Julep looked up at the sky, as if by admiring the cloudless blue she could ignore the ugliness of my words.

"Caprice was my friend once." I spoke to the old woman's back, desperate to make her understand. "But now she's something different—something evil." A heartbeat or two later, I added, "Mojo says she's a duppy."

I thought for a moment that Granny Julep would say nothing, that she'd make her careful way around the weathered headstones and down to the car. I'd already made up my mind to let her go. The woman deserved to grieve her granddaughter in peace.

Instead, she turned around, movements slow and measured. Silent tears wet her cheeks.

"I done told that girl not to mess with the Sect Rouge," she murmured. There was both guilt and sorrow in her raisin-brown eyes. "That kind of power comes with a terrible price." She gave a low moan, covering her face with gnarled hands that shook. I was at her elbow again in two seconds flat, easing her back toward the stone seat.

All I needed was to have an old lady with a dark side die on me in the middle of the graveyard. Talk about bad juju.

Now that she took me seriously, Granny Julep wanted to know all. She blew her nose into a scrap of yellowed lace while I told her everything that happened since I first saw Caprice on the street. It was a relief to talk about it with someone who didn't question my sanity.

"Caprice must have been powerful mad when she passed," Granny said. "Baron Samedi don't come when he's called unless he's promised a soul in return—she know that."

"Baron who?"

She flicked me a look of irritation. "Never mind, girl. All you need to know is that Caprice done sold her soul to the devil." She frowned into her lap, concentrating as she plucked at the string on her wrist. "She's bound herself here."

"How do I get rid of her? And why isn't she haunting Mojo instead of bothering me?"

"Her spirit can't go as far as the jail—it needs to stay close to where she died," Granny murmured, still absorbed in her thoughts.

I stood up, having had enough of doom and

gloom in the afternoon. The cemetery was beginning to close in on me, and it would be dark again in a few hours.

"I don't have the power to get Mojo out of jail," I said. "I'm not a lawyer. I'm not anybody. It isn't fair what Caprice is doing to me." I was getting angry, and desperate. "No offense, but this stuff scares me shitless. If you loved your granddaughter as much as she loved you, you'll help me put her to rest."

"'Course I'll help my Caprice," Granny snapped, "but I'll do it for *her*, and not for some snip of a girl that show me disrespect and use profanity here"—she made a quick gesture with one gnarled hand—"in the shadow of the name of the Lord." She sat as righteously straight-backed as the headstones surrounding us. "This is hallowed ground, girl. Watch your mouth."

I bit my lip and looked away, searching for patience. My eye landed on the church steeple with its triple crosses. I couldn't deny that there was a kind of Presence here on this quiet hillside, maybe even the same Presence that sent me back to do unto others.

Angels and demons? Voodoo? What the hell did I know?

"I'm sorry, Granny Julep." I bit my lip and stared at my shoes, the black leather walking boots that were my favorite. "I shouldn't have said that."

She glared at me a moment more, then gave a regal nod of her braid-crowned head. Then she gave me her hand, obviously willing to forgive me enough to help her up.

"Now, we got work to do."

She started down the hill, threading her way through the headstones slowly but surely. I followed in her wake. The old guy in the parking lot saw us coming, took a final puff on his cigarette and ground it underfoot. When Granny reached Caprice's grave she stopped, waiting for me.

"What you got in your purse?"

An odd question, yet one I answered without thinking. "My wallet, my car keys, a comb—you know, typical stuff."

"Lipstick?"

"Yes."

She motioned with her hand. "Let me see."

Hardly the time or place, if you asked me, but I dug in my Rosenfeld and dutifully held out the black tube. "Take the top off," she said, "and scoop up some of this here dirt."

"I am *so* not doing that." I looked down at the fresh pile of red Georgia clay and shuddered. Caprice's body was under there—talk about creepy.

"Yes, you is," Granny replied calmly. "I can't make you a *gris-gris* without grave dust."

I was either going to have to learn French or quit asking questions. Quitting was easier. I bent down and filled the top of my forty-five-dollar tube of Viva Las Vegas with ugly red dirt, trying my best to keep the gritty stuff off my fingers.

"Now, let's go." Granny had already started toward the parking lot. She called to the old man who was still patiently waiting by the car.

"Start it up, Albert. We's going to Indigo."

"Indigo?" I wasn't entirely certain I wanted to step foot in Caprice's old haunt.

"Got to," she said simply. "Only place to get what I need."

"I'll follow you in my own car."

She held out a hand for the grave dirt, and I gave it to her gladly.

"You go straight there, girl, and don't dally. This got to be done while the dirt is fresh."

I stared at her blankly as she turned and hobbled away, the moment surreal.

Then I headed for my own car. I got the feeling that when Granny Julep said don't dally, she meant don't dally.

CHAPTER 8

"Tell me that's not what I think it is."

An entire glass cabinet full of rat skulls? I tore my gaze from that macabre display and scanned the shelves full of bottles—rows and rows of them—that lined the small room.

Granny Julep ignored me, just as she'd ignored me since Albert unlocked the back door and ushered us into Indigo. It hadn't seemed to bother her that he'd locked the door behind us from the *outside*, leaving us alone in the deserted store. Just as it didn't seem to bother her when our footsteps rang loud on the old hardwood floors, sounding out of place in the quiet. Bins filled with produce,

shelves filled with foodstuffs, dust motes dancing
in the late afternoon sun coming through the front
windows. She'd led me to this hidden room, tucked
away behind the broom closet.

"*Ugh*. What's that?" An old doll with button eyes
lay on a bottom shelf, caked in dirt and smeared
with something unidentifiable.

"Don't touch it." Granny Julep spoke sharply,
obviously paying more attention than I thought
she was.

I shook my head, grossed out. "You don't have
to worry about that."

Granny turned away, reaching a gnarled hand toward the bottles, obviously searching for something.
I kept quiet and kept looking around, morbidly fascinated by the sheer weirdness of the room.

One corner held an altar of some sort. Photographs and bits of paper were stuck to the wall
with pins, a colorful mosaic backdrop for a carved
wooden snake about a foot high. Guttered-out
candles and shot glasses full of liquor ringed the
base of the statue. I looked closer, then drew back
with a shudder, wrinkling my nose at the scent of
stale rum. The wooden snake had an actual dead
lizard dangling from its open mouth.

Every inch of wall space in the room was covered
with something; feathers, dried snakeskins, strangely carved sticks, and scary-looking masks. This

was no made-up movie set for a bad B movie—this place was the real thing. I'd never imagined something like this could exist in the back room of a trendy Jamaican grocery store in Little Five Points, Georgia.

"Caprice actually practiced voodoo." I still couldn't quite grasp it, even surrounded by the proof. Playing at goth in my early twenties was one thing, getting lost in the world of black magic was another. Death had lost its glamour for me after my parents died.

I still clung to my heavy black eyeliner, but that didn't make me a ghoul, just a girl.

Granny was still gathering her ingredients.

"People believe what they want to believe, child." She took down another bottle, full of yellowed sticks that rattled against the glass. "If they ain't got the patience or the gumption to wait on the Lord to solve their problems, they turn to the Evil Ones. The Ones who are always waiting."

The matter-of-fact way Granny made the comment was the creepiest thing about it.

"I don't understand how you can be a Christian and still believe in this stuff." I was really baffled by the contradiction. The old woman whom I'd just watched pick up a dried chicken foot kept talking more like a Sunday school teacher than a voodoo priestess.

Granny stopped what she was doing and looked at me. "You have it backward, child," she said gently. "It's because I believe in this that I'm a Christian. As long as there's been evil, there's been good—an everlastin' war that'll go on long after we're gone." She winked, surprising me. "And this old woman is gonna be on the winnin' side. The Lord looks after his own." Hands full of bottles, she moved to a table along one wall and motioned me over with a lift of her chin. "Clear me some space here."

While I reached out with a grimace to move a bowl filled with balls of what looked like dried cow dung, Granny kept talking. "I know the old ways—learned 'em at my mother's knee. My mother, now, she a strong mambo woman back in Haiti. People were afraid of her, but they still come to her for help. She did what she could, and took care of me and my brothers and sisters real good that way."

A jar containing seashells and another with colored stones were easy enough to move, but no way was I picking up the skeleton of a dried toad, squatting like death itself in the middle of the table.

"I took care of my kids the same way, but I never did no harm, no matter what I'se offered." A half-burned stick of incense was the perfect tool to push the toad off to the side and out of Granny's way.

"Love potions, good luck *gris-gris*, charms to drive away sickness . . . all the realm of the Loa Erzulie." She nodded toward a small statue of a black woman, crowned and carrying a baby. To my surprise, the little statue reminded me of a black Virgin Mary. Granny put her ingredients down with a sigh. "But the darkness is always there, just the other side of that line you think you're not willing to cross." She shook her head sadly. "Caprice always too curious about the old ones for her own good. Always wantin' to know more, always wantin' to know *why*."

"The old ones?"

Granny Julep turned her head and looked toward the carved snake on the altar. "Damballah is the oldest, the most powerful loa." Then she indicated a picture on the far wall with a jerk of her chin. "Baron Samedi is the wildest, and the most dangerous. 'Eat, drink, and be merry,' he say, 'for tomorrow you mine.'"

The picture was yellowed and tattered about the edges, stuck to the wall with pins. A grinning skull in a tuxedo and top hat, complete with bow tie. It looked as if some skeletal dandy had chosen to reject Halloween in favor of New Year's Eve.

My cell phone rang, startling us both. Granny shot me an irritated look as I fumbled in my bag and pulled it out. The caller ID showed an unfamiliar number, but I answered it anyway, anxious to stop the ringing.

"Hey, precious." Evan's singsong voice was the one he used when he was especially happy. "Just wanted to let you know that I'm all settled in at Butchie's."

Butchie's? I wanted to laugh but I didn't dare. Laughter would have been out of place in this creep show of a room.

"That's great, Ev." I glanced at Granny Julep and saw her lips moving as she rummaged through her bottles. "I'd love to hear all about it but I can't talk right now—can I call you back later?"

Evan gave a heavy sigh, but it was purely for effect. "All right, but don't call too late. Butch is fixing us a romantic dinner for two and then we'll probably turn in early. He's positively insistent that I get some rest."

I had a feeling that rest was gonna be the last thing in the world Evan was gonna be getting tonight, but I kept that comment to myself, given present company.

"Why don't I just come by and see you tomorrow? Listen, I'll call you back."

"Wait, wait, wait—I have a message for you from Joe. You really should give the poor guy your cellphone number."

I glanced nervously at Granny again. Now she

was sprinkling powder on the table in some sort of pattern, knobby fingers curiously delicate. I turned my back to her, hunching over the phone as though that provided some privacy.

"You need to stay out of this, Evan. Joe doesn't need a fairy godmother."

"Ha, ha. Anyway, he said to tell you he's still up for the 'mambo woman' thing, whatever that means. He wants you to call him."

"Too late." I turned around to see a frown of annoyance on Granny Julep's face, and decided to get off the phone quick. "Already found one."

"What?" Evan's voice rose. "Nicki? Where are you?"

"I'm at Indigo, and I have to go."

"Indigo? What—"

"I'll call you later, Evan. Everything's okay. Gotta go."

I made sure I turned the phone off before I slipped it into my purse. When I looked up, Granny was watching me.

"I'm gonna need your help, girl."

Dammit. Why did everybody always need my help?

"My old fingers can't work this thing." She handed me a lighter, and with a sharp click, I brought it to life. She gestured toward a thick black candle, and I touched the flame to the wick.

"Now close those curtains while I prepare the altar."

Oh, I really didn't like the sound of this, but I did as I was told, pulling heavy drapes, already in place, over the room's one window. In an instant, I'd shut out the world and stepped into a nightmare.

Candle flame flickered over Granny Julep's ancient face, creating shadows where none had been before. The light licked at the walls, gleaming on the shelves of bottles and bones, and giving leers to the carved masks high above my head. I glanced at the poster of Baron Samedi and wished I hadn't— he looked positively gleeful at the thought of some entertainment.

"Light this incense and put it over there."

Granny handed me the stick, then bent over a bowl that sat right in front of the candle. I did as she asked, checking out the powdered design she'd made on the table. It made no sense to me. She poured a few inches of water into the bowl and added something from one of her bottles. Then she reached for my former lipstick case and sprinkled about half of the grave dirt into the water. I hadn't noticed a knife until she picked one up and passed it through the candle flame. Light gleamed along the sharp edge.

She faced me, knife in hand, while my heart began

pounding like a runaway train. Tomorrow's head-
lines flashed before my eyes—*Stupid Girl Found
Dead in Voodoo Shop,* or better yet, *Senior Citizen
Murdered—Crazy Woman Claims Self-Defense.*

"I need to cut a piece of cloth from your skirt."

"Sure," I answered weakly. Coward that I was, I
was so relieved Granny Julep only wanted my skirt
that I could care less if she ruined the outfit. I could
always get another black skirt.

Granny didn't waste any time, ignoring my involuntary wince as she stabbed through a section
of hem and sliced it away. She laid the section of
fabric flat on the altar, right next to the bowl of
water.

My lipstick case was emptied, the last of the grave
dirt dumped in the middle of the cloth. Mumbling
to herself, Granny Julep plucked an assortment of
items from the bottles and jars surrounding the
candle: a clear crystal, which she passed through
the flame as she had the knife; a pinch of herbs, a
pinch of brown powder, and a drop of something
syrupy; the tiny bone of some creature—maybe a
frog or a bird. She kept up a steady litany of what
I took to be French patois beneath her breath, her
mind obviously focused on the task at hand.

I watched, nervously silent, as she added a charm-
sized silver crucifix to the mix. It looked out of
place against the other, more natural ingredients.

Then she picked up a small pair of scissors and turned to me, gesturing toward my hair.

I wanted to ask why she hadn't just used those scissors on my skirt instead of scaring me to death earlier with the knife, but Granny's eyes were somewhere else, clouded with other thoughts. So I meekly bent my head, hoping she wouldn't completely butcher my cut. I was really happy with it these days.

Luckily, she took only two small snips of hair, making sure she got a few pink ones in the second snip. Then she tossed them on top of the little pile.

What looked like a beaded mallet turned out to be a rattle as Granny Julep picked it up and began shaking it over both the bowl and the fabric, stirring the coil of smoke from the incense and filling the air with a rhythmic shushing sound, like dry leaves underfoot.

It was then I smelled it—the sickly sweet odor of spoiled fruit.

"Granny Julep," I hissed, afraid to speak too loudly.

Granny ignored me, murmuring louder now. She gathered up the four corners of the cloth and twisted it into a ball, then tied it with a piece of string. I recognized the twine she'd worn on her wrist earlier.

The smell got stronger. I could almost hear the buzz of flies that would have accompanied the stench in the light of day.

Unfortunately, there was no light of day. Only one candle, now flickering in a chill draft that had come from nowhere.

Granny Julep handed me the little ball of fabric, and I took it numbly. There was a pounding noise coming from somewhere far away, and for a moment I thought it was just the drumbeat of blood in my ears. But there was something else, something I only vaguely recognized as shouting.

"We have to get out of here, Granny Julep. Caprice is coming—I can feel it."

Granny shook her head, half of her face lit by the candle, the other half in shadow. "No, she ain't, child." She leaned in and smiled, teeth gleaming. For a moment they looked red, as though covered in blood.

"She already here."

"Nicki? Nicki, are you in there?"

I could hear someone calling my name, but I didn't dare answer. I didn't dare make any sound at all that might draw the attention of the giant snake that swayed back and forth on the altar, seemingly hypnotized by the flame of Granny Julep's candle.

"Damballah know," Granny crooned, moving

the candle in a constant, rhythmic motion. "Dam-ballah know when one of his children in trouble."

It had begun when the table holding the altar started to shake, rattling the shot glasses and caus-ing the liquor they held to tremble. I'd watched, open-mouthed, as the snake statue coiled and lengthened, swallowing the dead lizard it held in its mouth in one smooth motion. The wooden snake had become a real one—one that slithered and hissed in a sibilant version of Caprice's voice.

"Shhhut up, old woman," the snake hissed, "this isn't your busssinesss."

Granny Julep never stopped moving the candle, and never took her eyes off the snake.

"Nicki Styx! Are you in there? Answer me!"

This time I recognized the pounding for what it was. Somebody was hammering on the front door of Indigo, looking for me.

"Let me help you, bebe. Let Granny Julep set you free," she crooned to the serpent, her voice warm and loving. "The Lord Jesus is waiting to save you."

I jerked backward as the snake feinted a strike at the candle. The scent of incense cloyed in my throat as I bit back a scream, but Granny didn't flinch.

"Sssave yoursssself," it hissed malevolently. "Ca-price isss mine, and ssso isss thisss ssstupid bitch."

"This stupid bitch" would be me.

Granny began to murmur in a language I didn't understand. It was a chant of sorts, as rhythmic as the sway of the candle.

"Ah la ya ma santi o, ele ya ma santi go . . ."

"Ssshriveled old witch." The tip of the snake's tale quivered, warning of another strike. "Your ssspellsss are ussselesss."

"Nicki! Nicki, where are you?" I could feel the reverberation of footsteps through the building's old hardwood floors. The voice was closer now.

Faster than I would have thought it possible for the old woman to move, Granny Julep snatched up the bowl of water and grave dust and splashed it all over the snake. It recoiled, writhing and twisting, knocking over shot glasses and spilling rum all over the altar. Then it twisted off the table and onto the floor.

That was it for me. I shrieked like the girl I was and bolted for the door—no way was I gonna stay in that dark, scary place with a demon-possessed snake slithering somewhere around my ankles.

I was in deep enough shit already.

Daylight flooded the hidden voodoo room as I ran shrieking into the store.

There was Joe with Albert, both of them shocked to see me come bursting into the store's main room. I was just as shocked to see Joe, but that didn't stop me from making a beeline straight for him. He met me in the middle of the main aisle and held me tight against his chest.

"Granny Julep . . . the snake . . . oh, God . . . the snake."

Albert strode past us, giving Joe an evil look. He disappeared through the doorway I'd just emerged from.

"*Shhhh,*" Joe murmured, gathering me even closer. He rested his cheek against my hair. "A snake? It was probably more scared of you than you were of it. Everything's okay."

I seriously doubted that, but I tried to get a grip, breathing deep. Joe didn't seem in any hurry to let me go. My heart was pounding in a way that frightened me—I could visualize all too well that loose valve flapping, struggling to keep up with the blood flow.

I lifted my head. "It wasn't just *a* snake. It was Caprice. Granny Julep was making me a *gris-gris* bag when the wooden snake came alive and started whispering things . . . ugly things—" I shuddered. "—in Caprice's voice. Granny Julep—"

"'Take unto ye the armor of God, that ye may be able to withstand evil.'" Granny shuffled into the room, leaning heavily on Albert's arm. In one hand she clutched the statue of Damballah, now a wooden effigy once more.

The old man glared at us both, then spoke.

"You two go on and get outta here." He glanced at Joe, meeting his eye. "You take care of yo' woman, and I'll take care of mine."

Joe didn't hesitate. He swung me toward the back door, giving the old man a quick nod. Then he hustled me outside and into the sunshine. I didn't object as he took me by the hand and pulled me up the alley, walking fast. The buzz of flies as we passed the Dumpster made me flinch, the stench of garbage reminding me of Caprice.

This late on a Sunday afternoon most of the stores in Little Five Points were closed, with only a handful of tourists wandering the streets and peering in store windows. My car was parked out in front of Handbags and Gladrags, and even in my shaken state I could appreciate how unique our storefront was—the lettering of the sign quirky but elegant, the mannequins and their outfits glamorous yet tongue-in-cheek.

"Let's get out of here quick—before the police show up to find out why screams were coming from a supposedly empty store." Joe hustled me toward his own car, which was closer. I didn't object—I didn't trust myself to drive right now, anyway. He held the passenger side door open and ushered me in. "I had to make a spectacle of myself to force that old man to let me in, and I wouldn't be surprised if somebody already called them. Cops might take extra interest in the scene of a recent murder."

Joe slid into the driver's side and started the engine before his door was even shut. The reassuring *chunk* of automatic locks never sounded so good.

"I can't believe it." I stared at the wad of black cloth I held in my hand.

"You saw a snake, that's all. Some mumbo-jumbo sleight-of-hand or something. An old store like that most likely has mice, and where there's mice, there's snakes." Now that we were safe inside the car, Joe seemed less inclined to be sympathetic. "Or else that old woman just wanted to scare you silly so she could up her fee. How much did you pay her, anyway?"

"It wasn't like that. I didn't pay her anything, and she didn't ask me to." I felt deflated suddenly, adrenaline rush ebbing away. "Could you take me home?"

Joe put the car in gear and checked his mirror grimly before pulling away from the curb. "I'm taking you home, all right. My home."

I suppose he expected an argument. A "mind your own business" or "you're not the boss of me" or something equally scathing or sassy or sarcastic. Instead, I just slipped my hand into his and held on tight, so he was forced to drive all the way to his apartment one-handed.

He didn't say anything else until we got there,

and neither did I, but he didn't let go of my hand, either.

His apartment didn't have much personality, but its tidiness would have made even Evan proud. White walls and beige carpet, ordinary furniture and a collection of black and white framed prints. The only unique feature was the view through the glass doors that led to the balcony. The apartment overlooked a beautifully manicured garden, rimmed by heavy woods.

I heard the click of the bolt as Joe locked the door behind us. "Why didn't you wait for me, Nicki? We had a deal, remember?"

"I'm sorry," I said absently. I was still pretty shaken by what I'd seen in that room. *How could such a thing be possible?*

"Come and sit down."

He touched my elbow and led me to the couch. I sat down, and caught him staring at the jagged tear in the hem of my skirt.

"What happened to your clothes?" I hoped he wasn't complaining . . . the tear left several inches of leg showing, which most men would appreciate despite the situation.

I showed him what I'd been holding.

"Granny Julep made me a *gris-gris* bag. It's supposed to keep Caprice away." I gave a little laugh. "I guess it didn't work."

Joe frowned, and somehow I knew he fought an impulse to snatch the homemade bundle and toss it in the trash. I could see it on his face. He confirmed it when he said, "Maybe you should leave well enough alone and forget this voodoo hoodoo."

"I can't." I fingered the ball of grave dust, tied with brown string. "It won't forget me."

Joe walked into the kitchen and pulled a half-empty bottle of scotch from the cabinet. As he splashed some of the liquor into a couple of tumblers, he asked, "What the hell did you think you were doing?" He stared at me across the breakfast counter as he put the bottle down and picked up the two glasses. "Did you even *know* those people?"

I shook my head as he walked toward me, and took the thimbleful of scotch he offered. "Not until today. I met them at the funeral."

"The funeral," Joe repeated. He took a swallow of scotch. I sipped mine with a grimace, feeling the burn from throat to belly.

"You went to your friend's funeral and you met some old couple who say they can drive away spirits." Joe listed the facts dispassionately. "Then you go off with these two total strangers to the scene of a murder and let them cut up your clothes to make you a good-luck charm?" He didn't even try to keep the skepticism from his voice. "C'mon, Nicki. This is crazy—even for you."

I shot to my feet. "Did you just call me crazy?"

"It was dangerous, Nicki. It was stupid. You put yourself in a vulnerable position—you could've been mugged . . . you could have been hurt! You ask me for help, and then you go off alone." Joe's voice had risen. He lowered it. "I was honest with you last night about Kelly, and you repay me by going off like a spiteful child. That's not fair, Nicki."

My mouth fell open. "Who are you, my father? No wait . . . you're my brother-in-law, right?" I could tell he didn't like the way that phrase sounded coming out of my mouth. "You think that gives you some kind of right to tell me what to do?" I swallowed the rest of my scotch and put the glass on the coffee table. "For your information, I didn't do this on purpose—it just worked out that way." I coughed a little at the burn of scotch. "I only meant to ask Granny Julep if she *knew* of an Obeah woman. I didn't know she *was* one. But then she said we had to use the grave dirt right away, so I went with the flow."

Joe looked at me incredulously. His eyes moved to the *gris-gris* bag.

"You've got to be kidding me."

My hand closed around the bag, which I was suddenly tempted to throw at him. My explanation might sound bizarre, but it was the truth.

"You know, for somebody who just recently told

me the most unbelievable little tale I've ever heard about a twin sister and a missing wife, you're a fine one to talk," I said waspishly.

Joe met my eye, refusing to look away.

I had him there.

"Touché," he said.

The almost imperceptible easing of his shoulders reminded me that this situation didn't need to turn into a fight. He really had done me a favor today, and I couldn't blame him for being pissed if he thought I'd blown him off on purpose.

He had a right to his opinion. Even if he was wrong. About everything.

"Look, Nicki . . ." His voice softened. "I was worried about you today. I was really . . . worried." He put down his glass and straightened, looking me in the eye. "I know we haven't known each other all that long, but I like you. A lot." He glanced away briefly, shaking his head. "When I heard you scream, I thought my heart would stop."

How was a girl supposed to resist that?

I flashed him a smile. "That's my department, remember?"

He apparently was in no mood for teasing, and didn't return my smile. Instead, he asked me the same question I'd asked him in the car last night, after I'd kissed him. "Who am I to you?"

I reached out and touched his face, barely grazing his cheek with my fingers. "You're a lot of things, Joe Bascombe." My hand slipped down to rest lightly on his chest. "Today you were a friend when I needed one. Even if you're being high-handed about it now." I gave him a tilt of the head. "Where'd you come from, anyway? How'd you know where I was?"

"Evan," Joe murmured. His dark chocolate smell was in my nose. My palm covered his heart. "Evan called me."

I let my gaze slide down to rest on his lips, and felt his heartbeat speed up beneath my hand. I swayed closer, leaning some of my weight against him. "Did he offer you a pair of glass slippers, by any chance?"

Joe had no idea what I was talking about, and obviously cared even less. His hands came up to catch me about the waist, and he took my lips with his, drinking in my teasing along with the smoky taste of scotch.

I met him more than halfway, arms twining around his neck, body pressed against him as close-ly as clothing allowed. He couldn't have hidden his arousal if he tried. He gasped into my mouth as I arched, rubbing him there with my body.

It was enough to turn me to liquid heat. I flowed over him, kissing and touching, and everywhere I touched I wanted more. I wanted his clothes off and us naked, warm and soft beneath each other's hands.

And before I knew it, I had want I wanted, accomplished in a jumble of feverish kisses and scattered clothes.

And when I was naked, hair mussed and lipstick smeared, I stopped kissing him and smiled. I took a step back, reaching for his hand. My eyes widened.

"Oh my." I gave him a devilish look, very impressed. "What *have* you been hiding, Dr. Bascombe?"

"Nothing you haven't seen before, I'm sure." Joe grinned, breathing ragged. He was obviously pleased by my pleasure.

"A nipple ring. Who woulda thunk it?" I murmured.

Joe stood still, giving me every ounce of his attention as I traced a fingernail over the tiny loop of metal.

"A college whim," he said, "the only sign of rebellion I've kept for myself all these years."

His skin prickled with goose bumps beneath my hand, the nipple erect and sensitive. I stepped closer, grazing his hardness with a hip, and felt him shudder. The feel of his male body was exquisite— an exquisite torture of forbidden fruit and cherry chocolate decadence, all mixed up in one mouthwatering package named Joe.

"You're full of surprises." I leaned naked against him in the middle of the living room. My head fit nicely into the space beneath his chin, and I nuzzled him there, punctuating each word with a warm kiss. "I could just"—*kiss*—"eat"—*kiss*—"you"—*kiss*—"up."

Luckily, Joe couldn't stand it anymore. He swept me up behind the knees and held me to his chest. I swooped and giggled, feeling light as a butterfly in his arms.

"You broke your last promise to me, woman," he growled, burying his face momentarily in my hair. He was strong, and very, very hard. "I'm not taking any chances on this one." He kissed me again, quick, before carrying me toward the bedroom.

I sighed, completely at ease being nude in his arms. I kissed his shoulder, then lay my cheek against it.

"*Mmm . . .* smart man."

CHAPTER 9

"Don't worry about the store, Evan—Jason and Heather have it covered. College students always need money, and they were happy to get the extra hours. Monday afternoons are never busy."

I sat in a deck chair, enjoying the fresh air as well as the view of the lake behind Butch's house. Despite Peachtree's cookie-cutter facade, the house was great. Evan was being doted on in the middle of some beautiful Georgia countryside.

"Huh," Evan snorted. "Jason will be smoking dope by the back door and Heather will be yakking on the phone to her boyfriend." He shrugged, resigned. "But whatever. You're the boss." He leaned

over from his deck chair and squeezed my hand.
"You look tired, Nicki. Did she—" Evan shuddered, and I didn't have to ask who he was talking
about. "Did she bother you last night?"

I shook my head, grateful for that, at least. I
hadn't told Evan where I'd spent the night yet,
or why I had a reason to look exhausted. "What
about you?"

Evan leaned back, smiling at Butch, who manned
the grill on the other side of the deck. Bald and
muscle-bound, Butch wore an apron that said KISS
THE COOK over his shorts and sleeveless tee, and
waved a spatula at us cheerfully.

"No, thank God," Evan answered. "I've only
seen her that one time."

"You should stay here with Butch for a while.
Granny Julep says that Caprice can't go very far
from where she died. She can't reach you out
here."

Poor Evan looked so relieved I thought he was
gonna cry.

"She did?" Relief immediately turned to annoyance. "Why didn't you call and tell me that last
night? I had a hard enough time sleeping in a
strange bed. It would have been easier if I hadn't
been so scared. Just look at the bags under these
eyes." Despite the whining, Evan looked much
healthier, more relaxed than the last time I'd seen

him. Love with the lovestruck bouncer obviously agreed with him.

"I'm sorry." I knew I should've told him sooner, but I'd been caught up in my own drama for a change. "I was with Joe."

Evan's eyes got big. He smiled, forgetting his complaints.

"As in the biblical sense?" he teased.

Unbelievably, my face heated. I ducked my head but couldn't hold back a smile.

Evan's mouth dropped open. He gave a delighted shout of laughter.

"You're blushing!" he gasped. "The naughty Nicki Styx is actually blushing!" He sat up and stared at me like I was an oddity from outer space.

I rolled my eyes but let him have his fun.

"What's so funny?" Butch wanted in on the joke, flipping our burgers expertly, making them sizzle. The scent of grilled meat came to me on the breeze, making my mouth water.

"Nicki's in love," Evan gushed.

"No, I'm not," I said quickly.

"Are, too."

"Am not."

Butch grinned and raised an eyebrow, looking back and forth between us. He shook his head and went back to his cooking.

"Stop it," I hissed.

Evan knew the signs of my temper well enough, so he shut up while he rearranged himself in the deck chair. But he grinned at me the whole time, and by the time he was comfortably settled on his cushions, I was reluctantly grinning back.

"Okay. Tell me everything."

"You're kinda nosy, you know?"

"I know. Tell me."

"Well, after Joe came riding to my rescue yesterday, I could hardly resist him, now could I? Thanks for that, by the way, you little tattletale."

Evan looked supremely pleased with himself.

"You should have given him your cell-phone number. Then he wouldn't be calling me."

"You called *him*," I clarified. "You told him where I was."

He waved a hand as if at a gnat. "Whatever."

I shook my head, knowing it was hopeless to reason with him. "We went back to his apartment. I shouldn't have, but I was too scared to go home. If you'd seen that snake . . ." It was my turn to shudder, remembering how the wooden statue of Damballah had begun to move, to slither, to speak. But I'd already told Evan about what happened in the back room of Indigo, and I didn't wanna go over it again.

"At first Joe was mad because he thought I went

off without him on purpose, but he got over it pretty quick." I smiled at the memory of Joe telling me he "liked" me. The man was so sweet—he'd been mad at me, but still came looking for me. "And I'm pretty sure he thinks I'm a nutcase. He made me an appointment with some shrink friend of his on Wednesday afternoon. But other than that . . ." I paused, trying to sum up my evening with Joe. " . . . it was . . . nice."

"Nice." Evan made a disgusted sound. "Getting a manicure is *nice*. Taking your grandma to lunch is *nice*. Are you telling me there were no sparks," his hands starting waving, "no fireworks?" The fairy godmother was beginning to look worried.

I thought about Joe's body, warm and firm beneath my hands. Of his long, hot kisses and the rasp of his hair against my legs. I thought of his hard length and what we'd done with it, and the cherry candy taste of his skin.

"It was sweet."

"*Sweet?* That's all?" Evan sat up, clutching the arms of the deck chair.

I looked at him and smiled, drawn away from my memories of the night just past.

"Oh," Evan drawled, comprehension dawning. He leaned back, smiling big. "It was *sweet*."

"Shut up."

"Burgers are ready," called Butch.

* * *

I drove back to Joe's apartment in the gathering dusk, joining the slow trickle of traffic on the outskirts of Atlanta. Loud music usually helped on the highway, but right now Siouxsie and the Banshees was too intense. I slipped some Sheryl Crow into the CD player instead, smiling as I remembered Evan's parting shot.

"Don't do anything I wouldn't do."

As if that cut down on my options. Evan was hardly a poster boy for restraint when it came to matters of the heart, and for some reason he'd decided I should give Joe a chance.

Maybe it was just the starry-eyed romance in Evan's life oozing over into mine that had me thinking the same.

It had been Joe's weight that woke me that morning, sinking onto the mattress as he leaned in to let me know he was on his way to the hospital.

"Don't get up," he'd murmured, nuzzling my neck. Dawn was filling the room, seeping past the blinds, and I remembered a sense of relief that the night was past, and regret for the very same reason.

"Stay here, get some sleep." His face had been against my hair, hand warm on my bare shoulder.

I'd smiled and rolled over, letting him kiss me despite my potential morning breath.

"I gotta go anyway," I'd told him drowsily. "Evan's taking a few days off and I need to open the shop."

Joe had kissed me again, and I sensed he wanted to stay, to climb back in the warm nest of covers and make love again.

"Come back tonight," he'd said. "I'll be home by eight, and I'll make us a late dinner. We need to talk." He'd paused, smoothing the hair back from my face. "You're welcome to stay here, you know."

"Thanks, but I'm fine."

"I know you're tough, Nicki," Joe had said. "But it's okay to be weak now and then."

There'd been a house key and a note on the table by the front door when I let myself out a little while later. "Just in case . . ." the note had said. I'd left the key there, unwilling to admit I might need it.

I wanted to stay detached, to stay objective—but in reality, I was touched. And the even bigger reality was, I was afraid. Here I sat in rush hour traffic with a *gris-gris* bag full of grave dirt in my purse and no desire to go home to a dark, empty house. I'd been there this morning to shower and change, clinging to Caprice's "Day for you, night for me" remark as comfort. But then I'd packed an overnight bag "just in case."

While Sheryl Crow sang "Are you strong enough

to be my man?" I couldn't help but wonder what the hell I was getting myself into with a guy who just might be married to my hitherto unknown twin sister. Except he wasn't just *a* guy . . . he was Joe.

Jeez, talk about a bad soap opera in the making.

"Throw in a few ghosts and I've got myself a regular *All My Children* meets the *Sixth Sense*," I muttered. Suddenly even Sheryl got on my last nerve, and I shut off the CD, leaving me cocooned in welcome silence.

And what about that hitherto unknown twin sister? I'd deliberately avoided thinking about her, but now—alone in the quiet—I couldn't help but wonder.

Was there really someone out there who looked like me? Someone who shared the same nameless, faceless biological parents that I did? The concept was bizarre.

Even more bizarre was the thought that someone existed who might have shared the very same womb with me . . . a yin to my yang.

Joe was right. We needed to talk.

When I finally made it to the apartment, it was full dark. I could see from the parking lot that the lights were on even though it was nowhere near eight o'clock. Joe's BMW was in its assigned space.

He opened the door with a smile, looking harried

and happy and sexy as hell in T-shirt and jeans.

"Not many men can pull off an apron," I teased, admiring the kitchen towel he'd tucked in his waistband. "But at least it doesn't say 'Kiss the Cook.'"

"No, but you can do it anyway," he answered, leaning in for a quick one. There was a streak of something white on his cheek. "*Mmm,*" I said, touching it with a finger and then licking it. "Whipped cream? Are we into the kinky stuff already?"

Joe pulled me inside and locked the door. "Only if you ask me very nicely." He grinned wickedly, obviously picturing something extremely naughty. "But for now, I'm using it on our dessert. Strawberry shortcake."

"Wow." Something smelled great, so I followed my nose into the kitchen, noticing the candles lit in the living room and the background music on the stereo. "Somebody's hoping to get lucky."

He handed me a glass of red wine, already poured. "Drink this, funny girl," he said. "It's good for your heart." Then he turned back to his cooking, lifting a pot lid and releasing a cloud of fragrant steam. "Do you like chicken cacciatore?"

"Love it," I lied, never having eaten it in my life. "Chicken cacciatore and strawberry shortcake— my two favorites."

An hour later the lie was true. I'd just enjoyed

one of the best meals ever, made by a man who couldn't stop smiling at me. The lighting was soft, the music was softer, and there were fresh flowers and candles on the table. I'd never been romanced like this before—none of my previous boyfriends had ever thought past a sappy card or a box of candy.

A girl could get used to this.

"I thought you said you wouldn't be back until eight."

Joe shrugged, swallowing the last of his short-cake. "I got someone else to cover my shift." He grinned, dabbing at his lips with a napkin. "I'm told I can do that sometimes—I'm the boss." Pushing away his empty plate, he added, "I couldn't concentrate today, anyway, and that's not a good thing in my profession—wouldn't want to order a hysterectomy for a man who needs his gallbladder removed."

I toyed with the stem of my glass, watching the candlelight gleam red on the remaining dregs of wine. I looked up and met his eye. "Tell me about Kelly."

Joe sighed, as if the conversation weren't something he were looking forward to. "What do you want to know? I've already told you most of it."

"No, you haven't." I leaned in, resting my elbows on the table. "What's she like? What kind of music does she listen to? What kind of person is she? If your theory turns out to be right, this could be my *sister* you're talking about. I don't know anything about her except her name."

"Ah." He smiled, looking relieved. "Feminine curiosity. Here I thought you were worried about what she might mean to me, but you just want to know how she wears her hair."

"Smart-ass." I grinned to let him know he was right.

"I'll save us some time." He got up and walked over to the bookshelf, pulling out a photo album. My heart began to pound as he came back to the table and laid it in front of me, resting a hand on the back of my chair. I hesitated, then opened the album.

The first pictures were of a younger Joe in cap and gown, arms around an older man and woman. "Your parents?" He nodded. A girl with blond hair held her fingers in a V behind his head as Joe clutched a diploma and tried to look serious. "My sister Julie," he chuckled, tapping the girl with a finger. "You'd like her."

I didn't answer, turning the pages slowly, fascinated by how Joe looked in these family photos— here he was bundled up against the cold in a heavy jacket and knit cap, throwing a snowball at who- ever held the camera. Here again with his sister and parents, posing on the couch next to some long-ago Christmas tree. He'd been skinny as a teenager, but there was still a hint of the handsome man he'd become. As for his hair, it appeared he'd always had a problem getting regular cuts—good thing the shaggy look suited him.

I kept turning the pages, looking for the image I sought.

And suddenly there she was, a girl with long dark hair parted in the middle and a serious expression on her face. She'd just looked up from the book she was reading and into the camera.

"That's Kelly," Joe murmured, "though I probably didn't need to tell you that."

I suppose there was a resemblance, though the girl in the picture wore no makeup and was barefoot, wearing a shapeless gray T-shirt that hid her figure.

Here she was again, smiling this time, face in profile and long hair tucked behind an ear. It was then I saw it, though I didn't want to. Her nose, her chin . . . they were *my* nose and chin.

I kept flipping through the album, saying nothing. I saw pictures of Kelly at her college graduation, smiling and happy yet still no makeup; in the crowd at a rally to end world hunger, hair in a messy ponytail. *My* hair—the way it would look if I'd never learned the value of a good cut and color. Then there was one with Kelly and Joe together, standing beside a moving van. Joe had his arm around her, and she held a sign for the camera that said "Boston Bound."

"On the way to start my residency," Joe murmured.

I'd reached the end of the album, so I closed it, having looked my fill anyway.

Thank God it was over before we got to wedding pictures.

"Well?" he asked, taking the photo album. He shelved it away while I answered.

"I guess she looks like me." I shrugged. "Kinda hard to tell."

Joe looked at me closely, but I couldn't quite meet his eyes. I'd just discovered that I didn't like looking at pictures of Joe with some other woman. A woman he'd slept with, loved . . . married. If I didn't know myself better, I'd have said I was jealous.

Of my own twin.

"Nicki, are you okay?" Joe's hand was warm on mine. He squatted next to me, frowning. "That had to be weird, looking at those photos." *Dammit. Did he have to be psychic, too?* "I want you to know that whatever feelings I had for Kelly . . . well, they were a long time ago. She's a stranger to me now." He squeezed my fingers, willing me to squeeze back. "Now there's only you."

I caught my breath at the look in his eyes, hardly ready to hear, or exchange, vows of undying love. I felt claustrophic all of a sudden, trapped in my chair.

"How about I clean up the dishes since you cooked?" I hoped my voice didn't sound as panicky as I felt. "That was a great dinner."

Joe eased back and stood, no dummy.

"We'll do them together," he said with a smile. I was grateful he'd let me change the subject so easily.

"But I have one final comment . . ." He picked up his own plate and reached for mine, giving me a nice view of male biceps in action. "You and Kelly may look the same, but you're very different. There's thunder, and there's lightning." He shook his head with a smile. "You're lightning."

On the other hand, maybe I'd been too hasty.

"We could do these dishes now," I said. "Or we could—" I cocked an eyebrow at him, laying a hand on his arm. "—do them later."

Joe gave me a lazy smile that made my toes curl. "Ah. You've thought of something else we could do together—you're a clever woman, Nicki Styx."

"Yes, I am," I agreed, stroking his arm and enjoying the rough rasp of hair beneath my fingers. "Is there any whipped cream left?"

CHAPTER 10

Granny Julep was waiting for me the next morning.

I'd just unlocked the front door to Handbags and Gladrags when someone called my name. I glanced over my shoulder to see the old woman making her careful way down the front steps of Indigo—the steps where Caprice died—with the ever-faithful Albert supporting one elbow.

Granny looked more ancient than ever, if such a thing were possible. She was using a cane today, too.

"What took you so long, girl? We been waitin' almost an hour."

I was in too good a mood to let the old lady's

crankiness bother me. It wasn't like I'd asked them to wait, now was it? Besides, it was barely eight o'clock.

"Good morning to you, too, Granny Julep. Albert."

That earned me a polite nod from Albert and no reaction from Granny Julep except a vague wave of her cane.

"You seen the paper this morning?" Granny held up a copy of the *Atlanta Constitution,* folded to an article I couldn't read. "Mojo confessed to killing my granddaughter, but he claimin' it was self-defense."

"Self-defense?"

"Let us in, girl. No need to spread our private business all over the street."

I hesitated. It'd been two days now since the incident with the snake, and no sign of Caprice. I'd be more than happy to let Granny Julep take care of things on her own from now on. Caprice was her granddaughter, after all, not mine.

"I need to sit down," the old woman said flatly. "And use the bathroom."

Albert gave me a look, and I suddenly realized why he hardly ever spoke. He didn't need to.

"All right," I said, ungraciously, "but I've got work to do." I held the door open. They went in and I came behind, flipping up a row of switches by the front door. The store came to life, and I felt a little thrill of pride. The mannequins, frozen in their glamorous poses, basked in the sudden blaze of light. Color and style were everywhere. Even the clothes racks were neat and orderly, contradicting Evan's forecast of disaster in his absence.

"*Hoo-ee,*" said Granny Julep, "ain't that pretty." She hobbled over to Audrey Hepburn, who looked elegant as always in a sapphire blue cocktail dress with a full organdy skirt. The flirty, feminine look was pure fifties, with the classic sheer sleeves and buttoned cuffs of the period. Granny fingered the huge blue flower on the matching sash.

"The bathroom's that way." I pointed. "And just so you know, Caprice has left me alone. She hasn't come back."

"Good, good," Granny said, nodding while she examined the organdy skirt. "That grave dust slowed her down some. Give you a few days, anyway."

A few days? My heart sank.

"Now we got to make sure she don't find a way back in."

"Back in?" I asked weakly.

"Back in your mind, girl. That's the only place she *is*—that's how she draw her power." Granny gave the blue dress one last admiring look and turned to face me. "As long as she can make you hear her, the Evil Ones can use her. They's always waitin', remember?"

Unfortunately, I did, though I'd have preferred to forget.

"What *use* could they possibly have for Caprice, and why? She's dead already!" I tamped down a sense of panic. "This 'evil one' stuff may make perfect sense to you, but I don't get it. The more I try, the crazier it sounds."

Granny Julep drew herself up and gave me an affronted look. "I may be many things, girl, but I ain't crazy." She wagged a gnarled finger at me. "You need to quit gettin' all bitchy every time I tell you somethin' you don't wanna hear. You gonna be wishin' you'd kept your mouth shut when Damballah start whispering in your ear."

Had a little old lady just called me "bitchy"?

As if reading my mind, Albert gave a solemn nod, outspoken as ever.

"Now get me a chair and let me explain things to you," Granny said. "Albert, there's one over there behind the counter."

The old man went to do her bidding while I fumed, biting my tongue. I couldn't resist one comment, however.

"I thought you had to go to the bathroom."

Granny didn't hesitate. "I lied." She turned and

hobbled toward the main counter, taking the chair Evan liked to call his "catbird seat."

"I just sit here and wait for the pigeons, sweetie," he'd say.

I sure wished he was sitting there now, instead of a wrinkled voodoo queen with a bad attitude. Or maybe I had the bad attitude. Somebody did. I took one look at the sour expression on Albert's face and decided to blame him.

"The way I got this figured," Granny said, "Caprice found out about Mojo and his woman. She done called on Baron Samedi before she died, and promised him a soul." I looked away from Albert and went to lean against the counter, resigned to hearing whatever it was Granny Julep had to say. "Either Mojo's or that tramp he was sleeping with—I don't know which. It take time to call up the Baron. Caprice was mad . . . real mad. She knew somebody was gonna die that night."

"You mean she was going to kill Mojo?" I was shocked. "Or the other woman?"

Granny gave me a level look and went on.

"But something went wrong, and the Baron, he take the only soul he can—Caprice's. Now Caprice know the risk before she call him, but she took it anyway. The Baron don't leave empty-handed." The old woman shook her head, looking sad. "The only way for Caprice's soul to be set free is if she give that wily old rascal the soul she promised him to begin with."

This was giving me a seriously creepy feeling. "Mojo's?"

Granny nodded. "That's right. He got to die."

"Whoa, whoa, whoa," I said, putting up my hands. "I'm not getting involved in anything like that! I don't even want to *hear* anything like that!"

I got identically impatient looks from Granny and Albert. I'm not certain, but I think Albert even sneered a little.

"*We* ain't gonna kill him, girl. He'll get his reward soon enough." For a moment Granny looked fierce, eager for Mojo to pay for what he'd done. "I'm just telling you why Caprice want him out of jail so bad. He'd go back to the store sooner or later, and when he did"—here she gave me a grim smile—"Damballah be waiting, with his friend the Baron. Together they send him straight to hell, and maybe—just maybe—they let my granddaughter go into the Light."

I gasped, the mention of the Light more than I could ignore. I don't know why, but I hadn't expected to hear that from Granny Julep. Christian or not, her ways seemed darker.

"You know about the Light?"

Granny looked at me curiously. "Not as much as you do, I think."

Uncomfortable, I looked away.

"Anyway, we got to keep Caprice away from you until nine-night. After that her soul will be at peace, and she can't do you no harm."

"Really?" I couldn't keep the hopeful note from my voice.

"Really." Granny fingered her cane, watching me. "*If* we can keep her away. If not," the old woman's eyes grew distant, "then maybe she offer *you* to the Baron instead."

Shit.

If I were going to dance with the Devil, I'd prefer the more romantic, slightly edgy version presented by Anne Rice in her novels. A grinning skeleton with delusions of royalty just wasn't my thing.

Knowing when I was beaten, I gave in. "Okay, Granny Julep. What do we do now?"

Granny rummaged in the straw bag she carried and brought out a handful of dried sticks. At least I thought that's what they were until I got a closer look. She held a jumble of tiny straw figures, intricately tied and knotted. "Put one of these over every door and window of your house," she ordered.

She gave me two handfuls of the stick figures, and I had to pile them on the counter before I could take what else she offered.

"Tobacco seeds. Sprinkle them on the windowsills and in front of every door before you sleep."

Lovely. Spread carcinogens in your home to keep out the zombies. Made perfect sense.

"And wear these." The last thing Granny pulled out of the bag was a necklace of jet black beads. "Wear it *all* the time," she emphasized, squeezing my fingers as she placed it in my hand. "Put it on now and don't take it off."

Now this was more like it. The beads were gorgeous—a double strand of multifaceted crystals—definitely vintage and definitely my style. I could hardly wait to show them to Evan.

"These are beautiful . . . may I buy them from you?"

Granny shook her head. "A gift, child. I done my part by wearing 'em all these years. They got most of the good in me, soaked up from my skin like a sponge. I'm almost dried up and done now, and you gonna need 'em."

I felt the unexpected sting of tears, and suddenly, keenly, missed my mother. I hardly knew what to say.

"There must be someone else who—"

"I was saving 'em for Caprice."

That silenced me.

"Put 'em on, child," Granny urged me gently. "Put 'em on."

So I did, the weight of the beads on my neck

both a comfort and a sorrow. Without thinking, I slipped the beads beneath my shirt, where they lay warm against my skin.

"Can I make you both some coffee?"

That earned me my first-ever smile from Albert, and one from Granny, too.

A half hour later I propped open the front door to the early birds on Moreland Avenue and waved good-bye to the old couple. Then I sat at the counter and did the books while I watched the store, trying to concentrate on the numbers instead of all the "jumbie" advice Granny had given me before she'd left. "Wear red," was the last thing she'd said, "duppies don't like that color." I wondered if red lingerie counted . . . I had plenty of that.

The phone rang, a welcome distraction.

"Handbags and Gladrags. This is Nicki."

"Good morning." *Speaking of red lingerie.* It was Joe. "You left awfully early."

I smiled into the phone, unable to deny a surge of pleasure. I'd never talked to him over the phone before. "I needed to go home and shower, and I didn't want to wake you. I know you're on call."

"Yeah. I have to be in the E.R. in less than an hour." His voice lowered, became intimate. "The bed seems empty without you."

"I've spoiled you already, *hm*?"

"Pretty much," he agreed. In fact, he sounded pretty pleased about it.

"Well, you'll have the bed to yourself tonight, pretty boy," I quipped. "I'm exhausted. I'm gonna sleep at my own place tonight."

I'd made that decision on the drive in that morning, and Granny Julep's visit left me even more determined to take back my life. Things were going so well with Joe, and so crappy with everything else. The whole situation made me nervous. Great sex was one thing, but I needed more. Right now, I needed more time to myself.

There was silence on the other end of the line. Then he said, "I can sleep on the couch, you know."

I closed my eyes, though he couldn't see me. What a sweet gesture from a guy I'd just discovered was an extremely sensual—and extremely virile—stud muffin.

"No strings, I promise."

I knew Joe was sincere. But for the first time in my life, strings didn't sound like such a bad idea.

Problem was, these strings were damned tangled.

"I need some time, Joe." Bluntness was always easier in theory. "Things are moving a little fast for me."

More silence, but not for too long.

"Are we okay?" Joe could be blunt as well.

"We're okay. I just need to sleep in my own bed tonight."

"You'll go see Ivy Jacobson tomorrow?"

"I will," I promised.

"You'll call me in the middle of the night if you're scared?"

I smiled again, cradling the phone to my ear.

"I will."

"You should've taken the key."

"I should've."

A brief pause, then Joe said, "I guess I better go. Have a good day, *hm*?"

"You, too."

I hung up feeling oddly wistful. He'd handled my decision even better than I hoped, but part of me wondered if he wasn't just a tiny bit relieved.

Girl dies, girl comes back to life, girl looks exactly like your wife. Oh yeah, and she hangs out with dead people.

The phone rang again, and I jumped.

"Handbags and Gladrags. This is Nicki."

"Hidey-ho," sang Evan on the other end, "how's business this morning? Do I need to come in?"

"It's Tuesday morning, silly. There's nothing going on. You and Butch go get a pedicure or something, and don't worry your pretty little head about me."

"Very funny. Worrying about you is a waste of

time . . . I'd never risk the wrinkles. Just thought I'd check in."

"Bored with suburbia already?"

Evan sighed. "Only a little. You'd think there'd be some decent shopping, but the upscale stores are pretty limited around here unless you play golf."

I smiled, knowing Evan considered golf clothes to be an insult to fashion unless paired with something utterly cool. To be trapped in a wasteland of plaid shorts and tepid Polo shirts was a fate worse than death.

"Let's have dinner tonight," I said. "Just you and me."

"No can do." Evan giggled, sounding quite pleased with himself. "I'm meeting Butch's mom. She's having us over for pot roast and mashed potatoes."

"What? If you're not careful I'm gonna start thinking you're really serious about this guy."

There was a very uncharacteristic moment of silence.

"You're in love," I gushed.

"Am not."

"Am too."

I heard a noise of impatience. "Don't start with me, Miss 'It Was Sweet' Thang. People who live in glass houses shouldn't throw stones. How's it going with Joe, anyway?"

Damn him for knowing me so well.

"It's going great," I admitted. "So great, in fact, that I spent the night with him again and then ran like hell. I told him I needed some space."

"Oooh, those little tootsies are getting cold, aren't they? Maybe I should bring over your pink fuzzy slippers."

"Smart-ass," I mumbled.

"You can't run forever, you know. This 'couples' thing isn't so bad with the right person."

"How the hell are you supposed to find the 'right person' in a world filled with millions of people? No matter which way you look at it, the odds are stacked against anybody living happily ever after."

"That didn't stop your parents." Evan wasn't cutting me any slack. "Even mine actually loved each other once. Now they do a great job of tolerating each other for the sake of their darling boy. Coming out of the closet was the biggest favor I ever did them—PFLAG gives them something in common."

Parents, Family and Friends of Lesbians and Gays was an organization that embraced diversity and emphasized tolerance.

"The fact that your parents broke up to begin with is further proof that true love isn't always true," I said.

"The point is, they tried, and created the miracle

that is me. You, on the other hand, are still making every guy pay for the idiot who broke your heart in high school."

Only Evan could get away with knowing me so well.

"We were engaged, Evan. Erik cheated on me, remember?"

Evan made a *tsking* noise. "Engaged. Who gets engaged in high school?" My silence warned him—we'd been over this ground many times, and I knew he'd never cared for Erik. I didn't need to hear that lecture again. "Anyway," he went on, "you need to check that baggage at the door this time, girlfriend. Joe is a keeper."

I knew he meant well, but I didn't need the pressure. As much as I hated to rain on Evan's love parade, it was time to change the subject.

"I heard some news about Mojo this morning. He confessed to killing Caprice. He said he had to, because she'd found out about his girlfriend, and *she* was gonna kill *him*." I'd read the newspaper article over coffee with the old couple. "There was a knife with Caprice's fingerprints, lying in the grass. Granny Julep believes him. Mojo's being charged with manslaughter now instead of murder."

"Caprice was gonna stab him? Out of jealousy? Wow." Evan's voice turned thoughtful. "But it doesn't surprise me. Not after what happened."

I knew Evan well enough not to let him dwell on his visit from Caprice. He was doing quite well out there in the burbs with Butch.

"Don't you have something better to do, like get your hair done?"

Evan gave a mock sniff. "Well, I never."

"Oh, yes you have. Many times."

We teased a little more, good mood restored, then I hung up with a smile and a promise to call him later.

Just after lunch I got hit with a wave of elderly ladies in red hats, bussed into Little Five Points on a shopping trip.

Southern ladies are all about the past. I enjoyed helping them spend their money while they revisited their youth through fashion and frippery.

"How much is this, dear?"

True Southern belles still believe in the genteel power of wealth. Many of them are apparently too wealthy to be bothered with reading price tags. I was happy to give them service with a smile, though I wished Evan were there to flatter his way into their hearts *and* their wallets.

Old ladies always loved Evan, and vice versa.

"I carried a beaded purse like this to Cotillion when I was seventeen. Daddy insisted we hold the party at the country club even if it *was* during the war."

In Georgia there'd only been two wars: the one between the states and World War Two. I tried my best to envision a wizened grandmother as a dewy-cheeked seventeen-year-old, boogeying to the big band music of the forties. "It must have been a lovely party. Would you like to see this purse out of the case? It's a Whiting-Davis with the original satin lining."

Another old woman was drawn to the jewelry counter. "You're about my granddaughter's age. She's a pretty little thing, just like you." Southern ladies were also sweethearts. "Do you think she'd like this bracelet?"

"I'm sure she would. Vintage Juliana, very collectible. Amethysts and citrines set in japanned lacquer."

By five o'clock I was beat. The last of the Red Hat ladies was gone, and foot traffic was beginning to die down on Moreland. Most people were heading for cocktail hour or home to their dinners.

Knowing I had nothing in my refrigerator that wasn't at least a week old, I decided to close up shop and run by the grocery store. I wasn't much of a cook, and even my stock of frozen dinners was running low.

By six o'clock I was pulling into my driveway. I had almost an hour to put my groceries away and spread voodoo charms and tobacco seeds all over my house before it started getting dark.

The wind rustled the leaves in the big tree that shaded the front lawn, reminding me of my childhood. I used to climb that tree and listen to the same rustling, pretending the tree was whispering to me. Or sometimes I'd make believe that fairies lived among the branches, imaginary friends no one could see but me.

"Welcome home, Nicki," whispered the leaves/fairies. "Welcome home."

I stood for a moment, looking at the house. It was *my* house, dammit, and no evil spirit was going to keep me away.

If Caprice wanted to dance, we'd dance.

So I did what I almost always did when I got home from work—I turned on the stereo.

"'You are the dancing queen, young and sweet, only seventeen,'" I sang. Disco music was one of my guilty pleasures, but never when anyone else was around. I had my reputation as a chick with a dark side to think of, after all.

I turned it up until it was blasting. Music always set the mood for me, good or bad. Right now I wanted to feel young and alive and upbeat.

The straw figures Granny had given me weighed almost nothing, and it was easy enough to tape them above the doors and windows. The tobacco seeds were black specks that reminded me of mouse poop, but I sprinkled them faithfully on every windowsill and over the thresholds.

If the seeds kept Caprice from slinking like a shadow into my house, I'd happily suck them up in the morning with a straw.

The final weapon in my arsenal: Ralph Lauren sheets, barn red, only slightly faded. They looked great with a denim comforter, but I left that off tonight. Between those and a red T-shirt and panties, if Caprice wanted to get me, she was gonna have to get past a lot of red.

Disco tunes carried me through until dusk, and then it was time to change the mood. I brought on the heavy metal, and ate a nuked vegetable lasagna while AC/DC growled out "Dirty Deeds Done Dirt Cheap." Soon it was full dark outside.

Every light in the house was on, and all my preparations were done. Granny Julep's beads were hard crystals of resolve around my neck.

I was ready to kick some duppy ass.

CHAPTER 11

Nothing happened.

An uneventful evening of listening to rock music and flipping through magazines. Of turning off the music to read a novel in bed, trying not to jump at every imagined sound. Around midnight I finally felt safe enough to close my eyes and try to sleep.

Scratching woke me at 2:43 in the morning. The bedroom was bright as day, the lights still on. I'd moved a few extra lamps in earlier.

Scritch scritch.

Something was scratching at my window.

The tree didn't reach the house, and the bushes were trimmed. I stayed in bed, listening.

Scritch scritch. A pause. *Scritch.*

There was a drawn-out deliberateness to it. Someone wanted me to hear, to know it was there.

Use your mind, girl. That's the only place she is—that's how she draw her power.

Granny Julep's words came back to me, and I realized what she meant. If I allowed myself to imagine what horrible creature might be scratching at my window, trying to find a way in—

The scratching became a rattle, as if something tested the strength of the window frame. Then came a tapping against the glass, quick and urgent.

I fingered Granny Julep's beads beneath the covers while I forced myself to breathe, to be calm, to ignore the noises at the window. I squeezed my eyes shut and snuggled deeper beneath the red sheets, trying to think of other things. Of safe things.

Like Evan and the store. Like our annual shopping trip to New York every spring. Like maybe getting a puppy. Having someone to come home to wouldn't be such a bad idea.

The noises stopped, and I breathed a sigh of relief. Maybe I'd won, after all.

But I wasn't gonna push my luck by dwelling on it. To stay distracted, I thought about Joe.

Why had I met him *now*? Was there some kind of cosmic joke I didn't get? I'd been offered a glimpse of eternity and then sent back, though I'd happily have stayed. I was a believer now—God had made His point. He didn't need to punish me.

I didn't want to talk to the dead. I didn't want to fall for a conventional, respectable doctor. I didn't want to have a twin sister who was married to the doctor.

Is married to the doctor.

A sister. Someone who could've taken the place of the stuffed animals I'd had as a kid, the ones I'd whispered my girlish secrets to and snuggled against so I didn't feel so alone.

I was drifting in that place between asleep and awake when I heard the drums.

Far away and steady—regular as a heartbeat but faster. The sound came in waves, like gentle ripples on a pond, rising and falling. The drums lured my dreams, beckoned my thoughts, urged me to hear nothing but their rhythm.

"No." I opened my eyes and rolled onto my back, staring at the ceiling.

The drums got louder. It was so comfortable there, listening to those drums. They were in my mind, and all around me.

"No," I said again, and sat up.

The drums were insistent, ruthless in their staying power. The rhythm never faltered.

I threw back the covers and got out of bed, heading for the bathroom. Cotton balls might help.

"Nicki?"

The drums stopped.

Someone rapped on my front door. "Nicki? Are you up?"

Who would come knocking on my door at this hour? I couldn't help but think of the night my parents died . . . that time, it'd been a pair of Georgia state troopers.

Suspicious, I eased down the hall toward the door.

The knocking came again.

Gathering my nerve, I looked through the peephole.

"Joe . . . what are you doing here?"

Even through the distorted lens I could see he was weaving a little.

"Nicki." He smiled beatifically, as if he could see me. "I think it's called a 'booty' call. I wouldn't know, because I've never had one . . . or given one . . ." Joe waved a hand vaguely. " . . . or whatever. The boys in Radiology said that's what it was."

The conventional, respectable doctor was drunk! It would have been funny if it hadn't been the worst timing in the world. I glanced down at the sprinkling of tobacco seeds on the floor and remembered Granny's instructions: *Once the house has been sealed, don't break the seal until dawn.*

"You went out with the boys in Radiology?" I was stalling, torn about what to do.

"I did." Joe nodded his head solemnly. "First time ever. Told 'em all about you."

I couldn't help but smile on my side of the door, cringing at the thought of how *that* might have gone.

"Great guys, should've gone out with 'em sooner. Dr. Dull has been a Joe boy."

Stifling a laugh, I said very seriously, "Joe, you have to go home now. You can't come in."

He leaned against the door with both palms, pressing his eye against his side of the keyhole. "You can't send me home . . . I've had too much to drink. I'm a menish to society." Joe sounded completely self-satisfied, and completely confident I'd let him in.

I didn't know whether to laugh or cry. I wanted to let him in, but I didn't dare break the seal. So far Granny Julep's advice seemed to be working.

"Joe, listen." I leaned up against the door, still peeking through the lens. "I can't open the door. I've sealed it for the night."

He leaned back, disappointed.

"Sealed it with what? Duct tape?"

"Never mind with what." I wasn't going to give Joe any more reason than I already had to doubt my sanity. "Sealed with seeds" just didn't quite get it. "I can't break the seal until dawn."

"Okay." Joe heaved a theatrical sigh, hands dropping from the door. "I'll just make myself comfortable here on the porch. We've only got"—he peered blearily at his watch—"three or four more hours."

"You can't sleep out there. You have to go." The porch light flickered, as though a shadow passed over it.

Could've been a moth.

"Please, Joe." He was glancing around as if looking for a place to sit. There was a porch swing, but it was in a far corner. A corner with lots of shadows. "Stay right there. I'll call you a cab."

"You'll call me a cab?" Joe was so disappointed. "The boys in Radiology will never let me live it down. My first genuine three A.M. booty call, and I'm shot down in flames." He lost his balance and stumbled a little. "Are you sure?"

Damn the man. Caught between fear and laughter, I didn't stand a chance against the hurt look on his face. Throwing caution to the wind, I unlocked and opened the door.

His smile was almost worth it. I grabbed him by an arm and dragged him inside, closing the door as quickly as I could. I let go of him, looking around for my remaining tobacco seeds.

"I knew it," Joe said, making a beeline for the couch. He threw himself down with a sigh and settled himself comfortably on his back, while I watched, open-mouthed.

"Sealed the door," he mumbled, eyes closing. "Worst excuse I ever heard." Within a few seconds he was out.

"Some booty call." I shook my head as I found the tobacco seeds and sprinkled more, hoping to fix any damage. I suppose I should've been pissed, but I wasn't. Even passed out, Joe made me feel safe. I was glad he was there.

I'd felt a lot of things for a lot of guys: lust, both reciprocal and unrequited; casual affection, casual sex; mad crushes and hurt feelings. But I'd never depended on any of those guys. *I* took care of me. I'd only known Joe for a week, but I already knew he was the type of guy I could always depend on.

And it scared the hell outta me.

Hoping there'd been no harm done in the few seconds it took to get Joe inside, I pulled a blanket down out of the linen closet and covered him with it. He looked younger when he slept, his seriousness relaxed. *It must be hard to make life and death decisions every day, to hold people's lives in your hands.* I touched his dark hair and he mumbled something.

The overhead light by the front door flickered.

I looked around the room uneasily, hearing the faintest *ping* as the bulb blew out.

It was only one light. The house was full of them.

Then the lamp by the chair went out.

"Joe." I ripped off the blanket I'd just tucked in and grabbed him by the shoulder, giving him a shake. "Joe. Wake up."

Needless to say, he didn't wanna wake up. I shook him harder, and he opened his eyes just as the third light, the one at the end of the couch, went out.

"Get up, c'mon, get up," I urged. I eased myself beneath his arm and pulled, hard. "We have to go to bed."

I'd never have been able to move him myself, but Joe caught the gist and tried to cooperate. Together, we stumbled from the living room and down the hall toward my room.

I couldn't leave him out there. I had to get us barricaded in the bedroom with every lightbulb I could find. Red sheets, tobacco seeds, straw charms, and *gris-gris* bags. Lightbulbs and old beads.

Heaven help me.

I'd done all I could. Joe was passed out in my bed, unaware of the fear creeping up my spine. I'd skittered like a nervous mouse throughout the house, snatching up lamps to add to my hoard until the resulting shadows became too threatening, then retreated to my room.

Caprice had made it inside. I just knew it.

I'd locked us in the bedroom, sprinkling tobacco seeds over the threshold and again on the two windowsills. Then I'd covered Joe with the red sheet, the only other protection I could give him.

Damn him for trying to play the bad boy.

Damn him for tempting me tonight, of all nights.

A faint echo of feminine laughter, just at the edge of my hearing, brought my head around uneasily. I scanned the room, nearly blinded by the ring of lamps.

"Oh no, you don't," I muttered. "You're not getting inside my head." If thinking of evil gave it power, then I had to think of something else. Caprice couldn't harm me if I were stronger mentally than she was.

Evan's Christmas gift was my salvation.

I snatched up the little white iPod and plugged the earphones into my ears. The power adaptor was already in the wall, ready for recharging. I sincerely hoped Caprice couldn't influence anything bigger than lightbulbs, but if she did, I had batteries. Then I applied my own antidote to evil by listening to The Cure and Ani DiFranco, letting the music drown out everything else.

When dawn finally came, I was lying on the bed, back-to-back with a still sleeping Joe, and down to my last three bulbs. I was completely exhausted. Caprice wasn't giving up, and either I had an electrical problem of epic proportions or she really needed the darkness to get to me. Thank God for Evan's recent fondness for bulk warehouse sales— I'd started with a stockpile of two dozen bulbs and used nearly all of them. The bulbs had blown out, one by one, all night long.

As sunlight lit the edges of the curtains, I pulled the earphones out of my sore ears and turned off the iPod.

Joe stirred, coming awake. I made room for him to roll over on his back, and when he did, I snuggled against his chest. He gathered me close with one arm and covered his eyes with another, groaning as my movements shook the bed.

"Oh, man. Now I remember why I quit going out with the boys," he moaned.

"Poor baby," I said, totally unsympathetic. I'd been dancing with the dead all night while he'd been sleeping like one. "Does your head hurt?" I asked, knowing full well it had to be pounding. Still, I couldn't be too mad at him—he felt good, warm and solid beneath my cheek.

Joe lowered his arm, wincing at the glare. He lifted his head with an effort and looked around the room, taking in the ring of lamps surrounding the bed. There were ten of them . . . I know, I'd counted them often enough during the night.

"Wow." He eased his head back to the pillow. "Did we make a porno movie?"

I giggled tiredly, realizing how it must look to wake up in a sea of red sheets, bright lights all around.

"More importantly," Joe licked dry lips, eyes already closing, "was I any good?"

CHAPTER 12

"So let me get this straight."

Dr. Ivy Jacobson was a no-nonsense woman in her early sixties. She offered private counseling at two hundred and fifty bucks an hour from an office on the second floor of an old Victorian on Piedmont. The house was in the heart of the Buckhead historic district, where Ivy no doubt did a thriving business among the desperate housewives and businessmen of wealthy Buckhead County.

"During the last ten days you've suffered a near-fatal heart stoppage, lost a friend to domestic violence, and learned you might have an identical twin sister." Ivy had pale blue eyes, a direct manner, and gray hair cut fashionably short.

"Um, yeah. Don't forget that I can talk to dead people and that I've started sleeping with my doctor. Who might also be my brother-in-law."

Ivy waved that away for the moment, unimpressed with my glib comments. After spending less than an hour with her, I should have known better. The woman wasn't easily shocked. She'd listened to my whole twisted tale without batting an eye.

For two hundred and fifty bucks an hour I wasn't wasting time. I was telling all . . . a total brain dump.

"One life-changing event would be traumatic enough, Nicki, but you've had to cope with several within a very short time. It could certainly be enough to cause some misconceptions in your thinking."

The window behind Ivy overlooked the backyard of the old Victorian. Moss-draped trees, azaleas, and a fountain, very peaceful and picturesque.

"Misconceptions?"

"Let's talk more about your near death experience." Ivy leaned over to check the tape recorder. "I appreciate you agreeing to tape our session, by the way." She gave me that direct gaze again. "Why is it, do you think, that you were sent back?"

I shook my head. "He said it wasn't my time."

"He?" Her eyes sharpened. "This is the first time you've mentioned a gender."

I was frustrated at my inability to explain. Gender wasn't an issue. "The Light. The Presence behind the Light."

"I see." Ivy scribbled notes while I stared out the window. The chair beneath me was a butter-soft leather, designed no doubt to relax the people who sat in it while they put themselves under a microscope. Ivy had taken the couch, a reversal of what I would've expected.

"Did he say anything else?"

I closed my eyes, remembering. "Something about life being a dream, and that I should do unto others as I'd have them do to me."

"The Golden Rule."

I opened my eyes. "Yeah."

Or row, row, row your boat. One or the other.

Maybe I *was* delusional. Maybe a few dying neurons had sparked childhood imaginings of heaven.

Maybe Irene and Caprice were both just figments of a fried brain cell or two.

I wanted to believe that, but I knew better. I had an empty box of lightbulbs to prove it.

"And why, do you think, can you now see and speak to the dead? Do you think these events are somehow connected?"

I was starting to get irritated. I'd come here for answers, not questions.

"Of course they're connected. When I woke up in the hospital, there was Irene Goldblatt. I thought if I helped her, I'd be 'doing unto others' and that would be that. But as soon as I got rid of Irene, there was Caprice." I sounded defiant, but I didn't care. "Spirits seem to know I can hear them—like they know I've been to the other side. Even Granny Julep said so. She knew it before I told her."

"I see." Irene tapped her lower lip with a pencil, face carefully neutral. "What does Granny Julep say about Caprice?"

"It's complicated, but she says Caprice draws her power from my mind."

"I see."

Those two words were rapidly becoming my least favorite phrase in the English language. Ivy scribbled some more while I tried not to fidget.

"You seem to admire this Granny Julep, respect her opinion."

I thought about that carefully. "I do respect her." *She'd accept nothing less, the old bat.*

"In all honesty, she sounds like a charlatan." Ivy gave me a carefully bland look. "But perhaps you should consider the possibility she may be right. Perhaps Caprice exists only in your mind."

I could see where this was going. "I'm not imagining things. I'm not crazy."

Ivy shrugged. "That word's not in my vocabulary."

"That's what you're saying, isn't it?"

"No, it's not." She put her pencil and pad aside and leaned forward. "I'm saying you should consider the possibility that your mind is creating its own reality."

Not bothering to hide the roll of my eyes, I said, "That sounds like typical psychobabble to me. I promised Joe I'd come and talk to you, but in all honesty, I can't see the point." Ivy's expression never changed. "Something happened to me. Something *changed* me." My voice quivered, almost broke. "It's not something I ever wanted, or anything I would've ever 'made up' for myself."

I dug my nails into the leather chair. "I don't *want* to see ghosts, or spirits, or whatever the hell they are." I was trembling, emotions building. I felt the tears coming, struggled to hold them back. "I don't *want* to 'do unto others'—I just want to be left alone." Ivy held out a box of tissues, impassive in the face of my meltdown. I snatched one, crying openly now. "And I don't want a twin." It felt good to admit it, so I said it again. "I don't want a twin, and I sure as hell don't want to fall in love with her husband."

Oh my God. Had I just said the L word?

Ivy said nothing, letting me cry. Crying wasn't something I normally did, and I wasn't very good at it. My nose quickly felt twice its size, making it hard to breathe. I felt like a wet fish, flopping and gasping for air, crying my heart out in a way I hadn't since my parents died.

Ivy turned off the recorder and leaned over to squeeze my hand. She waited, making sympathetic noises.

After destroying a few tissues and smearing my eyeliner beyond repair, I finally got myself under control. A shaky breath or two later, I felt better. Surprisingly so, for a woman whose nose felt swollen to the size of a grapefruit.

"I guess therapy might not be such a bad idea after all, huh?" A lame attempt at a joke, with a grain of truth.

"Everybody needs a good cry now and then," Ivy said, giving my hand a final pat. "I'd like to continue this next week, Nicki. Would Monday work for you?"

I was hesitant. "To be honest," *though only partly so,* "I'm not sure I can afford you. I don't even know if therapy is covered under my health insurance."

And I don't know if I want the word "therapy" to become part of my vocabulary.

Ivy rose and moved toward her desk. "I'm sure we can work something out, Nicki. Dr. Bascombe is a colleague of mine, after all. I wouldn't have agreed to assist him with a blind study otherwise."

"Excuse me?"

Ivy picked up her appointment book. Her pink and gray tweed suit was nicely tailored, Ann Taylor or Saks.

"I assumed Dr. Bascombe told you I've agreed to help him with his paper." She turned to face me, frowning.

How had I forgotten this? I was a test case to Joe, an oddity, made more so by the resemblance to his missing wife. He'd sent me to a handpicked psychiatrist to get more data for his report.

"The blind study relates strictly to the documentation of near death experiences and their aftereffects, nothing more. We present our findings separately, and compare conclusions." Ivy looked worried. "As far as the personal nature of your relationship with Dr. Bascombe, I'm bound by confidentiality. I would never share anything with him of a private nature—only my findings as they relate to your NDE. I thought you understood the situation when you agreed to let me tape the session."

I noticed for the first time the pin she wore on the breast of her suit—a tiered pink rhinestone flower, vintage Coro maybe.

"You won't tell Joe anything I say about him?"

"Absolutely not. Doctor-patient privilege."

I hesitated, considering. I couldn't deny I felt better after spilling my guts. "I don't mean to be rude, but what's in it for you?"

Ivy leaned back against her desk and crossed her arms. "Aside from a chance of having an article published in a medical journal?" She paused, giving me a wry smile. "Let me be honest, Nicki. You're a refreshing change from the typical mid-life crises and sexual dysfunction I see every day."

I grinned, knowing I looked like a sodden version of a raccoon with my mascara-smeared cheeks. She probably didn't get many clients with nipple rings.

"You seem like a nice girl," she added. "Let me help you through this."

"How'd it go with the shrink?"

Evan was happily ensconced in the catbird seat, flipping through the latest issue of *Vogue*. He'd called me that morning, just after Joe left, and informed me he'd decided it was safe to leave suburbia for Little Five Points during the day. Privately, I think he was just bored. The store was his lifeblood as much as it was mine.

He tore his gaze from Christian Lacroix's spring collection to take a good look at my face.

"Oh, dear Lord. It's Kelly Osbourne the morning after. What happened to your mascara? Your lipstick is all smeared."

"Kelly Osbourne's fat," I sniffed. "I'm not fat."

Evan was nothing if not clever. Clever enough to cease the questions long enough to offer me the catbird's seat and a soda from the little fridge we kept under the counter.

I plopped down with a sigh, opened the soda, then told him about Ivy.

"I like her. But I don't like that Joe didn't tell me she was helping with his paper. That part makes me feel like a specimen, a freak." I chewed morosely on a fingernail until Evan slapped my hand away. "I thought he sent me to her because she could help me, because he cared about me, not because he needed another expert opinion for his report."

"He should've told you," Evan agreed.

"I'd forgotten about the stupid paper anyway. Even thought it was just his 'opener,' you know?" Evan nodded, completely understanding where I was coming from. "I thought it just was an excuse to find out more about me, figure out if I was Kelly's sister—I didn't realize he was serious."

"He should've told you."

"Then why didn't he?"

Evan threw up his hands. "Honey, if I knew the answer to that I'd either be a straight man or a shrink. And I'd much rather have the two hundred bucks an hour."

"Two fifty," I said glumly.

The front door jingled as two teenage girls came in. Evan put on his show face and greeted them cheerfully, then gave me a final comment.

"Ask him."

I wanted to ask him.

I should've asked him.

But instead I did what any red-blooded American woman would do if given half the chance.

I snooped.

When Joe woke up in my bed that morning, hung over but happy, his solution to the problem with the lights, the drums, and the scratching was to insist I take the key to his apartment. He'd also insisted I go there when the sun went down, even though he was working the night shift. I'm not sure if he believed that Caprice was behind it all, but at least he believed *I* believed it.

So it was kind of his own fault if, when I opened the door to his empty apartment, I couldn't resist stepping inside.

It was quiet. Being there alone felt strange. I dropped my bag and keys on a chair and looked around.

His collection of black and white framed prints was the nicest thing about the place. I could easily envision how much better they'd show if he put an Oriental red on the walls and got rid of the bland brown couch. Black leather furniture might be a bachelor cliché, but it could work if done tastefully. With Joe's wholesome good looks, he could carry it off.

I walked around the living room, deliberately avoiding the bookcase with its photo albums. I admired the prints for a moment—all black and white nature photos, stark contrasts of light and shadow—and wondered if Joe would like Edward Gorey's macabre sketches.

Then I trailed into the kitchen, taking a peek inside the fridge.

Mostly empty; cartons of milk and orange juice, some apples and some yogurt, a few leftover strawberries. I popped one in my mouth as I moved on, enjoying the juicy reminder. No need to look for the whipped cream—that was all gone.

Joe's cupboards were equally spartan; some healthy cereals and canned soups, a shelf of vitamins and herbal supplements. Evidently, Dr. Bascombe practiced what he preached when it came to good health. He had the great body to prove it.

The apartment wasn't that big, so I had a decision to make. Joe's bedroom, or his office? The bedroom was tempting, but that would be going over the line. I wanted to find out what the man really thought about me, not rat out his stack of dirty magazines.

I'd never been in the second bedroom he used as an office, but the door was open.

This room had more of Joe's personality—framed photos of his sister and his parents, scattered papers and books, some stacked on the floor. A scuffed and battered recliner, dark blue, with a flexible reading lamp. Newspapers and empty cups, the foil wrapper from a protein bar. A big desk with a computer and printer.

Hoping his computer wasn't password protected, I turned it on. While it booted I took a look at the papers spread all over the desk.

Supporting NDE in the Health Care Setting. The Lancet. Scientific American. There was a small pile of books, nearly buried beneath the papers. *Lessons from the Light. The Division of Consciousness. Near Death Experiences: The Other Side of Life.*

Wow. There were actual books written about this stuff.

The screen flickered, then steadied as the icons

appeared. Next to the keyboard were pages of notes in what I assumed was Joe's handwriting, scribbled and barely legible. I figured I'd have better luck with the computer itself, and loaded up Joe's word-processing program. Sure enough, the last document he'd worked on was a file called *NDE#1*.

I pulled it up and began to read.

Eight million Americans have experienced near death episodes during medical emergencies. A near death experience is defined as clinical death accompanied by successful resuscitation.

As fascinating as that was, I was more anxious to read about how Joe's paper related to *me*. I found myself skimming quickly over boring things like "methodology" and "abstracts."

Near death experiencers often report a significant increase in belief in the afterlife, accompanied by higher spiritual awareness.

"Huh," I muttered. "That's putting it mildly."

Problems can occur with these increased
sensitivities. The sudden shift in thinking may be so drastic that the experi-
encer cannot adjust.

Uh-oh. Can't adjust? As in maladjusted? As in
screwed-up?

The perception of a different reality
other than that of the physical world
can have negative consequences as well
as positive. Some experiencers find it
hard to commit to relationships after an
NDE, citing an inability to "personal-
ize" concepts such as love and family.
What were once private emotions are now
seen as universal concepts . . .

"Blah, blah, blah." I hit the Print button, deciding to reread that part later. I wasn't too thrilled
with what I'd read so far.

While the printer spewed out paper, I skipped
ahead, searching for the good stuff. Lots of statis-
tics and theories, but nothing personal. I checked
the file menu on the word processor again and saw
a filed named SUB#1. I pulled it up.

Subject #1: Female, age 28.

Subject, huh?

Cardiac arrest due to secondary mitral
valve prolapse, previously undetected.
Spontaneous resuscitation after time of
death declared. Subject reports tunnel,
white light, feelings of euphoria.

All accurate, but reading it left me cold. Joe made
it sound so clinical, so dispassionate.

The experience had been anything but.

I leaned back in his chair, unsatisfied. There was
more; notes from what I'd told him in the hospital,
reference to the taped session we'd had in the coffee shop the day of Irene's funeral. It seemed so
long ago.

Suddenly, I felt like an absolute jerk. What was I
doing? What was I looking for?

I closed all the files as quickly as I could and
shut down the computer, though I did take the
pages from the printer. It wouldn't hurt to learn
more about NDEs. I even took a minute to write
down the name of a couple of Joe's reference
books, thinking a trip to the bookstore was in
order.

Joe hadn't done anything wrong here except not
tell me about Ivy Jacobson's involvement with his

paper. He'd been nothing but good to me—even offering me a safe place to stay until nine-night was over.

I was ashamed of myself. For about two seconds.

Then I went in search of his stack of dirty magazines.

CHAPTER 13

"You got a phone call while you were at lunch."
Evan stopped fussing with Marilyn Monroe's cleavage just long enough to fluff her yellow organza skirt.
"Somebody named Albert." He stepped back to admire Marilyn's new outfit, gesturing absently toward
the register. "I left his number on the counter."

The only Albert I knew was Granny Julep's Albert. "Did he say what he wanted?" I stuck my
purse under the counter and picked up the slip of
pink paper.

Evan shrugged, absorbed in his vision. Evidently,
Marilyn was going to a glamorous spring picnic,
straw hat, sunglasses, and all.

"Nope. Just asked for a call back. What do you think, the white rhinestone glasses, or the yellow ones?"

"The white," I answered automatically as I began dialing the number. "Very cool."

"I thought so, too." Evan always pretended to take compliments as a given, but my opinion mattered. We'd once gotten into a huge blowup over Jayne Mansfield's ability to carry off a somewhat demure cocktail dress from the fifties. I'd won, and now Jayne wore nothing but sexy and flirtatious.

Privately, I liked to think that if mannequins could talk, Jayne would've thanked me for it.

"Hello?" A rusty male voice—definitely someone elderly.

"Albert? This is Nicki Styx. I'm returning your call."

I didn't bother to ask how he'd gotten my number. Handbags and Gladrags was in the phonebook.

"Granny Julep wants to see you." Albert made it sound like a summons.

"Um . . . okay. I'll be here the rest of the afternoon if you wanna come in. But you can tell her that everything's fine—I'm staying with a friend until nine-night is over and I'm doing everything she told me."

Evan, who was listening shamelessly, rolled his eyes at me when I described Joe as "a friend."

Things were way beyond the friendship stage, and he knew it. In addition to living in his apartment and sleeping in his bed, I'd had lunch with Joe two days in a row.

There was silence on the other end of the line for a moment. "She too tired to go out. I'll come pick you up."

Too tired to go out? I unbent a little. She was old, after all.

"Thanks anyway, but I'll drive myself. Just give me directions and I'll come." I hesitated. "Is she okay? She's not sick or anything, is she?"

"No." Albert kept it brief, as always. "She just tired."

He gave me slow, precise directions to Granny Julep's place, which I wrote down on the back of a slip of paper. I promised to be there by four, knowing Evan wouldn't mind closing by himself tonight. Then I hung up, a sense of unease hanging over my head.

"Going to see the voodoo woman?" Evan clicked his tongue at me while he draped a scarf over Marilyn's hat and tied it loosely under her chin. "I wouldn't go looking for trouble if I were you."

He had a point—I'd had two blissful nights of duppy-free sleep at Joe's apartment. He was still working nights, so I'd been free to go to bed early, waking in the early dawn when he got home. He'd slip in the bed beside me, naked and freshly show-ered. We'd steam up the sheets, then I'd leave him to get some sleep of his own while I went to work.

"I'm not looking for trouble, just visiting an old lady."

"Oh my." Evan whipped off Marilyn's scarf, apparently dissatisfied with its effect on the hat, and flounced it at me. "Is it time for your good deed of the month *already*?" His eyes sparkled. "With all the"—a giant sweep of the scarf—"*love* in the air, I almost missed it."

"You are such a fairy."

Evan's answer was to drape the scarf over his head and neck, tossing the end over his shoulder in a dramatic flourish. "Thank you." He slipped on the yellow shades and struck an elegant pose, à la Grace Kelly. "No autographs, please."

In the next instant he'd whipped both off and was moving toward the accessory racks, obviously not finished with Marilyn's outfit. "So where did Dr. Yummy take you for such a late lunch today? Chinese? Italian?"

"Hospital cafeteria. It was breakfast for him, lunch for me."

Evan couldn't have looked more horrified if someone had told him spandex shorts were back on the runway.

I shrugged. "What can I say? A girl's gotta eat."

He opened his mouth to speak.

"Don't say it," I warned, only half joking.

We giggled like the girls we were, and spent the next hour designing a summer theme for the front window—checkered tablecloth, picnic basket, and all.

"If you're gonna go, go ahead and go," Evan said as flipped through the clothes racks, looking for a halter top that would fit Jayne's generous curves. He was going to pose her sunning on a blanket. "It's Friday night. Most everybody's more interested in what bar they're going to instead of what they'll be wearing tomorrow."

"I know." We hadn't had a customer since I'd gotten back from lunch. "You sure you're okay to close up?"

Evan waved me off. "I'm fine. I'm outta here at five o'clock sharp. I'm meeting Butch for drinks."

I waved my hand in front of my face as if mosquitoes were after me. "Sorry? I couldn't quite catch that—there's so much *love* in the air I almost missed it."

"Smart-ass."

"Takes one to know one."

Granny Julep lived in a shotgun-style house in the Decatur area of Atlanta. Shotgun houses are a very old Southern tradition. One room wide and three or four deep, they're called shotguns because a bullet fired from the front door can go straight through the house without hitting a thing.

The neighborhood Granny lived in was old, but a lot of the houses showed signs of tender loving care; fresh paint and nice yards. There were kids playing in the street, parents watching from their porches. Granny's house was as tidy and neatly kept as any, white with black trim, side garden filled with blooms.

Albert was waiting for me at the screen door. He let me in without a word and motioned me to follow him toward the back. I could hear a TV somewhere, but barely got a glimpse of the place before we were in Granny's bedroom.

Granny Julep was propped up on pillows, watching *Oprah*. Her gnarled hand reached for the remote, but Albert got there first. He turned off the TV and put the remote back on the bed next to Granny, closer to her than before. Then he turned around and left us alone, closing the bedroom door behind him.

"Albert doesn't say much, does he?"

The lighthearted comment was a cover. Granny didn't look well.

"We done said all we'll ever need to say to each other, my Albert and I."

I didn't like the sound of that.

"Are you sick, Granny Julep? Is there anything I can get you?" Her cocoa brown skin had a grayish cast, and her eyes were deeply sunken in their sockets. Despite Evan's teasing about my lack of noble qualities, I found myself worried about her.

She smiled at me, shaking her head. "I'm just tired, girl. Old and tired. Been up most nights for Caprice's setups, so I been takin' my rest during the days. It's hard on an old woman."

Granny motioned me toward a straight-backed wooden chair near the bed. "Sit. I need to talk to you."

The quilt on the bed was beautiful, a patchwork of bright yellows, reds, and blues. I knew without asking that Granny Julep had made it, because its colorful spirit suited her. If only she didn't look so gray beneath it.

"I did what you said with the seeds and the straw charms, Granny." For some reason, I wanted to make her feel better. I pulled aside my shirt collar so she could see the black beads she'd given me. "I haven't taken these off. It seemed like everything was working, but I messed up. Caprice almost got in." I shuddered, remembering the drums. "I couldn't take it anymore, so I'm staying with a friend until nine-night is over."

Granny Julep frowned, considering. "She must've

found a cottonwood . . . she's stronger than I thought."

Her statement made no sense for a moment. Then I realized what Granny meant, and at the same moment I saw, in my mind's eye, the tree in my front yard.

My special "fairy" tree. How dare she?

"She's in the tree?"

Granny nodded. "The roots are powerful. She can rest there during the day, underground, soakin' up their life force."

Great. Just great. A childhood joy corrupted, and a zombie in my front yard.

"It's good you stayin' somewhere else." Granny Julep sighed and closed her eyes, leaning her head back against the pillows. "It'll all be over soon."

I didn't like the way she said that. A sense of unease returned, pushing aside my annoyance. I waited, wondering if I should let Granny drift off and then slip out, or stay until she woke up.

I waited, but the wait wasn't long. Granny opened her eyes and lifted her head, then shifted herself higher on the pillows. She looked tired, but her dark eyes had lost none of their shrewdness.

"I wanted to ask you about the Light," she said.

The statement caught me off guard, though I quickly realized it shouldn't. For all her secrets and all her wisdom, Granny Julep was still human, and very old. I knew what she was asking.

She was asking if the beliefs she'd based her life on were worth having. Odd, how I knew her so well when I knew her so little.

Then again, maybe not.

"It's the most peaceful, beautiful place you could ever imagine," I said slowly. "The Light isn't a *who* or a *what*—it's a place, a being, a state of existence nearly impossible to describe. Everyone's there, and when I say *everyone*, I mean it, you know?" Granny Julep nodded, as though I'd just confirmed something she'd known all along. I knew I could tell her everything, freely, and she'd believe me. "Time, distance, age . . . they just don't matter there. There's music. Music like nothing you've ever heard . . . and you're a part of it. Part of it all."

Granny Julep reached out a hand and I took it, letting her squeeze my fingers while I told the rest of the story. "I understood *everything*. I *knew* everything. And it was all . . . beautiful. But then the Light said it wasn't my time." I allowed myself to remember that moment, right down to the pang of regret that I couldn't stay. "He sent me back and told me to 'do unto others as I would have them do unto me.'" I ducked my head, swallowing an unfamiliar lump in my throat. "Sounds cheesy, I know, but that's what He said."

I squeezed her hand gently, careful of the birdlike bones beneath my fingers. "But you're not going there yet, are you?" And I held my breath, hoping she'd say no, she was just tired.

"Not yet." Granny Julep's eyes were suspiciously moist, and so were mine. "I got to save my grand-daughter. And while I'm at it, I'm gonna save you." She smiled a sweet smile. "And now I know how."

What a relief. "How?"

"The Lord works in mysterious ways, child, and so do I. You don't need to know how. But you once asked me for a favor, so now I'm gonna ask you for one." Why was I not liking the sound of this? "You come to the nine-night on Monday. You be my hands"—she held both of them up in the air, letting me see their shaking—"and draw the *veve.* The pattern gotta be perfect, or Papa Legba won't help us."

There was that "lost in translation" feeling again. I didn't speak voodooese.

"The *veve*?"

"Every loa has a symbol, child. We draw it in cornmeal to call them down, like I did for Dam-ballah."

An ugly flash to that darkened room in the back of Indigo, where a wooden snake came to life.

Shit.

"And this Papa Legba? Is he a good loa or a bad loa?"

"Papa Legba is the guardian of the crossroads. He the One who has final say over whose soul goes where."

"The voodoo version of Saint Peter. I get it."

Granny Julep frowned. "Don't make fun of things you don't understand, girl." She lay her head back against the pillow, adding, "You of all people should know better."

Three hours later I sat in the middle of a big mess, cornmeal on my clothes and in my hair. Joe's formerly clean kitchen floor was now in desperate need of vacuuming.

Granny Julep had given me a complex diagram of flowery squiggles, and explicit directions on how to reproduce the pattern a pinch of cornmeal at a time. She'd even made me practice on a tray Albert brought from the kitchen, and she wasn't satisfied until she'd explained the symbolism of every swoop and curl. Like I'd ever remember.

Then she'd sent me off to practice on my own, content with my promise to come back on Monday afternoon to draw the *veve* for the ceremony. It didn't sound so bad, really, because Granny didn't want me to actually *attend* the ceremony.

"You'd just be a distraction, child, and make the others uneasy," she'd said. "We'll draw the *veve* early, while it's still daylight."

Thank God. I had no desire to meet any more voodoo deities, whether they slithered or walked upright. Once Monday night was over, I hoped I never heard the word "voodoo" again.

It was painstaking work, and I was on my third try at getting a good-sized *veve* just right. The sound of a key in the front door caught me off guard. I had a palmful of cornmeal in one hand and a pinch in the other, and the kitchen was a total disaster area. Before I could decide whether to claim that a box of muffin mix had exploded or just tell the truth, there was Joe.

"Well, well, well." Even wearing two days' worth of stubble and wrinkled green scrubs, Joe looked good. He grinned at me as he tossed his keys on the table by the door and came into the kitchen, cornmeal crunching under his feet. "Morticia Addams meets June Cleaver, perhaps? I thought you goth types were supposed to draw pentagrams on the floor with chalk, not bread crumbs."

I grinned back. "It isn't bread crumbs, it's cornmeal. And they're not pentagrams." It was easier to dispute the facts than explain them. "And I'm not goth. Not anymore, anyway."

"Well, in that case, maybe you should know that normal people usually prepare food on the counter, not on the floor."

"Why is everyone I know such a smart-ass?"

Joe laughed, obviously not upset to find his kitchen looking like I'd been feeding chickens while he was gone. "Takes one to know one."

He sounded just like Evan.

"I'll have you know that I'm practicing how to draw a *veve*," I said loftily. "It's a delicate art."

Joe's smile died. "A *veve*? That sounds like voodoo."

"Give the man a cigar." I tried to keep it light, not liking how quickly his good mood faded. "It's a favor for Granny Julep."

"Give the man a break," he answered flatly. "Don't you remember what happened the last time you helped that old woman with her 'voodoo'? She scared you to death with that snake . . . Haven't you learned your lesson yet?"

I stared up at him from my cross-legged position on the floor. "What lesson is that, Joe? Don't die and go to heaven because if you come back you might see dead people? Or don't tell people the truth because they'll think you're a wacko?"

My sarcasm was tinged with bitterness, surprising me as much as it apparently did Joe. He didn't answer immediately.

I was tired of people thinking I had some kind of *choice* in all this. I was fighting to regain control of my life, to get back to the relatively carefree existence I'd once had. And to do that, a girl's gotta do what a girl's gotta do.

"Nobody thinks you're a wacko." Joe's voice was very quiet.

"Oh, really? And who was it that insisted I go see Ivy Jacobson, huh?" *Oh my God . . . I was picking a fight.* Worse yet, I was beginning to enjoy it. "And by the way, don't you think you could've mentioned Ivy was doing a"—I used cornmeal-coated fingers to make hash marks in the air—"'blind study' on me for your precious paper? Don't you think I should've been given the courtesy of being asked if I wanted to be somebody's lab rat?"

He seemed genuinely surprised by my anger. "I didn't think you'd mind. It's a win-win for everybody—you get reduced fees, I get additional credentials for my paper, and Ivy gets another case study for her files."

"I'm not a case study!" I yelled. "And you could've told me!" I threw my hands up, disgusted with his lack of sensitivity. Unfortunately, I forgot about the handful of cornmeal I'd been holding. A cloud of dry crumbs flew up.

Joe blinked, clearly unsure how to handle an angry woman covered in cornmeal. Then the corner of his mouth began to twitch.

"Damn you, Joe Bascombe." My own lip was twitching in response, so before it got away from me, I scooped up a handful of cornmeal and threw it at him.

He ducked, but only halfheartedly, giving me a wicked look as he bent and scooped up a handful of his own.

"I think you missed a spot," he said as he tossed it over my head.

I shrieked with laughter, scrabbling backward on the floor and shaking dry crumbs from my hair.

"You're gonna pay for that, buddy," I warned between giggles. The next handful of dry crumbs went straight down the front of his scrub pants.

Joe tickled me mercilessly in an effort to fend me off, then grabbed me around the waist. We ended up on the floor, both of us now covered in cornmeal. He rolled onto his back and pulled me with him, so I lay on top, laughing down into his eyes.

"And for the record, you are not a case study." He wrapped his arms around me and squeezed. "Unless it's a study in individuality. Or spontaneity. Or whether a man can survive an erection with cornmeal in his pants."

"Quit teasing for a second." *I had to know*. "Do you believe me when I tell you I see spirits?"

Joe didn't hesitate, honest as always, warm and solid beneath me. "I don't claim to be an expert on the afterlife, Nicki. I believe you believe it . . . and I believe in *you*." He tucked a strand of hair behind my ear, letting his fingers linger.

Not quite the resounding yes I'd hoped for, but better than nothing.

Then he was actually brave enough to ask me, "Is the hissy fit over?"

Bravery should never go unrewarded. "For now."

"Good," he said. "Let's go dancing."

CHAPTER 14

What Joe lacked in technique, he made up for in enthusiasm, and luckily, he didn't look too much like a geeky white boy while he was doing it.

Not that it would've mattered at the Star Bar. It was just after midnight on a Friday night and the place was packed, loud music and free expression in the air. The stylish and the not so stylish rubbed elbows with tattooed metalheads and punk rockers. The dance floor was jammed, multicolored lights strobing overhead. Joe and I were minnows in a pulsing, gyrating pond.

Conversation was impossible, but Joe was obviously having a great time, and so was I. For just a moment I got a brief flash of him as I'd first seen him in the emergency room, all serious and intent, trying to save my life.

I hoped I'd repaid him a little by bringing some fun into his.

Joe pointed toward the bar and I nodded, letting him grab me by the hand and lead me through the crowd. In jeans and black T-shirt, freshly showered and shaved, Joe drew more than his share of glances.

Better luck next time, ladies and gents.

Luck was on my side again as we reached the edge of the dance floor and started threading our way through the tables. We snagged one near the back just as another couple was leaving.

"I'll get us something to drink." Joe's mouth was close to my ear, but he still had to speak loudly to be heard above the music. "Save me a seat."

"Diet Coke with lime," I answered. When he quirked an eyebrow, I added, "I'm pacing myself."

Joe smiled, and my heart did its little trip. He reached out and grazed my cheek with the back of his knuckle, letting his eyes do the talking. Then he turned and headed toward the bar.

Stop it, I told my heart silently. *I'm trying to keep you safe. You couldn't handle being broken, you wimp.*

I shoved aside thoughts of my defective ticker *and* my inability to follow my own advice, and turned to the ebb and flow of nightlife. People-watching had always been one of my favorite pastimes. The music switched from techno to R&B, just right for slow dancing.

"He your boyfriend?"

The question came from a girl standing beside my table, a girl I didn't know. She looked to be early twenties, with long blond hair, which would've been prettier if she hadn't gelled up her bangs within an inch of their life. Typical Georgia redneck chic.

Would the legacy of Farrah Fawcett never die?

I nodded, giving her a tight smile so she'd go away.

"Don't trust him," she said. "He's too good-looking."

The two words that came to mind weren't nice ones, but I contented myself with a dirty look. "Thanks for the advice, but nobody asked you." I angled myself away, making it clear I was done talking.

Evidently I didn't make it clear enough, because she slid into the seat across from me.

"Hey, you need to—"

It was then I saw her eyes. They were empty, empty and soulless as a bottomless pit.

"Billy was real good-looking, too," the girl said, as if I hadn't spoken. "He could talk you into, or out of, *anything* just by the way he smiled. 'Trust me, Tammy,' he'd say. And I was fool enough to believe him."

A chill crept down my spine. She stared right through me, lost in her memories, oblivious to the people and the music and the cheerful Friday night vibe. And suddenly I knew. No one heard her, no one saw her, but me.

"I try to warn the other girls who come in here, but they don't listen . . . they don't see," Tammy said. "But you do." Her eyes met mine, no curiosity at all in their depths as to how that could be possible. She didn't seem to care about anything except sharing her story.

"Everybody told me," she said. "But I didn't believe them. I thought he'd marry me when I told him about the baby, but he said he wasn't ready—that *we* weren't ready."

I listened in silence, an unwilling audience to what I was sure would turn out to be a tragic tale.

"So I did what he asked," the girl shrugged, "because he promised we'd have other babies. Lots of babies, he said. And I believed him."

She was pretty enough, in a "Southern comfort" kind of way. She must have laughed and smiled once, dreaming of a future with her Billy.

A future that obviously never happened.

"When I heard he was down here with another girl, bragging how he'd knocked me up and then talked me into getting rid of it, I had to come see for myself. I found him here with my younger sister, Sue Ellen." Her eyes moved listlessly over the crowd. "They were making out at a table in the corner."

I felt like an insect frozen in amber. I wanted to get up, to run away from the monotonous drone of her words, the relentless depression that radiated from her in waves. But I couldn't, and I knew why.

Because she had no one else. No one but a total stranger out looking for a good time, who'd come face-to-face with tragedy.

"What happened?" I asked quietly. It didn't matter how loud the music was. She could hear me.

"They laughed. Billy told me he was done with me now that I couldn't get him for child support. Sue Ellen was drunk—said she'd tell Daddy about the baby if I didn't leave them alone. He woulda killed her if he'd known she was out drinking with Billy—she was only seventeen. Daddy woulda killed us both for what we did with Billy, I think."

She raised those empty, soulless eyes to me again.

"I saved him the trouble, at least with me."

It was all so clear. Maybe my brush with death had left me with more compassion for those who had to deal with it. After all, if I needed help passing over, I'd want someone to help me.

"You don't have to stay here, you know," I said.

The girl looked at me dispassionately.

"This isn't all there is. You can go into the Light. You can be happy again."

The first emotion I'd seen flickered in her eyes. It looked like fear.

"No. There's no Light. There's only lies."

"But there is a Light. I've seen it."

"No!" She slammed her hands on the table, startling me. "Don't you get it? There's no Light for me!" Her voice started to crack, along with her composure. Her outburst should've been heard by everyone. "I killed my baby! I killed myself! I've seen what's waiting for me and I won't go!"

Shocked, I waited to hear what else she had to say.

"I hear them whispering. They say, 'Come with us, Tammy, come with us . . . it'll be okay . . . you don't need to be afraid, we'll take care of you.'" She glared at me now, frightening me. "But I've seen them from the corner of my eye. Dark, ugly little things. And there's a smell . . . an awful, putrid, stinking smell . . . they think I don't know they're lying. But I know. I know. If I go with them—" She looked away, glancing around as if someone were listening. "—then I'll burn in Hell for what I've done. Eternity in a juke joint don't seem so bad compared to that."

I had the oddest sensation. It took me a moment to realize what it was, and when I did, it nearly overwhelmed me.

Pity.

Pity for this poor girl who didn't understand that she'd condemned herself to a living Hell, not because of her actions, but because of her beliefs. She believed what she'd done was unforgivable.

Take unto ye the armor of God, that ye may be able to withstand evil.

Granny's words came back to me, as clear as if she were standing there, and I knew what I had to do to help this poor lost soul.

Feeling like a hypocrite, I asked, "Tammy, did you go to church when you were . . . well, when you were alive?"

Her anger was gone as quickly as it came. "'Course I did. Daddy was a preacher."

I'll bet he was. The fire and brimstone type, unless I missed my guess.

"Then you should know that if you ask for forgiveness, you'll receive it."

She shook her head stubbornly. "Some things are beyond that."

"No." I shook my head in return. "No, they're not." The glimpse I'd had of the afterlife showed me a place where guilt and self-hatred didn't exist. Neither did revenge or punishment. I'd hardly lived my life as a saint, yet I'd been taken someplace warm and welcoming. Surely this poor girl could go there, too.

"You *can* be forgiven. But I think . . . I think first you have to forgive yourself."

Tears filled her eyes but her expression didn't change.

"You're lying," she whispered. My brain registered the noise and music all around us, but my ears seemed tuned to her alone.

"I'm not."

Tammy stared at me, ignoring the tears that now slid down her pale cheeks. "But how can I? My baby's dead and—"

I interrupted her. "No, he's not. He's waiting for you."

She gasped, shaken from her apathy.

"Or she. I don't know." I spoke quickly, before she could refuse to listen. "It doesn't matter there. *Nothing* matters there, except joy and acceptance." She was trembling now, pressing a hand to her mouth. "You were young . . . you were in love . . . you made some mistakes." I tried my best to convince her of the truth. "Mistakes can be forgiven.

Be brave, and go past those little dark things. Ignore them, and go into the Light."

I had no idea if what I said was possible, but somehow I *believed* it to be so.

The Light had made me feel as if anything were possible. I wanted to keep feeling that way.

"Man, it took forever to get the bartender's attention."

Joe's voice broke through the odd bubble of silence, letting music and nightlife pour in with a rush. I jumped, startled, as he slid a drink in front of me.

"You okay?" he asked, moving around to Tammy's side of the table. Except Tammy wasn't there, and Joe slid into the empty seat with no hesitation. "You look a little spooked."

Oh, that's too easy.

"I'm fine. Just didn't hear you come up behind me. It's noisy in here, you know?" I drank half my Diet Coke before putting it down, both thirsty and thoughtful.

Poor girl. We all make mistakes. I wondered how many years Tammy had been paying for hers, here at the Star Bar.

Joe was smiling at me across the table, the music was loud, and I was young and alive—I didn't want him to lose that smile. There was no need to tell him about Tammy now, not when we were having fun. But I couldn't help but wonder if she'd taken my advice and gone into the Light.

"You're beautiful," Joe said. "Have I ever told you that?"

Now there was an attention grabber.

I rested my elbows on the table, feeling a rush of pleasure at the compliment. "I don't think you have."

"Well, I should've." He shook his head. "And you are. Sexy, too—did I mention that?"

"I don't think you did."

"Look at you." Joe's eyes traveled over my hair and face, roving over my body. "You're gorgeous and stylish and sexy and smart. And spunky."

"One more *s* word and you win the prize," I teased. "Where's all this coming from?" *Not that I minded.* "And I'm not spunky, I'm spirited." I grinned at him, ignoring my own double entendre. "Maybe *I* should get the prize."

"You *are* the prize."

My usual quick wit deserted me at that point. I leaned back, eyeing him with a smile as I drank the last of my Coke. He grinned at me, unrepentant, as he drank his own. I stood up and grabbed him by the arm.

"Let's dance, sweet cheeks."

Joe leaned close to my ear as he got up. "I love it when you treat me like a sex object."

I laughed, enjoying the way his body brushed mine. He took my hand and led me toward the dance floor. I slapped his butt with my free hand and gave it a quick squeeze. I was still laughing when I saw Tammy, standing by the door marked FIRE EXIT.

She was watching me, biting her lip.

I stopped laughing and dragged Joe to a stop.

"What is it?" We were almost on the edge of the dance floor now, right in the middle of a shifting knot of people, but I didn't care. I even ignored Joe for a moment as I smiled at Tammy, nodding my head encouragingly.

You can do it, I urged her silently. *Be brave.* Go.

And she did. Tammy closed her eyes and turned, walking straight through the fire door as if it were wide open. For just a second—one tiny, brief second—I thought I saw a flash of white, the tiniest glimpse of a brightness beyond description.

"It's nothing," I said to Joe. "My shoe was slipping, that's all." I smiled, glad to be there, now, with him. That life would be waiting, but I wasn't finished enjoying this one yet.

"Let's go shake some booty."

"How did that make you feel?"

Ivy crossed her legs, crisply tailored in gray pinstripe, and eyed me intently. The leather loafers were Prada, for sure. The tape was rolling and I was under a microscope again, but this time I didn't mind it so much. Ivy's question was the latest in a series about my encounter with Tammy the night before, and now she wanted to know how I felt about helping the girl pass on.

"Weird. Very weird. I mean, who am I to tell some poor, lonely spirit what to do?" I'd thought about this so much, and still didn't understand it. "I'm not exactly Virgin Mother material, you know. I went to church as a kid, but that's it. What I know about God could be written on the head of a pin."

Ivy smiled. "Interesting reference. A medieval theologian named Thomas Aquinas once posed the question: 'How many angels can dance on the head of a pin?'"

I'd never cared for riddles. It was just a saying, anyway.

"I don't know anything about angels."

"Don't you?" Ivy adjusted her reading glasses and read to me from her notes: "'There were others all around, bright shapes pulsing and flowing.'"

"I didn't say they were angels." I didn't know why, but I was uncomfortable with the thought of claiming I'd brushed elbows—or wings—with celestial beings.

But I had, hadn't I?

"It's obvious that this experience has had a profound effect on you, Nicki, whether you wanted it to or not."

Now there's an understatement.

"It would be easier, I think, if you just accepted that it seems to have heightened your psychic abilities." I blinked at her, surprised to hear it put so bluntly. At least she didn't think I was making up ghost stories because my brain was fried.

"Believing one has crossed the line of death and back again is enough to change anybody." Ivy took off her glasses and rested them in her lap. "And sometimes change can be a good thing. Sometimes not. But the ability to accept change, and move past it, will free you to better deal with the here and now."

I had a sudden, horrifying vision of a withered old woman in the back room of a run-down vintage clothing store, reading palms and holding séances. *Madame Styx Knows All, Sees All.* I shook my head, dispelling the vision. "I'm not sure I can do that."

"Let's get back to your near death experience." Ivy cocked her head at me like a well-groomed parakeet. "What is it that troubles you the most about the event? The fact that you almost died, or the fact that you didn't?"

Oh, man. Ivy was cutting me no slack.

I thought about it. "I'm not nearly as afraid to die now, but I can't say that I want to, either. What troubles me the most is, 'Why me?'"

Ivy waited, saying nothing as she slid her glasses back on her nose.

"I'm pissed off." I knew as I said it that it was truer than I realized. "I'm pissed off that anybody could think *I* should be sent back to make some kind of *difference* in the world." I held out my arms, knowing I looked like a vampy tramp in my oversized red silk shirt, red and black beads glittering over black tights, and chunky combat boots. I had to draw Granny's *veve* today, and I wanted to make sure I was ready for anything. If Caprice showed up, I'd either stomp her flat or hide my head under the shirt.

"I don't know if I even believe in God, so why should I be given any responsibility for cleaning up after Him?" Ivy's eyebrows went up at my snarkiness. "Blasphemy, I know, but I'm sure there's plenty of Little Polly Purebreads out there who would be better suited to this kind of thing."

A trendy Zen fountain trickled in the background, but I wasn't interested in being soothed. "And what do *I* get out of it? Scared shitless and sleepless, that's what. Dead people jumping up like Pop-Tarts to impose their unfinished business on me. Dying isn't what scares me—it's living like *this* that does." I leaned forward, hands clasped. "Do I look like Mother Teresa to you?"

Ivy's lip twitched, but her professionalism never slipped.

"Saving lost souls has never been on my 'to-do' list." I shook my head, rejecting the thought. "I just wanna run my store and live a normal life."

"Do you?" Only an idiot could've missed the skepticism in Ivy's voice. "It seems to me you've made a career out of avoiding a normal life."

Dammit. Why do smart people always make things sound so simple?

"You're obviously a free spirit, Nicki. You seem to have more than your share of self-confidence and self-reliance." Ivy's eyes twinkled. "You've done well for yourself. But if I may make an observation, you may also have a slight unwillingness to commit emotionally. You have no family, and the person you spend the most time with is a gay man. A normal life for most women would include thoughts of husbands and babies."

"I'm not even thirty yet," I said indignantly, "and who said anything about babies?"

"I'm just suggesting that there's a reason behind all this, Nicki. Maybe this happened to you because you needed to learn something you wouldn't have learned otherwise. Or maybe it happened to you because you're open-minded enough to handle it."

Despite the back-handed compliment, I wasn't satisfied.

"Just *what* I am supposed to learn from all this?"

Ivy shrugged a pin-striped shoulder. "Only you know the answer to that, my dear."

CHAPTER 15

As close as Evan and I were, and as close as Joe and I were becoming, I still couldn't bring myself to tell them everything.

So I didn't bother to mention to either of them that I'd seen another ghost the evening before I went to a voodoo ceremony to get rid of a duppy.

I'd tell 'em both later, anyway. The three of us—no, four, with Butchie—would have a great dinner over a bottle of champagne, celebrating the fact that Caprice had finally been put to rest. That's what I kept telling myself as I drove to Granny Julep's little shotgun house in the middle of the afternoon.

After all, if Granny's plan worked, Evan would be safe, and so would I. It would be over. Life could go back to normal again. I was only going to draw the *veve*—there was no reason to be scared . . . no reason at all. And no reason to worry anyone else.

Albert was rocking on the front porch, slow and steady, as I parked my car and went up the steps.

"Hello, Albert."

He got up and let me in without a word, and there was Granny in the living room, looking better than the last time I'd seen her.

"'Bout time you got here, girl."

Now I knew she was better.

"You been practicin' like I told you?" Her dark eyes were still sunken, and she seemed tinier than ever, but her crown of coiled braids was held high.

"Yes, Granny." I had the feeling this might be a hard day and night for the old woman, and I didn't wanna add to it by letting her provoke me. "I think I can make the *veve* just fine."

"No *thinking* about it," she grumbled, "show me."

And damned if she didn't make me prove it, right there in the middle of the coffee table. Albert was at my elbow with the cornmeal before I could blink. I took my time, concentrating, and managed to keep from spilling any. When I was done, Granny Julep gave a grunt that could've been taken either way.

"Have to do," she muttered. "Start up the car, Albert." She gestured for me to help her from the couch. Her fingers clutched my arm like the bony claws of a bird. A hoot owl, maybe, too old and frail to fly.

"You got to ride in the car with us, girl. This ain't a place where you'd normally be welcome."

Lovely.

Big Daddy's Bar-B-Q.

It would've read "Bar-B-Que," but the *u* and the *e* were missing. The end of the sign had been smashed, shards of glass still dangling from the metal framework. Two battered pickups and an old RV were parked out front.

Smelled great, though. Smoke rose from a dirty chimney on one end of the building, the tangy scent of hickory and roasted meat filling the air. Despite the squalid setting, my mouth watered.

I was in the backseat of Albert's car, feeling like an unwilling child on a road trip. We'd driven the dusty and bumpy Georgia back roads mostly in silence. Granny's mood had been dark since we left the house, while Albert had done his usual "Lurch" routine.

Albert's car rocked to a stop in a cloud of red dust, and a black man in a torn shirt stepped out the door of the barbecue joint. He took a look at

Granny and Albert in the front seat, then eyed me impassively. After a second or two he went back inside.

Albert opened the car door and got out, then went around to open the door for Granny Julep.

"Umm . . . I'm not hungry," I said. Only my stomach knew what a liar I was.

"We're not here to eat."

That was all Granny said before Albert reached her and helped her out of the front seat.

I slid out and joined the old couple, sticking close.

Granny Julep had been right. I didn't feel very welcome.

She and Albert made their way around one corner of the porch, and I followed, glad we weren't going inside the place. I reconsidered, though, when I saw the alley that ran alongside the building. A rickety tin overhang was held up by a slatted fence, shading the alley from the sun and creating a dim tunnel that led to who knew where.

I'd never cared for horror movies, but I suddenly saw the scene as a director might see it: the gateway to a deliciously gory splatter film.

"C'mon, girl. Stay close." I was so shocked to hear Albert speak that I nearly missed the significance of what he said. Apparently even the unflappable old man was a bit nervous.

We walked through the alley, dappled sunlight breaking through rusted tin and broken boards here and there, and made our way to the back of the building. We came out beside a huge fire pit, surrounded by bare, packed earth. Scattered among the scrawny trees on three sides were picnic tables. The fire pit was cold and the tables were empty.

"Here," Granny Julep said to me. "Here's where you draw the *veve*." We'd reached a wooden post on the far side of the fire pit. I looked down at the dirt, eager to get it over with, and didn't bother examining the crude carvings on the wooden post; I didn't wanna know what they meant.

"Take a sip of this before you start." Granny had a miniature bottle of rum in her hand, the kind you see next to the cash register in a liquor store. "You callin' down a loa, and Papa Legba likes his rum."

I wrinkled my nose. "No, thanks."

It appeared Granny wasn't asking. She glared at me, offering the bottle without another word. I took it.

What the hell. A little artificial courage couldn't hurt.

"One sip," Granny repeated.

When I gave the bottle back, the sip of rum was burning its way from my throat to my belly.

The back door of the barbecue joint opened and two older guys came out, each with a small drum tucked under an arm. They didn't look at me at all, merely giving Granny Julep a respectful nod and taking seats in the dirt on opposite sides of the fire pit. Without speaking, they started thumping out a steady rhythm that immediately raised the hair on my arms.

Drums had once nearly been my undoing. Caprice had used them to lure me from my sleep, to make me let her in . . .

"Never you mind them," Granny murmured. "They's here to help. Get to it." She took a bag from Albert and handed it to me. "Make it big. At least two feet wide."

I knelt down and put the cornmeal to one side, untying the twine that kept the bag closed. The drums were distracting me already, and I didn't like it.

Concentrate. The outer circle of the *veve* began to take shape as I sprinkled it into being, pinch by grainy pinch. It wasn't that hard, but it would take time.

Granny Julep moved away, but I hardly noticed in my effort to ignore the drums, to get this weirdness over with. I wanted to go home.

The pale yellow curves of cornmeal looked nice against the reddish-orange dirt. The ground was perfectly flat here in front of the carved post, as though it'd been swept clean many times.

The drums seemed different now, faster, but I didn't care 'cause I was almost done. I kept working until the *veve* was finished, every sprinkle laid with care, every swoop as precise as I could make it.

"Guardian of the crossroads." Granny Julep walked to the other side of the carved post, directly in front of me. She carried a small bowl before her with both hands. "Legba, guardian of the way. *Ago, Ago, si Ago la.*"

Granny Julep hadn't mentioned there'd be anything more to this *veve* thing, but that was okay. I was finished.

"Papa Legba, come." Granny held the bowl up toward the sky, her thin arms shaking as though they could hardly bear the weight of it. She'd changed her clothes while I worked on the *veve*, and now wore all white, including an elaborately tied cotton headdress.

I sat back on my heels and brushed the cornmeal off my hands.

Then I got hit with a wave of exhaustion unlike anything I'd ever felt in my life.

I couldn't stand. I couldn't speak. I could barely keep from falling over. In shock, I looked at Granny, and saw that she watched me, her expression somber. She seemed to grow taller before my eyes as she raised the bowl higher. Her arms were no longer shaking.

Granny Julep began to talk to Papa Legba again, but this time I understood none of it. The drums weighed me down, chaining me to the earth. I didn't have the strength to get off my knees, much less run like the gullible fool I was. I could only gasp in disbelief, pinned like a deer in the headlights as Granny lowered her arms and started walking toward me, still carrying the bowl.

The sweetish-sour scent of rum flooded my nose as she held it out to me.

You've gotta be kidding me, was my first thought, and, *How could you do this to me?* was my second. This wasn't the Granny I knew. This Granny Julep was younger, harder, the raisin-brown eyes no longer sunken and the cheeks less lined.

And then I knew what she'd done.

She'd tricked me, used me to get what she wanted. The rum wasn't for me, it was for Papa Legba, who'd taken my strength and given it to her.

"No." I managed one word, and tried to say more with my eyes. I was furious, hurt. The drums were louder now, and I knew without looking that a third drummer had joined the other two.

Granny Julep turned away and poured the rum around the base of the wooden post, where the thirsty ground soaked it up. She raised both arms high in a vee symbol, empty bowl clutched in one hand, standing as straight and tall as a young woman.

The drumming changed abruptly, the rhythm more demanding. My legs were numb now. I tried to drag them but couldn't, arms shaking in an effort just to hold myself off the ground.

The drums echoed in my ears, pulsed in my blood.

"Eleguya go, eleguya go, ah la ya ma go . . ."

My head was so heavy. So heavy. The earth itself throbbed against my palms, in rhythm with the drums.

I'd trusted her . . .

So heavy . . . I had no choice, really. The ground came slowly up to meet me, and I surrendered and lay my cheek in the dirt.

And that's when things really got weird.

People. Lots of people, most dressed in white. Some of the women wore white kerchiefs over their hair. They spilled from the back door of the barbecue to form a circle around me, Granny Julep, and the pole, all them shuffling along with the drums.

No one spoke. That alone was terrifying.

Twenty, twenty-five, thirty maybe. Men and women, not one of them looking at me. They must've gathered—or been waiting all along— inside the barbecue joint while I drew the *veve*.

I lay helpless in the middle of the courtyard while they moved and shuffled in the shadows beneath the trees, caring only where they put their feet.

I couldn't speak or scream, and for a moment I wondered if I'd become my own ghost—but the ground was hard and there was an ant crawling on my hand. I was still alive.

"Eleguya go. Santi ah la oh," Granny chanted.

The crowd took up the chant, raising the hair on the back of my neck. *It was broad daylight—this kind of thing wasn't supposed to happen in broad daylight.* It was always dark when the girl in the horror movies gets whacked.

The chanting got louder, the circle of strangers going round and round, shuffling and stomping in time with the drums. A cloud passed overhead, and the sky seemed to darken. Either that or I was about to pass out. The reek of spilled rum was in my nose, the carvings on the post in front of me wet from Granny's splashing.

She was still standing in the center of the courtyard, arms held high. Her eyes were closed, face turned toward the sun.

I couldn't move. I could only watch and wait and try to stay calm. Squeezing my eyes shut didn't help—*not* watching was worse—and when I opened them again, the nightmare was still there.

There were more drummers, at least six men now, dark faces shiny with sweat. Granny Julep lowered her bowl to the ground, and a woman swooped from the crowd and took it away. Then Granny bent and picked up something else, moving with surprising ease. It was a rattle, an old gourd hung with feathers and beads. She lifted it above her head and began to dance, the rattle's dry hiss a whispery counterpoint to the thump of drums.

The old lady who'd been barely able to leave her sickbed was gone. In her place was a wiry black woman who moved as if she were in the prime of life. Granny Julep jumped and swayed and shook her rattle, a steady stream of patois coming from her lips.

"Le bon ton roulette, ye ye ye."

The chanting became a song, led by several women in the crowd, whose voices rose and fell in rhythm with the drums. Shuffling became dancing, and someone lit the fire pit. The flames leapt high, their crackle buried beneath the sound of drums and chanting as the group got louder and louder.

We were in the middle of nowhere for a reason. No one would hear them—I doubted the cops even knew this place existed.

It was the perfect place to hide the body of a stupid white girl who'd gotten herself into deep voodoo.

Women in white kerchiefs moved through the crowd, offering sips from bowls of rum, paying particular attention to the drummers. I blinked back tears, trying as hard as I could to believe that Granny wouldn't let anyone hurt me, that there was a reason for this I didn't yet understand. I'd almost convinced myself until I saw the knife.

A man stepped from the group, weak sunlight glinting off the edge of the blade he held in his hand. My only consolation was that he wasn't looking at me, but at Granny Julep. My heart should've been pounding, but whatever was in the rum had slowed everything down—including, it seemed—time itself.

Then I saw the chicken. It was alive, dangled by its feet, wings flapping weakly. The woman who carried it was fat and wore a white kerchief. As horrified as I was for the bird, I felt a secret sense of relief.

Better it than me.

I lay on the ground like a rag doll and watched what happened next, knowing it wasn't gonna be good.

Granny passed her rattle over and around the bird, making the poor thing flap its wings in terror. The fat woman had a hard time holding onto it, and I saw smiles and approving nods from the crowd, as though this were a good sign. Then Granny moved to a spot closer to the fire, putting down the rattle and scooping up another bowl. She knelt, sprinkling cornmeal on the ground in graceful arcs that put my clumsy efforts to draw a *veve* to shame.

She was summoning something—someone, another loa like Damballah, the snake that came alive in Indigo's secret room. Only this time I couldn't run away, and if there was animal sacrifice involved, it was gonna be ten times worse.

And it was. As soon as Granny brushed the last of the cornmeal from her fingers, the fat woman swung the chicken, caught it by the head, and snapped its neck.

I wanted to scream. I wanted to vomit. I closed my eyes, and when I opened them again, the man with the knife was holding the chicken high in the air. Its head was missing.

The ground seemed like a good place to be right now. I clung to the gritty feel of dirt beneath my cheek as the only proof of sanity in a world gone insane.

Blood dripped as the man took the dead chicken, limp-winged and dangling, over to where Granny Julep still knelt over the new *veve*. She took the headless bird by the legs and let it drip over the pattern, muttering something I couldn't hear over the pounding of drums and chants. Finally, she held it out to the man, giving it back. He melted into the crowd while Granny Julep rose from her knees, picking up her rattle once again.

When she turned to face me, I was afraid. Her expression was hard, dark eyes glittering amid the sharp planes of her face.

The rhythm of the drums changed; two high, quick thumps followed by a deep one, over and over and over again. A ripple of excitement seemed to course through the crowd as the dancing became more frenzied. The slow and steady tempo that marked the gathering before now was gone as self-expression took over, each man and woman following their own creative urgings. The crowd became a living, breathing mass of black faces and white clothes, bare feet thumping and bare arms waving, everything dappled by the shade of the scrawny oaks.

Shrieks of laughter rose into the air, coming from a corner of the courtyard. The crowd parted, and a man whirled into view, women scattering and giggling as they avoided his halfhearted attempts to grab them. Dressed in black, the man wore a top hat and a pair of sunglasses. His tuxedo shirt was untucked, his bow tie was crooked, and he was smoking two cigarettes, one on each side of his mouth. Most shocking of all, he wore white powder on his black skin, giving him the look of a corpse. He grinned and thrust his hips at the women, inciting howls of laughter.

I didn't find his obscene antics funny. Not that I could've laughed anyway . . . my body continued to betray me. No matter how hard I tried, I couldn't move. It was like being dipped in cement and remaining fully conscious while you slowly turned to stone.

The man in the top hat made an exaggerated turn, pretending to notice me for the first time. He straightened, giving me a leer as he tipped his hat, and my heart sank. As he blew out a cloud of cigarette smoke, it suddenly dawned on me who the man was supposed to resemble—Baron Samedi, the demented skeleton who'd grinned at me from the poster in Caprice's voodoo room— the loa of the dead.

Granny's words from a few days earlier came back to me. *Maybe she offer you to the Baron instead.*

Oh, shit. Maybe Granny was saving Caprice's soul by making her own deal with the devil. Sure enough, as the man in the top hat flicked away his cigarettes and took a step toward me, still leering, Granny Julep reached out and caught him by the sleeve of his black coat. She whispered something in his ear. He grinned and laughed and slapped his knee, grabbing Granny and twirling her around like she was a young girl again, and she let him do it.

Then he put his mouth to her ear and whispered something of his own before spinning off again, pelvis thrust forward, chasing lewdly after another woman who'd stepped too close in her dancing.

Granny Julep stood alone, the flames from the fire pit making her face glisten with moisture. She looked furious, angry in a way I'd never seen. She glanced at me from the corner of her eye, and my heart began to pound, the sluggishness that gripped it earlier overcome by pure, primal fear. For a moment I couldn't breathe, as though my chest were squeezed in a vise.

I'm not sure what would've happened next. What *did* happen is that Granny Julep's face contorted into an expression of agony. She stumbled, clutched at her chest with a cry of pain, and crumpled to the ground like a wilted flower. Her cotton headdress flew off as she hit the ground, leaving her crown of braids dragging in the dust.

The drums stopped.

Albert gave a shout and was at her side in an instant. Just as quickly, whatever hold she'd had over me was gone, and so was the pressure in my chest. My body was my own again, and I dragged in a deep breath, feeling like it was the first oxygen I'd had in hours.

I scrambled to my feet, hearing uneasy murmurs all around. The people who'd been ignoring me as if I were invisible now backed away from me as if I was contagious. Many shot me dirty looks, muttering behind their hands.

My knees were shaking. I wanted to run, but I

couldn't leave an old woman lying in the dirt. Besides, where would I go? Albert had the car keys and we were in the middle of nowhere.

I went to Albert's side and saw that Granny's eyes were open. Her lips were moving. She was alive, but her mahogany skin was an ashy gray color.

"She needs an ambulance!" My throat was so dry I could barely get the words out. It didn't matter . . . the people around looked at me as if I spoke another language.

"Julep Joan Johnson, don't you go nowhere without me." Albert's words were fierce but his hands were tender, holding the old woman's head from the ground. He had eyes for no one but her.

There wasn't gonna be any ambulance, that much was obvious. And I wanted *out* of there. "Let's get her in the car," I dared to snap at the nearest guy, a younger man wearing a ball cap. "She needs a doctor."

Surprisingly enough, three guys stepped from the crowd and did as I said. The first man approached Granny and Albert, and when Albert gave him a warning glare, the man touched his fingers respectfully to the bill of his cap. Then he bent and eased himself into Albert's place. Another man slid his arms beneath Granny's knees, careful to preserve her modesty by scooping up her dress. The third man went ahead of us and opened the car doors, helping to ease the old woman into the backseat.

A few seconds later we were pulling out of the parking lot of Big Daddy's Bar-B-Q, Albert driving like a bat out of hell. I was in the back with Granny, cradling her head in my lap.

"I'm sorry," she rasped, eyes closed. Her face looked sunken, like someone who was already dead. "I had to do it."

I blinked back tears, but I didn't know if they were from rage or sorrow. It was too hard to tell.

"I needed your strength to do what I had to do. You was never in any danger," she murmured.

I swallowed hard and took the high road, not wanting the last words an old woman heard to be profane ones.

"It's okay, Granny Julep," I murmured, brushing a bit of dirt from her forehead. "It's okay."

"Now I know," she whispered. "Now I know." Her hands were veined and gnarled, laying limp against her chest. "My Caprice was a good girl. They's someone else got her, name of Felicia." In a voice so faint I could barely hear it, she said, "I done told her not to mess around with them Sect Rouge."

I had no idea what she was talking about, and was too shaken to care.

She was quiet for a little while. We rocked along the back roads in silence, leaving a cloud of red clay dust to mark our speed. If it weren't for the even rise and fall of her scrawny chest, I'd have thought she was gone, and I was panicky at the thought that she'd die in my arms before we could reach help.

"It's up to you now, child," Granny Julep murmured. "You gonna have to do it."

"Leave be, woman." Albert's voice came from the front, gruff with emotion. "You done give enough of yourself to help Caprice. Hush up." The old man kept glancing in the rearview mirror as he drove. He'd angled it down at Granny Julep. I just hoped the battered old Lincoln could keep it together until we reached the highway.

Granny ignored him, I'm sure not for the first time. Her eyes were open but she was staring blindly at the roof of the car.

"Chains, child. You got to bind her with chains."

Surely the old woman was delirious.

"You the only one who can do it."

I had a hugely inappropriate urge to laugh, and then wondered if maybe *I* was the one who was delirious. The situation was surreal enough to be a dream, wasn't it?

But since one didn't tell a dying old woman that she was crazy, I said, "*Shh*, Granny Julep. Save your strength." She weighed almost nothing against my thighs. The back of her skull was cradled in my palm.

"I'm better now," she murmured. "The pain's gone." Her eyes fluttered shut. "Just tired."

I knew the feeling, and I hadn't forgotten what Granny'd tried to do to me.

"Guess you didn't count on me having a bad heart when you tried to steal my strength," I muttered, knowing I shouldn't.

Granny Julep smiled, eyes still closed.

"No. I counted on a good one."

"Which hospital was she taken to?"

Joe had his arm around me, and while I appreciated the snuggling, I was better now. I buried my nose against his chest anyway, breathing in man, medicine, and hand soap.

"Grady Memorial." I'd called Evan, and he'd come to get me, listening to me rage and cry all the way back to Joe's apartment. He'd doctored me with tea and sympathy until Joe got home from his shift, and now that he was gone, I was all cried out. "We found a walk-in clinic near I–85, and they called an ambulance. It got there quick."

"Grady's got a first-class E.R. I'm sure they'll take good care of her."

"*Mmm-hmm.*" I didn't bother to tell him it would do no good. Granny Julep's light was dimming, and soon it would go out.

She wouldn't have been so desperate to use me otherwise. Somehow, I knew that was the truth. But it hurt nonetheless.

I'd only known the old woman a little over a week. She'd lied to me, tricked me, scared me half to death. I still didn't know if she'd be going to the "good place" or the "bad place."

I should dust her from my hands like cornmeal, I thought, but I couldn't help but hope that the old woman's twisted, double-sided spirituality paid off, and she'd be "home with Jesus" in the end.

"How about I order us a pizza?" Joe was rubbing my back. It felt great.

"Will there be beer?" I asked.

"Absolutely. Ice cold."

"*Mmmmm.* You talked me into it." I let go of him reluctantly. He kissed the top of my head and slid from the couch, then walked toward the kitchen, looking for the phone.

I'd never noticed before how sexy surgical scrubs could be, particularly from the rear. When the kitchen counter hid my view, I turned my eyes toward the sliding glass doors that led to the balcony. It was twilight now, the sky a mixture of gray and orange.

I could hear Joe ordering pizza, but my thoughts were on the future. Where would I sleep tomorrow, now that the rest of Granny's plans for nine-night would never happen? Her efforts to put Caprice to rest were over. Had they been enough?

Joe came back. "You okay?"

I gave him a halfhearted smile. "Yeah, I'm okay."

"I can't believe you drove off into the boondocks with that creepy old couple, Nicki. You could've been robbed, raped . . . murdered. You have no idea the kind of things we see in the emergency room." Joe's face was grim—the tea and sympathy were obviously over.

"It was stupid of me, I know. I'm sorry."

"I want you to stay with me for the next few days." He pulled me up from the couch and wound my arms around his neck. I went willingly, leaning my weight against him. "And don't try any of that 'tough chick' routine with me this time . . . I want you to stay here for a while. We'll go to your house and pick up a few of your things, and anytime you absolutely have to go back there I'll go with you . . . no more running off by yourself."

"Who died and made you boss?" I didn't really mean it, of course. It felt good to know he cared enough to get bossy.

"Nobody's dying if I can help it," he said grimly.

"That's why I want you to stay here, with me."

"Granny Julep's dying," I said thoughtfully. "I should probably talk to her one more time, before it's too late."

"No."

Despite the warm fuzzies I got from being held in his arms, I didn't care to be told what I could or couldn't do. "No?"

Joe gave me an exasperated look but didn't let go of my waist. "She's a liar, Nicki. She put you at risk today, big-time. God knows what she put in that rum to cause temporary paralysis—things like that are not the kind of stuff you mess around with." His voice softened. "I'm running tox screens on you tomorrow, by the way."

Bossiness could be kind of cute. "I'm only giving in because I want to, Joe," I said with a smile. "I'll stay here for a few days, but that's it."

"Uh-huh." He was unimpressed with my reasoning. "Because you don't need anybody to protect you, right?"

"Because sleeping with you beats the hell out of sleeping alone. And I'm not hiding from the world forever—you can't protect me every minute, and I have a shop to run."

"I'll take what I can get." Joe reached out and smoothed my hair behind an ear, kissing me to take the sting from his words.

A sweet kiss, devoid of passion, yet one of the best I'd ever had. I buried my face in his neck and held on, feeling safe for the first time that day.

"You're a lot of trouble, Nicki Styx."

"I am."

"You make me crazy."

"I do."

I would've agreed to anything as long he held me like this, his body warm and strong against mine, his heart thumping steadily against my ear.

Joe sighed into my hair. "What am I going to do with you?"

"I can think of several things," I said, voice muffled against his chest.

"Later," he murmured, continuing to hold me close.

CHAPTER 16

As usual, whenever something significant happened in my life, I used music to work myself through it.

Today it was Bob Marley and the Wailers, and the song was "People Get Ready." By the time Bob and his backup singers got to the "train to Jordan" part, I was bopping and singing all over the store. I opened the front doors and let the music spill out into Little Five Points, knowing it would blend and melt into the crowd just like the incense from Crystalline Blue, the metaphysical shop on the corner.

Indigo was still closed. I had no idea what would happen to it. Somebody would probably buy it and turn it into a Smoothie Queen or something.

It didn't matter. I was done with that dark chapter of my life. Now all I wanted was the upbeat side of the Caribbean experience. No more bad mojo for me.

Maybe I'd even take a Jamaican cruise.

"Must you be so cheerful in the mornings?" Evan's eyes were still a bit puffy with sleep, but I'd never be so cruel as to tell him so. He walked in the front door while I was opening the register.

"There's fresh coffee in the back, Mr. Grumpy. Get us both a cup and come help me celebrate."

Evan's eyes opened marginally wider. "What are we celebrating?" The Wailers wailed in the background, and my body moved to the beat even as my mind kept track of the cash I was handling.

"One week of duppy-free, spirit-free existence," I said with satisfaction. "No ghosts, no zombies, no boogeymen, no bumps in the night." I laughed, thinking of Joe, and added a provisional, "No bumps I didn't ask for, anyway."

Evan shook his head, clearly not up to envisioning straight sex before caffeine, and went in the back room. He came back out a few minutes later with two steaming mugs of coffee and a slightly better attitude.

"So tell me again . . . you're all bright-eyed and

bushy-tailed because the dearly departed are leaving you alone, or because you're getting laid regularly? Which is it?"

I took the mug he offered. It was my favorite, black with red lettering: VENI, VEDI, VISA. I CAME, I SAW, I DID A LITTLE SHOPPING.

"I've reached a milestone, don't you see? A whole week!" I grinned at him over the rim of my cup. "Maybe I just had some temporary thing switch on inside my brain and now it's switched off again. No more dead people."

"Don't say that so loudly," Evan said. Our first customers were browsing the racks already, two middle-aged women in jeans and tie-dye.

"No whispers, no smells, no strangers asking for favors." I lowered my voice but went on talking. It was my third cup of coffee this morning; I'd been up since four-thirty. "No lost souls seeking redemption."

If I could just get rid of a weird sense of unease, everything would be perfect.

It was like having a hangnail after an otherwise flawless manicure. You could pick and chew at the problem until you'd ruined the shiny polish, or you could ignore it by drenching yourself in caffeine and reggae music.

Or something like that.

"Can we help you ladies with anything?" I stayed behind the counter but made myself available. Most people liked to have their space when they were browsing.

Evan beamed at them, then settled himself in the catbird seat.

"So you're back to normal, then. Thank God." He crossed his legs and flicked an imaginary speck of dust off his favorite Cavalli jeans. The lime green T-shirt he wore was tight, showing off his upper body. I felt a little guilty when I realized I'd never seen it before. When had Evan gone shopping without me? Just showed how far I'd had my head up my. . .

"Have you been working out?"

Evan's mood immediately perked up. "Can you tell? Really?" He preened a little, obviously pleased. "Butch has an exercise room set up in the basement. We've been using it together pretty regularly."

"Oooh." I gave a mock shudder. "Two handsome, sweaty men giving their muscles a workout. Sounds like heaven to me."

"You know it." Evan winked at me as he swallowed a sip of coffee. "And the showers are to die for."

"Excuse me." One of the tie-dye ladies was holding up a pair of jeans. "Is there a dressing room?"

"Absolutely," I said. "I'll show you."

I left Evan in charge of the register while I took care of business. By the time the two women were finished shopping, I'd sold them each a pair of jeans and unloaded some funky Lucite earrings I'd picked up at a garage sale about a month earlier. That was one of the great things about garage sales: one man's junk was another man's treasure—particularly if you had an eye for vintage treasure.

"With hair that red, she shouldn't be wearing purple tie-dye," Evan commented absently as soon as the door closed behind the two women. "And a hot oil treatment wouldn't hurt . . . did you see that frizz?"

"I liked the color, though." I smiled at the cash register, glad the day's profits had begun, and added, "Nothing a good stylist couldn't fix. I'd forgotten about those earrings . . . I think I'll go rearrange the jewelry in the display case."

"Ooh, that reminds me." Evan popped up from his seat and headed toward the back room. His voice drifted to me as he rounded the counter. "Butch and I were in Buckhead this weekend and we saw a sign for an estate sale. I got some great stuff—you're gonna love it." He came back with a box, still talking. "Those rich people sure know how to live. You should've seen the size of this house . . . it was *gy*-normous. We could've lived happily ever after in one of their bathrooms."

I laughed at the image. "Particularly if the showers are to die for, right?"

"You know it, devil doll. Now come look at this."

Evan opened the box and started laying costume jewelry out on the counter.

"You're right . . . this is great stuff." I picked up a delicate filigree necklace and admired the workmanship, turning it toward the light so the rhinestones sparkled. "Pure forties glam. I love it."

"Check out these cameo cuff links," Evan said. "I can see them on Butch."

I bit my lip, trying not to laugh. While the black and white cuff links were great, their vibe was a little feminine, and so *not* Butch. "Oh, just admit it. They'd look great on *you*, not Butch . . . you're coveting the merchandise."

Evan sighed, eyeing the cuff links again under the light. "They *would* look great on me, wouldn't they?"

"We've had this talk before," I teased. "There's only so much jewelry a man can own before it just gets downright weird. Back away from the cuff links."

With a moue of regret, Evan put them aside and went back to digging in the box. "I know. I can't help it. Shiny things make me lose my head." He pulled out a bracelet and held it up for me to see. "Remember this?"

I did, actually. Vintage Juliana, very collectible. Amethysts and citrines set in japanned lacquer. It was a valuable piece, and looked just like a bracelet I'd had in the fine jewelry case for a while.

"That can't be the same one." I took it and examined it closely. "I sold that bracelet a couple of weeks ago to one of those Red Hat ladies."

Evan shrugged. "It was an estate sale, Nicki. Somebody died, and they were clearing out the house. I don't know if it's the same bracelet or not, but it sure looks like it. Anyway, it's a great piece . . . somebody else will want it."

A involuntary shudder rippled through me, as though someone had walked over my grave.

"I got the whole box for less than a hundred dollars. I could hardly believe it," Evan said. "I'll take all this in the back and start cleaning it up. I just wanted you to see it first."

"Leave the bracelet." I wanted to look at it again—the one I'd sold had been worth twice that. "I'll clean it later."

Evan turned away with his box of shinies, obviously looking forward to his jewelry cleaning session. Nothing made him happier than to make pretty things sparkle.

"You did good, Queen Supreme."

"I did, didn't I?"

"Must you always be so smug?"

"I must."

And he was gone, having made me laugh again. My eyes fell on the bracelet, and I stopped laughing. It was definitely the same one—there couldn't be two with a tiny nick in the lacquer at the exact same place. The nice old lady I'd sold it to was probably dead, and that made me sad.

It also made me think about another old lady, Granny Julep, whom I'd been trying to avoid thinking about all week. I'd checked the obituaries in the paper once or twice, that was all.

"Those were my husband's cuff links."

I nearly jumped out of my skin. There was a woman standing right in front of me, and I hadn't heard her come in.

"Whoa . . ." I took a step back, clutching the bracelet to my chest. "I didn't know anyone else was here . . ." Then what she'd said dawned on me. "Did you say something about cuff links?"

The woman smiled reassuringly. "Don't worry, dear. I don't care about them." Her wrinkled face and gray hair looked familiar. She winked at me like a young girl sharing secrets. "Can't say I cared much for my husband, either. Luther was a hard man, but never in the ways that counted, if you know what I mean."

I did, but I had no idea what to say in response. Did I know this woman?

"Don't you remember me, dear? I was in here a few weeks ago with my friends from the Red Hat Club."

The top of my head started to tingle.

"You were sweet enough to help me pick out a gift for my granddaughter." She gestured toward the bracelet I was still clutching. "But I never got a chance to give it to her."

She was standing two feet away from me, as solid as I was, but something wasn't right.

"Here you go. Take it." I held out the bracelet, a terrible suspicion forming. "I'm really sorry about the mix-up . . . my friend Evan went to an estate sale in Buckhead, and even though I'm sure he's got a receipt, there must've been a mistake . . ." I was babbling, and I knew it. "It must've been in the wrong box." *Take the bracelet and go, lady*.

She shook her head sadly, and my heart sank. "I need your help, dear."

I shook mine. "No, thank you."

Even though my response was technically the wrong one based on her statement, it was the right

one for me. Her wrinkled face showed disappointment, and when she refused to reach for the bracelet, I knew for sure what was happening.

Another unquiet spirit, asking for help, and after
what had happened with Caprice, I was *so* not interested in helping.

"I'm sorry, dear. We haven't been properly intro-
duced, have we, and here I am asking you for favors." She looked at me sorrowfully. "Do you have
a grandmother, dear?"

When I didn't answer, she kept talking as if I
had. "My name is Violet Van Dyke, of the Morgan
County Van Dykes."

Of course. The Morgan County Van Dykes. For
one wild second I wondered if she expected me to
curtsy.

"I know it's a lot to ask, dear, but if you could
see that my granddaughter Cindy got that bracelet
back, it would mean a great deal to me."

"Lady . . ."

"It's Mrs. Van Dyke, dear, but you may call me
Violet." She fixed her faded blue eyes on me, smiling sweetly. Her tea-length dress was a creamy satin damask, formal enough for a wedding . . . or a
funeral.

"Violet," I hoped my voice didn't shake, "are
you . . ."

"I'm dead, dear." She seemed oddly content with

it. "And I'm ready to go. But the last words my granddaughter and I had were harsh ones"— Violet looked away, misty-eyed—"over that worthless husband of hers. I died with her thinking I didn't love her anymore, and I'd like to fix that before I go on."

I must have been getting used to dead people, because as freaky as this was, it was kind of interesting. She knew where she was going, but she wasn't ready to go. How did one get to choose?

"If you could find it in your heart to help me, I'd be ever so grateful." Violet knew how to play the gracious Southern belle card. Throw in a dose of grandmotherly guilt and only Rhett Butler himself would be able to not give a damn.

"You want me to give your granddaughter this bracelet." I kept my voice flat, deciding to get right to the point.

"That's right, dear."

"Or what?"

Violet looked confused. "I beg your pardon?"

"What will you do if I *don't* give your granddaughter this bracelet?"

Forget Rhett Butler . . . Scarlet O'Hara herself would've been proud of the old lady's response. Her face fell, lower lip trembling. "I guess I'll just fade away—heartbroken and unforgiven. It's very tiring to stay, you know."

No, I didn't know, but I was glad to hear it.

"You'll go away . . . you'll leave me alone." I was beyond the niceties. I mean, I was sorry she was dead and all, but I had my own life to live.

She perked up. "I will, dear. I promise." Violet looked me straight in the eye, giving me a decisive nod. Her carefully coiffed gray hair fit her head like a helmet.

"You won't ever bother me again."

One penciled eyebrow arched. "There's no need to be rude, dear. I said I'd leave you alone . . . a promise is a promise."

I flushed, hating how quickly my manners kicked in. "I apologize. It's nothing personal." Old habits died hard, unlike certain little old ladies; I may have been going through a rough time in my personal life, but at least *I* was still alive and kicking.

Violet gave me a nod, graciously accepting my apology as her due. She smiled encouragingly, looking hopeful.

This particular favor didn't sound too hard. I could make up a story to tell the granddaughter about the bracelet. With any luck, I'd never have to mention a visit from her dead grandmother. "Tell me where to go," I said, resigned.

Violet let out a refined chuckle, her "pitiful" routine forgotten. "Oh dear," she said, "don't ever ask anyone to do that."

"Do what?"

"Tell you where to go."

For a society grande dame, Violet had quite the naughty sense of humor.

"The address, Violet." I couldn't help but smile, just a little. "Give me your granddaughter's address."

CHAPTER 17

A half hour later I was in the extremely upscale Atlanta neighborhood of Buckhead, craning my neck at some beautiful homes. It was hard to read the house numbers through the jumble of dogwoods and azaleas, and would be nearly impossible in the spring, when the shrubs would be covered in masses of pink and white blooms. The rich liked their flowers, and their privacy.

The neighborhood was gorgeous . . . big estate homes nestled on wooded lots, gently sloping lawns and stone fences. Some went for the rustic look, while others went for show; there were quite a few red brick Colonials, tall white columns, and shaded porches, elegant throwbacks to the grand old plantation homes.

"This is it," Violet said from the passenger seat. "This is Cindy's house."

The private drive was marked with a discreet sign: 1800 BROOKWOOD. It looped up to what appeared to be a monument to concrete and glass, a squared-off block of stone made only slightly less imposing by some decorative cornice work above the front door.

"Nice," I said, only to be polite. I much preferred a home with a little character. This one looked like a museum.

"Yes." Violet sighed, as though disappointed. "That idiot husband of hers does seem to know how to make money." She gave a little sniff. "Though I know for a fact that his daddy gave him the down payment."

I kept my mouth shut, as I had for most of the drive. Violet was very chatty, and I'd already heard all I needed to hear about her darling granddaughter, Cindy, and Cindy's "idiot husband."

My cell phone rang. I pulled my car to a stop in the driveway, then got my phone from my bag. The caller ID said JOE.

I looked at Violet and put up a finger, then flipped it open.

"Hey there, handsome. I've missed you."

"Is that how you always answer the phone?" he teased. "Do you even know who this is?"

"It's Paolo, right? The cute guy from last night?"

"Excuse me," I could hear the smile in Joe's voice, and it made me smile, too. "But *I* was the cute guy from last night." Still playing along, he added, "You must've forgotten how many women were hitting on me."

"I only remember one," I said, "and she would be me."

"There ya go, then." Joe sounded completely satisfied with that answer. "Where are you? I called the shop and Evan said you were out."

I didn't want to tell Joe where I was. I felt guilty, but this was only going to take a few minutes, and it was no big deal. Joe and I had spent a fun, peaceful week together, and I was in no hurry to spoil it by telling him about Violet.

"I'm just running an errand." That wasn't a lie—it was the truth. I knew he wanted to keep an eye on me, but I was perfectly safe out here among the lifestyles of the rich and famous. Some private security guard probably already had me under surveillance.

What was Violet's granddaughter going to do . . . snub me to death?

I'd tell Joe all about it later, over a glass of wine.

"I'm heading back to the store as soon as I'm finished, and Evan's coming over for wine at my place later. Wanna come?"

Hard to believe Evan hadn't tattled about Violet already—he hadn't been happy to find out the Juliana bracelet had a spirit attached to it, but he sure hadn't argued about taking it back. I'd told him where I was going and what I was doing, and then I practically ordered him to keep his mouth shut if Joe called.

"I'm still not crazy about you going back to your house, Nicki. Stay with me another night."

"Joe," I said gently, trying to ignore Violet as she fidgeted beside me, "it's my home. It's where I live. And it's been a week without . . ." Glancing at my elderly passenger, I decided to quit while I was ahead. "You don't need to worry. Everything's okay."

There was a brief silence, then Joe said, "I have something to tell you. I've hired a private investigator to find Kelly."

I blinked at the sudden change of subject.

"You did what?"

"I want it over, Nicki, done. For the last four years I haven't cared, but now I do. I want the divorce finalized."

Hearing those words made my stomach knot and my heart leap. Joe was moving forward, and that was good. On the other hand, when and if he found

Kelly, everything—*everything*—would change.

"I only wanna be with you, Nicki."

Despite the fact that I'd been staying with him, his comment was as close to a declaration of commitment as we'd gotten. We hadn't even discussed exclusive sex yet.

"But what if . . ." I wasn't even sure myself what the *but* was, until I said it. ". . . what if she really *is* my sister?"

"Then we'll deal with that, too." Joe hesitated, then added firmly, "Together."

The front seat of my car became claustrophobic. Violet was staring through the window toward the house, head turned away, but it felt as if she was a third party to our conversation. This was a discussion I wasn't sure I was ready for, and I didn't need an audience.

I unbuckled my seat belt and slid out, grateful for the rush of crisp air. "Listen, can I call you later?" Gravel crunched under my feet as I shut the car door. "I don't have a lot of privacy at the moment."

One crisis at a time.

Joe didn't ask any questions, but I could tell he was disappointed. "Sure. You'll have to leave me a message—my shift doesn't end until eight."

"How about a late dinner, then? I'll cook something."

His answer was slightly more cheerful. "You got a deal."

"I'll be waiting."

I hung up and looked around for Violet but didn't see her. She wasn't in the front seat anymore, but since she seemed able to come and go as she pleased, I figured she was already inside. I checked my purse for the bracelet, and with a shrug, headed up the steps to the front door.

Big stone planters with precisely trimmed topiaries flanked the steps. The doorbell chimes sounded like the prelude to the Mormon Tabernacle Choir.

The door opened, and time stood still.

"Yes?"

The man in the doorway was about thirty, good-looking in a preppy kind of way, except for the pouchy bags beneath his eyes and the beginnings of a potbelly. He was holding a Bloody Mary in one hand, wearing khaki shorts and a striped Polo shirt. I watched, momentarily speechless, while he did a double take and said, "Nicki? Nicki Styx?"

My old boyfriend, Erik Mitchell. *Correction: My old fiancé, Erik Mitchell.* The one who'd broken my heart when I caught him in the backseat of a car with that skanky blond cheerleader, Cin—

"Who's here, Erik?"

And there she was, the skanky blond cheerleader herself, looking anything but skanky, unfortunately. Fashionably thin, blond hair in a pageboy, blue cashmere sweater set with matching linen pants. She looked like a model for Ann Taylor . . . one of the "bitchy rich" kind.

"Nicki?" Cindy's perfect little nose twitched before she caught herself and pasted a fake smile on her face. "Is that *you*?"

No, it's the Avon lady, you dumb shit.

Out loud, I said, "Wow. Erik and Cindy. Is this awkward, or what?"

Erik had the grace not to answer, but Cindy's fake smile just got faker. She took a step forward, resting her hand on the door. "You look great, Nicki," she gushed, effectively blocking Erik from opening the door any farther. Her gaze flicked over my hair and clothes. "Still the rebel, I see."

My white ruffled blouse was ruched with see-through strips of lace, a sexy yet modest look from the fifties that still worked today, as far as I was concerned. Judging by the looks Erik was sneaking behind Cindy's back, it worked for him, too. And while my hip huggers were a far cry from Cindy's linen capris, they were original Paris Blues, and fit me in all the right places.

"You know me . . . a regular rebel without a cause," I said, giving fake smile for fake smile. "Can I come in?"

Cindy looked surprised I'd even asked, and I

couldn't blame her. Visiting with a woman you'd stabbed in the back twelve years ago didn't seem like a pleasant way to spend the morning.

I, on the other hand, didn't care if it was pleasant or not. I was on a mission. But I'd be damned if I'd stand on this woman's doorstep like a delivery boy while I completed it. "I'm here about your grandmother, Violet Van Dyke."

Cindy's fake smile faltered.

"I have something she wanted you to have."

"You knew my grandmother." It was impossible not to hear the skeptical note in Cindy's voice.

"For God's sake, Cindy." Erik brushed her aside, impatient. He held the door wide. "Let her in."

Cindy shot her husband a look that promised there'd be trouble later, but Erik ignored her. He gestured with the hand that held the Bloody Mary, welcoming me to his home. "Come in, Nicki, come in."

The foyer was huge, rising two stories to a bright bank of upper story windows. A curved balustrade and wide staircase led upstairs. The floor beneath my feet was creamy vanilla Italian tile.

"Yes, Nicki, come in." Cindy was obviously not to be outdone in the hospitality department. Her heeled sandals clicked on the floor, echoing weirdly in the cavernous foyer. "Let's go into the morning room."

The morning room? Please.

I followed Cindy's size four ass into an area just off the front door, a big room with overstuffed Elizabeth Ashley furniture and bay windows on three sides. The whole time, I was conscious that Erik was right behind me, no doubt checking out *my* ass.

I took some consolation from the fact that I had nothing to be ashamed of, and deliberately added a little extra sway in my walk.

Eat your heart out, you faithless bastard.

Cindy perched herself on an overstuffed chair, gesturing carelessly toward the couch. She didn't bat an eye when Erik sprawled next to me, still clutching his damn drink.

It was barely ten o'clock in the morning, for heaven's sake.

"So what's this about my grandmother?" Cindy's eyes were hard, her fake smile firmly in place.

"She came into my store a couple of weeks ago with a group of Red Hat ladies," I said, reaching into my purse. I brought out the ribboned box I'd put the bracelet in and held it toward her. "She bought this for you."

Cindy stared at me, making no move to take the box. Her hands were clasped in front of her, ankles crossed and to the side, a perfect example of perfect posture.

"She meant it as an apology," I added. "She said you'd had a fight."

For a moment, a slight catch in Cindy's breath was the only sign she'd heard me. Erik moved restlessly on the couch, taking a sip of his drink.

I glanced toward the bay window, and there was Violet, sitting quietly on a window cushion, watching us.

"You have your own store?" Erik had apparently decided to fill the silence with small talk. "That's great! Good to know you're doing well."

Cindy obviously wasn't interested in whether I was doing well or not. She shot Erik a quelling look, lips thinned, and practically snatched the box from my hand.

"Why would my grandmother confide in you?" The suspicion in Cindy's tone was unmistakable. "And why would you do anything nice for me?" Her gaze flicked again to Erik, but she kept her spine straight and her head high.

I guessed that was as close to an apology as I'd ever get.

"Quit grilling her, Cindy," Erik said irritably. "She brought you a present."

"Of course you'd take up for *her*, wouldn't you?" For a second we were back in high school, missing only Cindy's cheerleader uniform. "Forgive me for thinking that my husband's ex-girlfriend might just be here to cause trouble. Kind of like when your *last* girlfriend showed up at the Martins' garden party."

I looked over at Violet, ready to kill her for getting me into this. Of all the things that had happened in the last month, sitting in the morning room of my ex-fiancé's mansion with him, his wife, and her dead grandmother seemed by far the most bizarre.

Hello, Ms. Styx, and welcome to the Twilight Zone.

Violet spoke, though no one heard her but me. "Tell Cindy you know what our fight was about." She flicked her hands at me, urging me on. "Tell her."

Sure, why not?

"You and your grandmother had a fight over your idiot husband."

Cindy's mouth fell open. It wasn't a good look for her.

"Hey, now," Erik protested, "there's no need for name calling, is there?" He gave a little laugh. "For all you know, I'm a great husband."

"I'll never know, now will I?"

Erik's smile vanished.

Proud of my self-control, I smiled sweetly and added, "I'm just repeating what Violet said, Erik, so that Cindy will know I'm telling the truth."

Cindy stared at the box, saying nothing.

I waited while she untied the ribbon, trying to ignore Erik's hairy knee, so close to my own. *I'd thought that knee would one day bounce my children.*

The little noise Cindy made when she saw the bracelet told me a lot. Her mask slipped, and for a moment I saw genuine grief on her face.

I glanced toward the window seat to see Violet smiling, obviously pleased by Cindy's reaction.

Cindy lifted the bracelet, turning it so the lacquer gleamed and the amethysts caught the light. "If my grandmother bought this from you a couple of weeks ago, why do you still have it?" I thought her voice shook a little, but it was hard to tell.

"It came back to me." I'd decided a partial truth was easier to sell than a total lie. "My partner and I own a vintage clothing store, and he went to an estate sale last weekend. This bracelet was in a box of costume jewelry, wrapped and ready to mail . . . that's how I knew your address." Not entirely true, but good enough. "I remembered the bracelet, and I remembered your grandmother, and I thought giving it to you was the right thing to do. I didn't make the connection about who you were until you came to the door."

Cindy's eyes flew to Erik. "An estate sale? You must be joking."

Gee, Cindy, you're welcome.

"My grandmother's only been gone a little over a week . . . her service was just last Thursday." She stood, clutching the bracelet. "Erik?"

Erik was surprisingly relaxed for someone whose wife looked ready to eviscerate him, and whose ex-fiancé was looking at him like he was the scum of the earth.

Which he was.

"You were in Myrtle Beach, hon," he said, shaking his now nearly empty cocktail so the ice rattled. "Recuperating. I just got the ball rolling, that's all. Got rid of the junk so the appraisers can come in." He tipped his glass, searching for that last sip. "It's our house now, after all. No big deal."

"No big deal to you!" Cindy's voice was rising. "You let total strangers come into my grandmother's house and paw through her things? I can't believe you!"

Cindy didn't seem to care that I was listening to every word. I looked at Violet again, unsure what to do, but she wasn't paying any attention to me. She was looking at Erik and nodding her head, a satisfied look on her face.

"My grandmother was the only person in the world who really loved me!" Cindy shot to her feet, still holding the bracelet. "You know how hard this has been on me!"

"For God's sake," Erik said irritably, rising from the couch, "stop being such a drama queen, would you? If you hadn't insisted on going to the beach house for the weekend we could've gotten a lot more of the estate paperwork taken care of by now. I was just getting a head start on things."

"*My* things!" Cindy was nearly shrieking now. "My grandmother left that house and everything in it to me. Me! How could you be so insensitive, you selfish bastard!"

"Um . . ." I got up, mumbling, "I'm gonna go now."

And I did, scooting out of the morning room and heading for the front door. Nobody tried to stop me. Erik and Cindy were both yelling now, their anger echoing through the foyer.

"You hated her because she saw you for who you really are!"

"For God's sake, Cindy, go take a Valium or something! You're making a total ass of yourself!"

"*I'm* an ass? At least I'm not a . . ."

I shut the door behind me with relief, practically running down the steps.

Violet was standing by my car. A faint aura of brilliance surrounded her, an aura I'd seen once before, with my Yiddish friend Irene. "I'm sorry you had to witness that, dear," she said, "I do hope you'll forgive me."

My shoulders slumped a little as I unlocked my car door. I wanted to get out of there, get another cup of coffee, and get my head straight. "Violet, it's time for you to go. I did what you asked, and as you said, a promise is a promise."

"Oh, I'm going, dear." She smiled at me, a sweet smile that made my heart stop, just for a second. "I just wanted to say thank you, and tell you that you did a good thing."

I smiled back, feeling lighter. That was nice to hear. Straightening my shoulders, I opened my car door, ready to get in. "Enjoy the Light, Violet. It's pretty amazing."

"So are you, dear." Violet turned, her aura getting brighter. A single step, into the brilliance, and she was gone.

I felt my spirits lift. I sucked in a deep breath, appreciating the rush of air in my lungs, the smell of wood smoke and wet leaves.

Time to move on.

"Nicki." The front door opened and Erik came out, nearly tripping down the front steps in his haste. Either that or he'd had one too many Bloody Marys.

"Don't rush off," he said, hurrying over to my car. "We haven't had a chance to catch up yet."

"You're kidding, right?" I stared at him, really *looking* at him for the first time since I'd arrived.

Those bags under his eyes made him look like he had a permanent hangover, and his hair was already thinning.

"I know the timing's bad." In five years he'd be chubby and bald, and in ten he'd be a total fatty. "I'd love to see you again . . . how about you give me your number?" He smiled at me, the same boyish smile that used to make me weak in the knees when I was seventeen. "We could meet for lunch."

"Erik!" Cindy threw open the front door and stood there, mascara streaming down her cheeks. "We're not finished! Tell your girlfriend to leave!"

What the hell? I slid into the front seat and tried to slam the door closed, but Erik's hand was on the handle.

"I'll take the kids and go, Erik, I swear it! Get back in here!"

"She's such a bitch, isn't she?" Erik's tone was casual, as if the sight of an hysterical Cindy didn't bother him in the least. "You see what I have to put up with?" He leaned in, so close I could smell the tomato juice and vodka on his breath. "I should've chosen you, Nicki."

I briefly considered spitting in his face, but this was Buckhead, after all. I'm sure they had their standards. I put a hand on his Polo-clad chest and shoved him out of my car and out of my face.

"Violet was right, Erik. You *are* an idiot."

* * *

"You won't believe what just happened."

I called Evan on my cell phone as soon as I pulled out of Erik's driveway.

"Hang on a minute." I could hear the beep of the cash register in the background, so I waited until I heard Evan give a cheery, "Thanks so much. Come back and see us."

"I was just at Erik Mitchell's house," I blurted. "Erik and Cindy. They got married. They live in a mansion in Buckhead and she's a total bitch. *She's* the woman Violet bought the bracelet for."

"No way," Evan breathed. The phone would be glued to his ear.

"She's one of those phony, pinch-faced society types." If I wanted to exaggerate the situation to get some sympathy, I considered myself perfectly within my rights. "Instead of being grateful that I brought her the bracelet her grandmother left her, she accused me of being Erik's girlfriend! She actually thought I was there just to cause trouble!"

"What about Erik? What's he look like these days?"

"He's a bloated playboy-wanna-be." I was fuming, barely paying attention as I drove. "Stupid jerk actually tried to hit on me."

Evan burst out laughing. "Did he have to pick his balls up off the floor?"

I grinned in spite of myself, eyeing an impressive French Colonial mansion as I passed. "He probably has a maid to do it for him." I couldn't wait to get out of this neighborhood and back into the safe, comfortable haven of Little Five Points. If I'd ever needed a lesson in how money couldn't buy happiness, I'd had one today.

"I can't wait to hear all the juicy details," Evan said. "Are you on your way back?"

A girl in a white convertible pulled up next to me. She had blond hair, just like Cindy.

"Yeah, I'll fill you in when I get there." The image of Cindy shrieking at Erik from the doorway, mascara dripping down her cheeks, was seared in my brain. "You won't believe it."

The light turned green, and the girl in the car next to me took off with a squeal of tires. I shot her a nasty look, her air of wealth and privilege reminding me of Cindy, too.

"Are you okay?" Evan asked.

"I'm okay. It was just so *strange*."

"I'll fix us some tea," Evan said. "Chamomile, maybe . . . it's supposed to be soothing."

Right then the white convertible veered into my lane. She flashed her brakes, forcing me to slam on my own.

"You can handle this, Nicki." Now Evan's voice took on a comforting note. "You've been dealing with zombies and voodoo and dead people . . . you can handle this."

"Huh." I gave the girl in the white convertible the finger as she made her turn. *Thanks for using your blinker, asshole.*

"Dead girls are easy. It's the live ones who give me trouble."

CHAPTER 18

"Man, it's good to be home."

Evan wiggled perfectly manicured toes free of his leather slides and plopped down on the couch.

The fact that he was talking about *my* home made no difference. It would always be his, too. We'd both grown up in this house.

"I thought you loved playing 'wifey' out there in the burbs," I teased. "I'll bet all the neighbors called you Mrs. Carson."

I'd missed this; just the two of us unwinding with a glass of vino after a long day's work, the store locked up tight and the day's receipts already in the night deposit.

"Adored every minute of it," Evan said, "except Butchie's snoring." He smiled, clearly not even minding that too much. "Sometimes my big ol' teddy bear sounds like a cave bear, hibernating."

"How romantic." I turned on the CD player and put on some Concrete Blonde. I loved those soulful tones. "I take it things are still going well."

"Blissfully. He's such a sweetheart—I'm in heaven." Evan took the glass of wine I handed him. "What about you and Joe, *hm?*" His voice took on a sly note. "How's the good doctor going to handle it now that you're back in your own bed?"

"He's okay with it. It's not like we were living together or anything." *Surely that touch of defensiveness didn't come from me?* "He asked me to stay, but I needed to come home."

Evan's radar was finely tuned. "Trouble in paradise?"

"No. I just wanted my house back."

Evan glanced uneasily toward the darkened windows. "You're sure it's safe? Caprice is gone?"

"Yep." I hadn't felt that nagging sense of fear, that feeling of something evil peering over my shoulder, since the night Granny Julep performed her ritual. "I think it's over."

"Hallelujah." Evan's fervent comment went down even better with a clink of wineglasses and a sip of chardonnay.

"So what's with Joe?" Trust Evan not to leave well enough alone.

I sank down on the couch, tucking my feet beneath me. "Nothing." A sip of wine. "I just don't wanna get too used to depending on him. The 'maiden in distress' thing is getting old. I can take care of myself." Another sip of wine. "I *like* taking care of myself."

"I thought you liked him."

"I do." *Too much*. "I'm telling you, there's no problem. He's coming over for dinner later."

Evan's eyebrows went sky high. "You're cooking?"

The way he said it might as well have been, *You're poisoning someone?*

"No, I thought I'd just jump naked into some Jell-O and call myself dessert."

"Don't forget the whipped cream and cherries. You do remember what a cherry is, don't you?"

I nearly choked on wine and laughter, appreciating as always how easy it was to be myself with Evan.

"Vaguely."

Evan put his feet up on the old chest I used as a coffee table. We sipped our wine and listened to music in companionable silence, letting the knots that bound us loosen.

"You're different these days." Evan was uncharacteristically serious. "Is everything okay, Nick?"

I wished I knew myself as well as Evan did. Then maybe I'd have an answer for him. I put my feet up next to his and reached for his hand.

"I think so. For now, anyway. It's been quite a month."

"You said it, sister." Evan nodded solemnly, squeezing my fingers.

"Seeing Erik today was so weird, but what's really weird is how little I cared. I've got so much other stuff going on, and then there's Joe . . . everytime I looked at Erik I felt nothing but contempt." I shook my head. "What was I *thinking*?"

"You should never have let him near the secret garden," Evan said complacently. "Women tend to romanticize the first guy who plucks their fruit."

"You should know," I teased him, well aware of his fond memories of a certain Manny Vittoro.

Evan grinned, not bothering to argue. "The guy swept you off your feet with that puny little promise ring—I told you never say yes to anything less than a full carat, didn't I? But did you listen to me? No."

I still had that puny little promise ring in a corner of my jewelry box. It was *so* outta there.

"He and Cindy deserve each other," Evan added.

"After what I saw today, I think Cindy's paid a pretty high price for what she did. Despite the mansion and the money, I almost felt sorry for her. I would have, if she hadn't been such a bitch."

"Then why so thoughtful?" Evan was still holding my hand, solid as ever.

"Do you remember when I told you about my near death experience, and how it felt like everything in the world—everything in the universe—was somehow connected?" I took another sip of wine, trying to find the words for what I was thinking.

"You mean like 'Six Degrees of Kevin Bacon'?"

I squeezed his fingers, knowing humor was a defense. Evan didn't like to talk about my dying.

"Yes, actually." I grinned at him. "Exactly like that, only on a mind-boggling scale."

"And your point?" Evan lay his head back on the couch, moving his bare feet in time to the music.

I let go of his hand to tuck my toes beneath me again.

"I can't believe it's just a coincidence that I would end up at Erik's house because I sold a woman a bracelet." I touched the tiny tattoo on my left breast.

"It wasn't because you sold the bracelet, it was because you were doing a good deed." Evan was always a stickler for detail.

"So I end up at their house because I was doing a

good deed for a dead woman?" I shook my head. "What if I hadn't decided to help Violet? Would I have spent the rest of my life thinking I'd missed out on a good thing by not marrying Erik?"

"Oooh, I get it." Evan's head came off the couch. "It's like that butterfly thingie."

I rolled my eyes. "I'm not talking about sex toys, Evan."

"No, no." Evan flapped a hand in my direction. "The 'butterfly effect' or whatever. They made a movie about it, with Demi Moore's boy toy. Chaos theory, ripples in a pond kind of thing."

I looked at him with new respect. "By Jove, I think he's got it."

"So that's why you're cooking dinner for Joe!"

I blinked at the sudden leap of logic.

"You're finally over Erik, and you're taking it to the next level."

"The next level?" I unfurled my legs and sat up straight. "Don't get carried away."

"Of course, I see it all now," Evan said, holding his wineglass aloft. "It was your destiny to be in Joe's E.R. that night. It's a match made in heaven."

"That's not it at all." Or was it? How was I supposed to follow my own convoluted thoughts if I couldn't follow Evan's? "And what do you know about heaven?"

"Oooh, and what about the whole karma thing?" Evan was really getting into it now. "You do something nice for someone, something nice comes back to you. Maybe Joe's your 'something nice.'"

Nice didn't seem a big enough word to describe Joe. He'd brought me back to life, in more ways than one, but it was a different life than the one I'd known, and I was still having trouble figuring out how to navigate it. Evan's theories were making my head spin.

Was it okay to have a different life? Was it okay to have one with Joe?

"Joe hired a private investigator to find his wife. He wants to finalize their divorce."

Evan's feet hit the floor with a solid thunk.

"And you're just now telling me this?" His outrage was only partly for effect. "First floor elevator, going up to the next level."

"Shut up and drink your wine."

As tempted as I was to live up to my earlier threat to jump naked into Jell-O and call myself dessert, I'd decided to cook something for Joe.

And it had nothing to do with Evan's stupid theories.

Spaghetti was easy, and I had everything I needed in the pantry and the freezer. Once Evan left, I got to work, and by the time Joe rang the doorbell at half past eight, the house smelled like tomato sauce and garlic bread.

"You look good enough to eat," Joe said as he came in. *"Mmm,"* he added, burying his face in my neck, "smell good, too."

"It's the basil," I said teasingly, hugging him tight. "Gets 'em every time."

Joe laughed and let me go, following me into the kitchen. "I brought you something," he said.

"You did?" *How sweet.*

"I brought you some pictures." Joe was holding a small envelope. He waved it at me before tossing it on the counter. "I thought you might like to see more pictures of Kelly." He shrugged, playing it cool. "Not right this second, I mean, but whenever you want to. In private."

The reminder of Kelly made me nervous, but the gesture really was kinda sweet. If Joe was going to track down his ex-wife, I'd have to deal with the possibility of her being my sister sooner or later. Might as well prepare myself.

"Thanks." I gave him a sideways smile as I took the bread from the oven. "Have a seat in the living room, handsome. I'm making spaghetti."

I'd already opened a bottle of red wine and left it on the coffee table with two glasses.

Joe poured while I went back for a final stir of tomato sauce, then I brought out a plate of sliced apples, knowing he liked fruit more than cheese.

"This looks great. What's the occasion?" Joe was smiling, relaxed and happy. He'd gone home and showered after his shift—his hair was still a little damp. I couldn't help but mentally compare his whole-some good looks to Erik's self-indulgent, middle-aged flabbiness, and *know* I'd dodged a bullet.

"No occasion." I shrugged, sliding next to him on the couch. "I just wanted to do something nice for you, that's all." It was true, I did. "I ate your food and lived in your house for a week. I washed the sheets before I left, by the way." My mom al-ways said a guest should leave a place neat.

"That's too bad," Joe said, shaking his head rue-fully. "I loved the way those sheets smelled." He took my hand, giving me a slow grin that set my heart tripping.

I grinned back, squeezing his fingers. "They'll smell that way again."

Joe surprised me by kissing my hand. "I wouldn't mind if they smelled that way all the time."

Things got really quiet. All I could think about was the feel of his skin as he rubbed his cheek against my hand, the firm heat of his lips as he kissed it again. It felt like a defining moment—almost like when Erik proposed—yet I didn't know what to say.

"Something really weird happened to me today," I blurted. Joe lowered my hand. "Nothing bad," I hastened to add, "but really weird. It started a few weeks ago, when I sold this sweet little Red Hat lady a bracelet."

I told Joe all about the bracelet, Evan's estate sale, and Violet's unexpected visit. He said very little, sipping from his glass as he listened to the first half of the story, including some completely unnecessary details about vintage jewelry. I was working my way up to telling him about Erik, but his continued silence had me worried.

"I'm stuck with it, Joe."

He looked at me, not saying anything.

"It's official . . . I see dead people. They come to me and they want me to solve their problems. Sometimes I can and sometimes I can't, and sometimes I wish I could crawl into a hole where they could never find me—but mostly I just wanna live my life." Here was the big question. "Do you think you can be with a person like that?"

Joe put down his glass and leaned over so our faces were close. He reached out and very gently smoothed a strand of hair behind my ear. "I *am* with a person like that." Then he kissed me, a kiss that told me all I needed to know.

After that it was easy to tell him about Erik and Cindy. He didn't judge, or ask why a seventeen-year-old goth girl would ever have been attracted to a preppy high school jock to begin with, much less gotten engaged to one. He laughed when I described Cindy's uptight size four ass, and by the time I finished the story, we were both laughing at the picture I'd painted of two miserably married yuppies, screaming insults at each other on the front steps of their Buckhead mansion.

"Your ex-fiancé, who cheated on you, actually hit on you right in front of his wife, the woman he cheated on you with." Joe gave a bark of laughter, shaking his head. "Unbelievable."

"You should have seen the look on his face when I shoved him out of my car." I giggled. "Calling him an idiot was just icing on the cake."

"He *is* an idiot." Joe poured us both more wine. "If the guy chose some blond bimbo cheerleader over you, he deserves whatever hell she puts him through." A clink of wineglasses sealed that statement, while I relaxed, feeling much lighter for having told him.

"He's the reason for the tattoo?" Joe glanced at my breast, where a broken heart still beat, stronger than ever.

"It was stupid." I flushed, embarrassed by that bit of childhood drama. "There's a tattoo artist down in Little Five Points who does really good work . . . I think I'll see if he can remove it."

"I don't know." Joe stretched out a finger, tracing it lightly over the tattoo, even though he couldn't see it. My nipple sprang to life. "I kinda like it." He bent over, leaning in close. "Maybe he can just—" He kissed the spot through my shirt. "—mend it."

"Maybe he could," I murmured, caressing his dark hair. Neither of us was talking about the tattoo artist.

Several wine-flavored kisses later, I pulled away. "Uh-uh-uh." My shirt had mysteriously come unbuttoned and my hair was messed up. "No dessert before dinner." I stood up, leaving Joe mock-groaning on the couch.

"You're a cruel woman, Nicki Styx."

"Yeah. Good thing I'm cute, huh?"

He laughed, then stood up, the bulge in his jeans evidence of my cruelty. "That reminds me, you left some girly stuff at my apartment. I left it in the car."

"Girly stuff?" I gave him my archest look.

"Face lotion, or something like that. You left it in the bathroom . . . I thought you might want it."

My moisturizer . . . how sweet. "I do want it. Thanks." I didn't like to go to bed unmoisturized.

"I'll go get it."

"Hurry back," I said, getting down plates and grabbing silverware for two. "Dinner's almost ready."

I heard the front door open as Joe headed to his car.

"Nicki." The way Joe said it didn't sound right. "Nicki, come here."

Putting down the plates, I went through the living room to find Joe standing by the door. He pointed down at the welcome mat.

"Look at this."

My blood ran cold.

It was a knife, very sharp and very shiny. A wide blade, with a red cord crisscrossing the handle, ending in a tuft of feathers.

Just looking at it made me nauseous.

"This isn't good," I said blankly. The knife had voodoo written all over it. "It wasn't there when you got here."

Joe bent to pick it up.

"Don't touch it!" I was absolutely certain that touching it was a bad idea.

Without stopping to think, I knelt, trying not to look at the knife as I picked up the welcome mat. I carried the mat, knife and all, over to the edge of the front porch and flung them into the yard.

"What are you doing, Nicki? I wanted to have a closer look at that!"

I shook my head, hugely relieved to have that thing off my porch. "I don't want it in my house. I don't want it *near* my house."

"We have to call the police."

"Call the police and tell them someone left a butcher knife on my welcome mat? It's some kind of voodoo . . . am I supposed to explain to them how I know? Or should I just cut to the chase and tell them I'm being terrorized by an evil spirit?"

My skin was crawling. I took Joe by the hand and pulled him inside, only too happy to lock out the darkness. I'd deal with that knife in the daylight, with a big pair of tongs and a garbage bag.

"Voodoo?" Joe was frowning, watching me slide the dead bolt home. "I thought it was over." *So did I.* "You're shaking like a leaf, Nicki . . . c'mere."

I slid into his arms, holding him tight as I pressed my cheek against his chest.

"Somebody's trying to scare me."

"Gee, ya think?" Joe had never snarked at me before, but I knew it was only frustration speaking. The way he rubbed my back confirmed that he was angry at the situation, not me. "You're coming home with me, right now."

Despite the icy tendrils of fear that snaked their way down my spine, I smiled a little against his chest. Typical male response—grab your woman by the hair and drag her to safety.

"I made dinner."

"We'll take it with us."

"I wanna do some research about the symbolism of the knife."

"You can do it at my place," he said implacably.

"Joe," I raised my head, "I know you're worried, but I can't spend the rest of my life at your place."

Why not? said his eyes, but I avoided the question.

"This is my home, and I'm not going to be driven out of it. Besides, if somebody really wants to get to me, they'll find me wherever I am. Should I stop going to work, too?"

Joe was frowning, not liking my arguments. "What if there's some guy out there in the bushes right now, Nicki, waiting until I leave?"

I seriously doubted it. Voodoo was based on symbolism and secrets. Evil desires were gained through ritual and spells, not direct methods. Aside from whatever potions were used—like whatever Granny had used on me when I'd drawn the *veve*—the real power of voodoo lay in the mind.

As scary as that knife was, I'd bet it was more of a warning than a threat. Still, I wasn't a *complete* idiot.

"Okay," I said, "I'll call the police and file a report. If we're lucky, they'll send somebody out to shine a flashlight in the bushes."

Joe sighed, clearly unhappy. "You do that. We can talk about where you're spending the night after you've made the call." He took me by the hand and led me into the living room, settling me on the couch. "But first, I'm checking every inch of this house." I'd never seen Joe look so grim. "You stay right there."

"Okay."

He looked at me suspiciously. "I mean it, Nicki. Stay there."

"I will," I said, despising my own wimpiness. My knees were a little shaky. I'd rather have stuck to his side like glue, but this was one time I didn't mind being told what to do.

Joe reached over and picked up the phone, which I'd left lying on the coffee table, and handed it to me. "Nine-one-one. Very easy number."

"Ha ha." I took it, not looking forward to the call. It wasn't an emergency, for one thing, and I didn't think the police would be able to help.

They'd be tilting at shadows.

"What's that godawful smell?" Joe raised his head, sniffing the air. "Is something burning?"

I started off the couch, but Joe stopped me cold. "Stay right there, I said."

Giving him an exasperated look, I said, "My tomato sauce probably needs stirring."

"I'll check it." Joe walked into the kitchen, tossing his keys on the counter. He went straight to the stove and turned off the heat.

I watched him, surprised to find I liked the way he'd taken charge—the macho man thing was both annoying and sexy at the same time.

"The spaghetti sauce is fine." He'd lifted the lid, releasing a cloud of steam. He was frowning, puzzled, as he put the lid back on.

"Something stinks." He moved to the refrigerator and opened it. "It really smells awful."

The hair rose on the back of my neck.

Joe rummaged around in the fridge, then gave up, turning to the garbage can as the culprit. "Don't you smell it?" I was frozen to the couch. "It smells like something rotten. It smells like . . ." He glanced up and met my eye.

"Like bad fruit?" I asked. "Like something dead?" My face must've shown what I was thinking.

Joe shook his head. "Nicki, it's okay."

"Nicki, it's okay," came Caprice's mocking whisper, slithering into my ear as neatly as a lizard. I shrieked and jumped up from the couch.

"Did you hear her?"

"Did you hear her?"

Before Joe could answer, I gabbled, "She's here. Caprice is here!" I was frantic—she wasn't supposed to be here.

"She's here. Caprice is here." The whispers were louder now, swirling around me.

Joe expression was priceless.

"What's that?" he asked sharply.

"What's that?" Caprice mocked, but her voice

was different now, full of spite. *"You hear some-thing, white boy?"*

Joe and I stared at each other, in shock, as Caprice went on, addressing Joe directly. Her vicious whispers filled the air.

"You wanna hear more? The screams of the damned, maybe? They gonna be like music to your ears."

"If you're dead," Joe said firmly into the air, "you can't hurt anybody."

"You think so? That old woman can't stop me no more . . . her day is done!"

Joe flinched suddenly, as though someone hit him. He stumbled backward, throwing out a hand.

"Stay there, Nicki!" He shot me a warning glare, palm upraised, scanning the empty kitchen for his attacker.

"Stay there, Nicki. Stay there." Caprice's nasty falsetto sounded like a child who'd been denied one too many times on the playground. *"Your girl-friend didn't bring me my man like I asked her. Maybe the Baron will like hers."*

"Go away," I shrieked, nearly at the breaking point. "Go away, Caprice! I never did anything to you! I thought you were my friend!" I was sobbing now. "I tried to help you, but I can't! Leave us alone!"

"You ain't never been my friend. You been try-

ing to keep me down." Caprice's voice was an evil whisper, all sound and no substance.

Joe stumbled backward again, this time clutching his throat. I rushed into the kitchen. Joe was leaning against the counter wheezing, fighting for breath.

There was no one and nothing to fight.

Then I remembered.

"'Take unto ye the armor of God, that ye may be able to withstand evil.'" I said Granny's scripture out loud, and then I said it again, louder. "'Our Father who art in Heaven, hallowed be thy name . . .'" I spouted every religious reference I could think of, as quickly as I could, while I squeezed Joe's arm and looked into his face.

He was gasping for breath. He gave me a desperate look, then understood. There was no one to fight, except the images in our minds. We kept an eye lock as I kept talking. "'Amazing grace, how sweet the sound . . .'" I ignored the stench that surrounded Joe like mildewed jelly. "'Thou shalt honor thy father and mother. Thou shalt not steal.'"

Joe took a deep breath, expression easing, then another. I held him tight. "'Thou shalt not covet thy neighbor's wife,'" I babbled. His arms came around me, his breathing easier. I could feel his heart pounding against my ear.

"'Mother Mary, full of grace . . .'" I wasn't sure if

Joe's gruff contribution was a fragment of memory or a statement of disbelief about what just happened to him.

"'Give us this day our daily bread.'"

"'Do unto others as you'd have them do unto you.'"

I sighed. "That's what got me into this mess."

Joe moved fast, grabbing my hand. He snatched his keys off the counter. "Let's get out of here."

I didn't argue. Two seconds later we were gone with the wind, and on our way to Joe's car. We didn't talk about where we were going until we'd driven several blocks.

"What the hell was *that*?" Joe kept checking the rearview mirror. He looked more pissed than scared.

"You know what it was," I said wearily, too drained to even say her name.

"How the hell do we get rid of it?"

"I have no idea." An unwilling thought came to mind. "But I'll bet I know who does."

Joe glanced over, apparently able to read my mind.

"No. Uh-uh." He was frowning, shaking his head decisively. "You're not going near that old woman again."

"Joe!" My nerves were shot, or I'd never have yelled at him. "Quit telling me what I can and can't do! It's not like I wanted any of this, you know!"

His frown got blacker. "I don't know what you want, Nicki, and half the time I don't think you know, either." Before I could come back with a retort, he added, "I'm just trying to keep you safe." He glared at me. "This is pretty serious stuff."

Using his own earlier snark against him, I snipped, "Gee, ya think?"

Joe sighed, clearly unwilling to fight. "Nicki, I . . ." another sideways glance, "I don't want anything to happen to you."

My anger drained away as quickly as it came. It'd been quite a day. I reached out and laid a hand on Joe's thigh in unspoken apology.

He covered my fingers with one hand and drove with the other, while the next mile or so went by in silence.

"I'm sorry I yelled."

"You should be." Joe's rueful grin took the sting from his words.

"Granny Julep is the only one who knows what's going on."

His grin faded. "This is crazy," he muttered.

How could I make him understand? "Listen . . . despite what she did at the barbecue place, I don't think she meant to hurt me. I'm here, aren't I?"

"Only because she collapsed," he shot back. "You don't know what would've happened otherwise."

"True." It wasn't worth arguing over. "But even if Granny Julep isn't necessarily looking out for my best interests, she has personal reasons for wanting Caprice to be put to rest. What she wants is what I want." The more I tried to convince Joe, the more I convinced myself that I had to talk to her. "She knows things I don't. Why shouldn't I use her the way she's used me?"

"Because you're not a user, Nicki." Joe sounded resigned. "If anything, you're too nice."

"I am not!" Indignant, I straightened. "I'm one tough cookie, and don't you forget it."

Joe let go of my hand to take a corner. "Yeah, like a Fig Newton . . . one with a mushy center."

CHAPTER 19

We were almost too late. One look at Granny Julep's face, almost as gray as her hair, told me that. Her eyes were closed and a thin strip of tubing ran under her nose.

"It's way past visiting hours, so make it quick," Joe murmured. "If you can get past *him*, that is."

"Him" would be Albert, already rising from his chair beside Granny's bed, glaring at us both.

"I need to see her, Albert." I wasn't going to waste time arguing with a man who never had anything to say. "Someone left a knife on my doorstep, and Caprice was in my house."

At her granddaughter's name, Granny's eyes fluttered open. Her fingers twitched. "You got to do it, child. You the only one who can do it," she murmured.

I came into the room, daring Albert with my eyes to try and stop me. It helped to know that Joe was right behind me, lending me courage. I knew I'd won when Albert shifted so I could get closer to the bed.

"Granny Julep." I wanted to be sure she recognized me and understood what I was saying. "It's Nicki." The little nod she gave me was enough—she was weak, but still there.

"Caprice attacked Joe tonight." I knew she understood when her eyes flicked to Joe, then back to me. "She's stronger now," I shuddered, "very strong. Evil, angry. I don't know what to do."

"Knife?" Granny's voice was feeble, but I could understand her.

"A big one. With a red cord tied around the handle. Someone left it on my doormat."

She closed her eyes again, and for a moment I thought she'd gone to sleep. "G'day," she murmured. "*Bokor.*"

Huh? I was so frustrated I could cry. Gibberish wasn't going to help me.

"The knife is the Mark of Guede." Albert's voice made me jump. He'd moved to the opposite side of the bed and stood facing us over Granny's blanketed form. Grizzled and scowling, disapproving as ever, his face softened as he gazed down at the woman on the bed. "Someone wants to steal your soul."

The room seemed to tilt a little, righting itself at the touch of Joe's hand on my shoulder. *Steal my soul?*

"Sir . . ." Joe's voice was mild, but I could hear his impatience. "What exactly are you saying?"

Albert lifted his eyes to mine, and in their raisin-black depths I saw something I didn't like.

Pity.

"Felicia," Granny murmured, drawing our attention back to her. "The chains." Her eyes fluttered open, finding and focusing on the old man who hovered over the bed. She moved her hand toward Albert, and he took it. "Tell them, hon."

Confused and scared as I was, I blinked back tears, touched by the obvious devotion between the old couple. They wouldn't be a couple much longer, and they knew it.

"Do you know a woman named Felicia?" Albert's words were abrupt, but his face was resigned. He didn't let go of Granny's hand.

I shook my head, drawing a total blank. "I don't think so."

"A black woman, who sells organic soaps and lotions."

I caught him with that skinny piece of trash who supplies us with that damn organic soap! Caprice's voice rang in my head, making me shudder. *Go see that skinny 'ho, Felicia. Tell her you'll go to DFCS about them kids of hers.*

Felicia—the woman Mojo had been having an affair with.

Joe tightened his arm around my shoulder as Albert kept talking.

"We didn't know she was *bokor*." Whatever *bokor* meant, it must have been pretty bad—Albert was frowning even more than usual. "Or she . . ." He glanced down at Granny. " . . . Julep would have done things differently. Now it's nearly too late."

I seized on that one word. "Nearly?" Joe squeezed my shoulder, silently urging me to let Albert finish.

"It isn't good to speak of these things."

I was still surprised Albert was speaking at all, so I bit my lip and just listened.

"The knife you found on your doorstep is proof this woman seeks to 'create *serviteur*' with our Caprice. She torments her spirit, keeping it separated from her body, until her soul becomes corrupted"—he lowered his voice, face strained—"a different thing entirely."

I glanced at Joe, knowing he remembered only

the evil spirit who'd attacked him in the kitchen, not the smiling, upbeat Caprice whose laugh used to carry all the way into the street.

"The knife has marked you as the *cheval*, the horse. If this woman can force Caprice's spirit to enter into you, she wins."

"Whoa there, Nelly." If I were going to be compared to a horse, I'd respond in kind. "'Force Caprice's spirit to enter into me'? That's impossible."

Albert just looked at me.

"Isn't it?" Getting no response, I turned to Joe. "Am I the only one who finds this conversation completely bizarre?"

"Call it what you like," Albert said. "But a death has occurred, and a bargain has been struck. The Baron must have his soul. He is not particular whose he takes."

Either all that time on the Internet had paid off or I must've been learning "cryptic" through osmosis, because what Albert said suddenly made some kind of weird sense.

Felicia had made a deal with the devil to get Caprice out of the way, but now that her rival was dead, she wanted the ultimate voodoo revenge—total control of Caprice's soul. In order to do that, she had to give the Baron another, and for some reason she'd picked mine.

"Why me?" I asked, gripping Joe's hand with fingers gone suddenly icy. "I don't even know this woman!"

Albert blinked, looked away. "You put yourself in front of her when you tried to help Caprice." His voice was so low I could barely hear it. "Just like my Julep."

I'd no sooner wished for a chair before Joe was guiding me to the one at Granny's bedside. Thankfully, I made it before my knees gave out. I stared at Granny's gray head on the pillow, knowing in my heart it was old age that claimed her, but wondering nonetheless.

Did this Felicia person really have the power to do what Albert said?

"You'll have to forgive me, Mister . . ." Joe waited for Albert to supply his last name, but Albert was back to being close-mouthed. " . . . um, sir. This Felicia is the one who left a knife on Nicki's doormat? What's her last name? Maybe the police should have a little talk with her."

Albert demonstrated his remarkable ability to drip contempt without saying a word. The silence in the room was broken only by the hum of the fluorescent light above the bed.

"What do I have to do, Albert?" I was so tired of fighting shadows. I wanted it over.

"She done told you, girl." He was talking about Granny, whose hand he still held. "You got to bind Caprice with chains. And you got to do it tonight, before the sun rises."

Caprice was in her coffin.

CHAPTER 20

Home improvement stores have everything.

By the time the moon was rising over the triple steeple of Trinity Baptist Church, Joe and I were well prepared to dig up a grave and chain down a corpse.

"This is insane," Joe said. We were sitting in the parking lot of the church, looking out at the darkened cemetery where I'd first met Granny Julep.

It looked very different tonight.

"Tell me again why we're doing this." Joe wasn't happy, and neither was I. The car was still idling. There were no lights on inside the church. The place was empty except for the permanent residents under the lawn.

"Because if we don't, Caprice will never rest. She'll be doomed to walk the world at night as an evil spirit, doing whatever Felicia wants her to do." I looked away from the spooky graveyard and into Joe's eyes. "Scare people, hurt people—like what happened in the kitchen." My real fear was that she'd kill someone—like me—and that person would end up just like her.

To comfort myself, I repeated what little I knew from a brief stop at a cyber café on the way over. The coffee had cleared my head as I'd surfed the Net, leaving room for the sketchy details to engrave themselves on my brain.

"Caprice's body and soul are still connected, but not for much longer. We have to bind them forever, symbolically, with the chains." It sounded like something from a bad episode of *The Twilight Zone*. "The weight of the chains ties the spirit to the body." I looked out over the shadowed headstones and shuddered.

"It's a last resort, and our last chance to get rid of her."

"Shit."

"Exactly."

Joe had gone from skeptic to believer. It was a relief to know he didn't think I was crazy.

Yet here I was, about to test that theory to the limit.

"Let's get this over with." Joe turned off the engine and the lights. We got out and gathered our gear from the trunk: two shovels, two heavy-duty flashlights, and a length of chain, the sturdiest we could find. Joe draped it over his shoulder, then took both shovels and turned on his flashlight.

I lit up a beam with a trembling finger and led the way into the sea of headstones, glad the place was nowhere near a main road. This was a pretty rural area. We'd still have to keep an eye out for the occasional passing car.

It was quiet. Dead quiet. I found myself wishing for crickets, even an owl. Anything besides the sound of my boots swishing through the grass, anything to cover the scared rasp of my breathing.

"I think it was over here," I murmured. We were in a shadowed maze of crosses and stone slabs. I tried hard not to let my flashlight rest on the names inscribed on them. It was easier not to think about who or what they sheltered.

"Kill the flashlight," Joe hissed, "a car's coming."

We snapped off the lights and ducked, Joe crouching behind a headstone as I slipped behind a stone angel. He was a shadow in the darkness, and I hoped I looked the same.

The headlights of a car swept over the stones

to our left, casting a moving silhouette of squares and crosses over the graves. A crunch of gravel reached us.

Someone had pulled into the church parking lot.

I ducked as low as I could go, daring to take a peek around the angel's robed feet.

A sheriff's cruiser. *Dammit, dammit, damn it all.*

Joe scuttled toward me, dragging me down with an arm around the shoulders. He pointed silently at a large double-stoned grave site about twelve feet away, a little deeper inside the cemetery.

A mist was beginning to rise from the grass, and the moon was shrouded. If we could stay out of sight, maybe the cop would go away. What was he gonna do, search an entire cemetery in the dark?

I nodded to let Joe know I got it. He slipped off the chains with hardly a rattle, and we left them there with the shovels. I followed him as he crept toward the big headstone.

The blare of the cop's radio startled me. He'd opened the cruiser's door and was getting out. Joe and I froze for a split second, then moved even faster. We stayed with the shadows, keeping low.

Then we were safe behind the stone, pressed against each other shoulder-to-shoulder, and breathing fast.

Just in time, too. Another sweep of headlights, another crunch of gravel.

"Oh, shit," I whispered. *Not another one.*

"Whatcha got, Dan?" The second car rolled to a stop, still idling. The man's voice carried clearly up the hillside.

"BMW 325i, looks like. Nice car."

Oh shit oh shit oh shit.

"Stolen?"

"I dunno. Haven't run the plates yet. Hood's still warm and it's locked, I checked. No sign of any damage."

One of the cops hawked and spit. Tobacco, probably. What else was there for a lawman to do in rural Georgia besides hang out in church parking lots and chew tobacco?

"Reverend Cobb's brother is in town. Some fancy lawyer from Boston. Could be his."

The other cop answered, "Yeah. Could be. Looks like a lawyer's car."

Even in the dark I could see Joe's insulted expression. I controlled a sudden urge to giggle.

"I gotta take a whiz," said the first cop.

This time I had to clap my hand over my mouth to keep from laughing. Joe's teeth gleamed in the darkness as he smiled. He slid an arm around my shoulders and held me, our backs to the tombstone.

"Well, hurry up, then. Coffee's getting cold."

"You got my bear claw?"

Doughnuts. It was too much. Joe and I rocked with silent laughter despite the tricky situation. After all, what else was there for a lawman to do in rural Georgia besides hang out in church parking lots, chew tobacco, and eat doughnuts?

"Yeah, I got your bear claw. Now hurry up . . . it'll be closing time at the Dew Drop Inn soon, and Earl asked us to swing by and patrol the parking lot. Government checks came in the mail today."

Mentally adding "breaking up fights between drunken rednecks" to my roster of sheriff's duties, I buried my face against Joe's chest to stifle any giggles.

He smelled great; male sweat and Tide. There was something to be said for a guy who knew how to do his own laundry.

"*Shh,*" Joe whispered. His breath in my ear made my nipples tingle. "We may be here awhile."

I lifted my head and he lowered his. My lips were next to his ear now. "Ever make out in a graveyard?" I kissed the rim of his ear, letting my tongue just touch it.

Joe's breath caught.

Behind us, the two cops slurped their coffee and ate their bear claws. They'd begun to argue goodnaturedly about the best bait to use in bass fishing.

"You're a very bad girl, aren't you?" Joe murmured.

"You have no idea." I had, in fact, made out in a graveyard once. Junior year of high school; Daryl Metcalf. Daryl had been bony and brooding, perfect teenage goth material.

Joe's lips were inches from my own. It was dark, his eyes unreadable. But when I slid my hand down his pants, the surge of maleness I felt there told me all I needed to know.

"*Shh.*" I kissed him, slipping my tongue inside his mouth, and he surged again beneath my hand.

I felt a bolt of heat inside that surprised me, given the circumstances. Making out was one thing, but. . .

What the hell.

So while the cops finished up their coffee break and the moon reduced the world to shades of gray, I brought Joe over the edge to the dark side. We barely even noticed when the first cop slammed his car door shut and the two cruisers drove away.

And when it was over, and Joe lay gasping for breath, me nestled beneath his arm, I looked up at the night sky and smiled. The line between life and death was a fine one. Throw in some sex and everything got blurred.

"Oh, my God." Joe sounded dazed but happy. "What just happened?"

"If I have to explain it to you then I must not've done it very well." I kissed him on the chin, feeling the rasp of stubble in the darkness. "But don't get too comfy . . . we've got work to do."

I sat up, raking the hair out of my face with my fingers. Joe straightened his clothes, only pausing once to lean over and kiss me, softly, on the lips.

"Never a dull moment. One of the things I love about you."

He stood up, leaving me sitting there with a stunned look on my face. Thank God it was too dark for him to see it.

I heard the quick rasp of a zipper, then Joe reached for my hand and pulled me to my feet.

"Let's get the shovels," he said.

Caprice's grave was easy to find, even in the dark. It was buried under a mass of white flowers, all of which we'd use to cover the signs of our digging when we left this place.

As I stood there staring at the pile of flowers, I heard a whisper, like a sigh on the breeze, swirling through the darkness. *"Nicki, please."*

"Did you hear that?"

Joe froze, gauging my reaction. He shook his head, but with a quick shrug let the chains fall to the ground, clinking and clanking. Then he moved closer, gripping the shovel in one hand, scanning the shadows.

I shone the flashlight beam over the nearby headstones, hoping against hope I'd see nothing, yet knowing something was there.

"She's here, Joe. I heard her."

"*Nicki.*" How could a whisper be so frightening? "*Help me.*"

Help me? I'd help her all right—I'd help her get the hell away from me. Even though the flashlight was shaking, along with my voice, I said to Joe, "Let's dig."

"I don't hear her this time." Joe's voice was somber. "What if she tries to stop us?"

The memory of Joe choking, gasping for air, made me touch the black beads beneath my shirt, and when I did, another memory came back to me.

"Granny says spirits are weaker on hallowed ground."

"Let's hope so," Joe muttered.

And so we started digging, me doing my best to ignore the whispers that continued to swirl in my ears.

"She keeps asking me to help her." I wanted Joe to know what was going on. "She doesn't seem angry. Do you think it's some kind of trick?" I kept my voice low, continually looking over my shoulder. "Every other time Caprice asked me for help, it was a demand, not a request."

Joe shrugged, digging for all he was worth. "I'm

just following your lead, Nicki. You're the voodoo expert."

"Don't say that!" I glanced around uneasily. "I only know enough to be dangerous."

"*Please, Nicki, please.*" As scary as the whispering was, there was a note of pathos in it I couldn't ignore. "*Help me.*"

"What if we open the coffin, and . . ." I didn't even wanna finish the thought, much less the sentence, but I'd seen my share of zombie movies.

Joe stopped digging, leaning on the shovel. "If you're having second thoughts, we can go home right now."

Home. That's what I was fighting for, wasn't it? My parents had laughed, loved, and lived in that house, filled it to the brim with memories and affection. It was all I had left of them, and I wasn't gonna give it up. There was also the small matter of soul-stealing, which I didn't really understand and didn't really want to. My soul was going nowhere but the Light, thank you.

"Keep digging."

The whispering stopped, and I wasn't sure whether to be relieved or concerned. We'd dug a nice-sized hole by the time the drums started.

"What the hell is that?" Joe murmured.

Frozen mid-shovel, I gave him a hopeless look.

"We're getting out of here." Stabbing his shovel

tip into the dirt, Joe snatched up the flashlight and grabbed me by an arm. He spun me in the direction of the parking lot.

But it was too late.

A woman stood behind a nearby tombstone, directly in our path. Behind her, far enough away to be only pinpoints in the darkness, at least six torches flickered. Shadows moved in the feeble light they cast. The drums went on, stronger now that we'd seen the woman. At her back, flanking her like an honor guard, were four men, dark shapes in the dimness.

Joe turned the flashlight fully on her face, but she never flinched. Black she was, black as midnight, skin shiny with sweat. She wore a snowy white kerchief like a turban, earrings of shell and feathers. I couldn't help but think of Granny, though this woman was at least fifty years younger and a total stranger.

"Don't stop now." The woman smiled a broad smile, her teeth a slash of white in her face. "You're not finished yet."

"Who the hell are you?" Joe stepped in front of me. "What do you want?"

The look she gave him was calculating, impersonal, as if she were sizing him up for something. "Don't make me hurt your girlfriend, white boy. You in over your head."

Silence, but for the drums. I took Joe's hand, lacing my fingers through his, feeling the tension through the muscles of his arm. His protectiveness was comforting, but he couldn't hope to win against four men. Who knew how many more were out there among the headstones? He couldn't fight them all.

"Finish what you started, girl, and get the bitch dug up."

If I needed any confirmation of the woman's identity, that was it.

"Why, Felicia?"

One black eyebrow rose at my use of her name.

I had nothing to lose by stalling a little—maybe the cops would come by for another doughnut. "Why don't you dig her up yourself?"

She stared, then gave me a sly smile.

"You think you know so much about the mysteries." I *really* didn't like this woman—she was bony and tough, all edges. "The body of an enemy is powerful *gris-gris*, honey, but you don't wanna be the one making it mad."

"Don't wanna get your hands dirty, is that it?" Joe edged us both one step closer to the shovel.

Felicia ignored him, addressing her remarks to me. "Your friend Caprice thought she was better than me . . . liked to flaunt her store, her powers, and her man. I stole her man, I stole her powers, and the bitch won't be so arrogant when I use her skin for a coin purse, now will she?"

She ignored my horrified gasp.

"I ain't gonna let her rest, and I ain't gonna let you or that old woman save her."

My knees were knocking, but I wanted to keep Felicia talking. Every minute I stalled was a minute closer to closing time at the Dew Drop Inn.

I squeezed Joe's hand so hard it hurt. "You shoved Caprice down the stairs, didn't you?"

Felicia's smile turned ugly. "Mojo told me you seen her duppy right after she died. If that's so, you already know the answer to that." She was enjoying this game of cat and mouse, playing with Joe and me both, while the drums kept pounding and my heart tripped double-time. "I watched you, seen you meet with that old mambo woman, and knew you was trouble. Every time I raised Caprice's shade, I talked trash in her ears about you and the old woman both. Once she turned against her own, she put herself in my power. She's been fightin' me, but I always win." Felicia wore a look of triumph. "After tonight, Caprice is damned to Hell and her power is mine."

"Why would you do something like that?" The mind boggled.

Felicia laughed, cocking her head. "Power is money, honey."

Of course. All of Caprice's "back room" voodoo business would now fall to Felicia—true believers would be afraid to go anywhere else.

A sudden shout came from the darkness, then a gabble of voices. The drums stopped. They began again, raggedly finding their rhythm, but not before I'd seen a look of fear cross Felicia's face.

Joe still held the flashlight, but he flicked it off. He whipped me around and gave me a shove. "Run," he said, but I was afraid to leave him, afraid I'd never see him again. Instead of doing what he said, I latched onto his arm, clinging like a leech.

A chanting began, seeming to come from all around us, keeping time with the drums. Joe gave in and pulled me closer, and I cowered in his arms, heart pounding in my throat.

Someone was coming, wending their way through the headstones. A line of torches moved steadily in our direction, bobbing and swaying.

Felicia flicked her hand, and one of the men who was with her melted away into the darkness.

The torches came on without a pause.

"Let's go," Joe muttered, but it was too late.

Felicia gave a sudden gasp, shielding herself behind a tombstone. Alarmed murmurs came from the men behind her.

And no wonder, because the apparition who

stepped from the shadows was frightening. If I hadn't seen him before, I might've gasped, too, but as it was, I clutched Joe's ribs so tight I'm sure he could barely breathe.

A black man, with a white face, in top hat and tuxedo. No hint of laughter this time, no crooked bow tie or leering looks. Torchlight flickered eerily over his features, bone-white cheeks and deeply pitted eyes—the perfect imitation of a well-dressed skeleton. He held a shovel, blade up. Gone was the clown who made the crowd laugh, and in his place was a walking corpse with the air of an undertaker. Other torches flickered behind him, giving him a backdrop of fire.

Joe shoved me behind him, freeing his hands. "Who the hell is that?" he whispered fiercely.

"Baron Samedi," I hissed, clinging to his belt while peeking around his shoulders. "Lord of the dead."

Eat, drink, and be merry, for tomorrow you be mine.

The men with torches came to a stop a few yards away, then the skeleton man in front took a few steps forward. The chanting stopped, but the drums went on and on.

Baron Samedi ignored Joe and me completely, engaged in a stare-down with Felicia.

I almost felt sorry for her—the woman didn't

stand a chance. Even without the face powder and torches, the guy was damned scary.

"I haven't called le Baron," Felicia said, her voice quivering, but she drew herself up, one hand on the tombstone. "The *veve* has not been drawn, the sacrifice has not been made."

The skeleton man stared, and the drums never faltered.

Felicia turned to the three men behind her and hissed something I didn't understand, but the men glanced first at the Baron. The whites of their eyes gleamed as they shook their heads and stepped back, into the shadows. Of the first man, there was no sign.

Felicia was alone.

"I owe you nothing!" she spat, as if boldness would win the day. "But I give you these two." She pointed at Joe and me, but never took her eyes off the skeleton man. "Two souls in exchange for one."

Baron Samedi shook his head.

"I demand it!" Felicia raised a hand, and in it gleamed a knife, much like the one I'd seen on my doorstep earlier. "If you don't kill them, I will!" She sprang at us, but Joe was ready for her.

He grabbed her by both wrists and gave the one holding the knife a sudden twist. There was a sickening crack—the sound of bone snapping—and an agonized cry from Felicia. The knife fell to the ground, and Joe kicked it away, drawing another agonized shriek from Felicia.

Murmuring came from the dark knot of men who held the torches, sounding suspiciously like approval.

Silence from Baron Samedi.

Felicia stumbled back, cradling her wrist, and Joe let her go. Her face was contorted with pain. After a moment she slumped to her knees against a tombstone, the fight gone out of her.

"Please," she whispered to the skeleton man. "I've served you well. I will make you an altar, bring you gifts of rum, fine cigars—let me prove myself to you, Old One."

Whoever this guy was, Felicia was obviously convinced of his power. The drums, the flicker of torches, the shadowed headstones—it was an incredibly creepy moment.

Baron Samedi never took his eyes from her. He raised the shovel and pointed it in her direction.

Felicia gasped as though she'd been stabbed. "No."

Two men detached themselves from the knot of torches and came forward, one on either side of Felicia. They were bare-chested, black skin gleaming in darkness. She didn't resist as they pulled her to her feet. The look on her face made me turn away, just for a second.

When I looked back she was allowing herself to be led into the night, slumped between the two men.

Finally, Baron Samedi turned his gaze on Joe and me. I held on tight, having no idea what might happen next.

"Finish it," the man said.

And just like that, I recognized him.

It was Albert.

Stunned, I couldn't help but wonder if Felicia had been tricked into believing something that wasn't true, or if I was the one who'd been deceived all along.

Albert's living dead routine obviously went a lot deeper than I'd thought.

Tension left my body in a rush as he turned to go, and the others followed. His top hat bobbed through the graveyard, weirdly lit by the flickering flame of the torch, as he followed the voodoo woman to her fate.

Whatever that fate was, I was certain I didn't want to know. Felicia was evil, and she was on her own.

Within a few moments the drums stopped and the torches disappeared down the slope of the hill.

"What the hell was all that about?" Joe whispered. We were still standing by the open grave, listening to our own breathing.

"That was the devil taking his due," I murmured. "Let's finish this and get out of here."

In the end, there was no flesh-rotted, pus-dripping zombie waiting to pull me into her evil clutches.

There was only Caprice, silent and unmoving on her bed of white.

I was streaked with dirt, as was Joe. We were exhausted, having dug for at least two hours straight. Thank God the ground was still soft. The moon was right over our heads, evidently curious to see what we were doing.

"Caprice," I whispered. She'd been cleaned up after the accident, obviously. Her cornrows lay neatly on her shoulders, reminding me of an Egyptian mask I'd seen in a museum once. No blood-covered face or twisted neck to haunt my dreams.

Joe wasn't wasting any time. He bent and picked up the chains.

I helped lay them over Caprice's chest and belly, careful not to touch her. Tears of grief pricked my lids, for this was the Caprice I remembered. Not the pure white dress she was wearing, for that wasn't her style; the sash around her head is what got to me. The bright oranges and yellows were muted by the moonlight, but I knew that sash. I'd seen her wear it many times.

"You don't have to stay in the dark, Caprice," I said, not even sure where the words were coming from. "Granny Julep wouldn't have wanted you there." I tucked one end of the chain around her and stepped back.

Joe would've covered her up again, but I made him wait.

"Just a second."

I was tempted to give Caprice the black beads Granny Julep always intended for her, but I had a feeling I might need them more than she did. Instead, I pulled out the *gris-gris* bag I wore beneath my shirt and untied the twine.

"Caprice, if you can hear me . . ." I dug into the mingled dirt and bones until my fingers found the tiny silver cross. I rubbed it clean against my tights and slipped it under her hand. " . . . you're free now. Go into the Light—look for it. Look for the Light."

Then we covered her up again and climbed out of the pit, me having to step on the coffin to reach Joe's outstretched hands.

By the time the sun came up, we were sitting in a truck stop near the interstate, drinking coffee and watching the sky turn orange and pink. *We* were the zombies; filthy, exhausted, unspeaking. I had blisters on both hands.

A sheriff's cruiser pulled up, and I gave Joe a tired smile.

"If he orders a bear claw, we're outta here."

CHAPTER 21

The afternoon sun filtered through the blinds, casting slanted shadows high on the wall. The room was dim, the bed soft and warm—waking up in my own home next to Joe was like being the marshmallow in a cup of hot chocolate.

"Hey, you." Joe was awake already. His arm slid around my waist as he drew close, chest to back, and I felt his lips, warm on my shoulder. The clock beside the bed said it was almost five o'clock—we'd reclaimed the house that morning when we shared a shower, lingering only to wash before tumbling naked into bed.

"*Mmmm.*" I didn't want to move, didn't want to think. I was safe and warm and comfortable, and I didn't want it to end.

"I have to go to work," Joe murmured. "Grave-yard shift this week."

"Didn't we just do that?" I mumbled, thinking fuzzily of the night just past.

Joe kissed my shoulder again, drawing his legs up beneath my thighs. The feel of him against my bottom made me smile.

"Always the funny girl," Joe said softly, lips moving against the back of my neck. "Even when you're sleepy." He breathed deep of my hair, while I lay unmoving in his arms, still smiling. "Are you okay? Last night was pretty rough."

I shifted beneath his arm, turning so we faced each other. His face was flushed with sleep, the bare skin of his shoulder warm beneath my fingers.

"It was awful," I said. "I'm just going to treat it like a bad dream."

Joe's eyes crinkled when he smiled. "Dream? More like a nightmare." His hand came up to stroke my hair away from my face, then came to rest on my hip. "But it's over now."

When I didn't answer, he quirked an eyebrow and added, "Isn't it?"

"I think so. I hope so. I don't know." I wished I

could guarantee our troubles were over, but "trouble" seemed to be my name these days.

"You know—" I hesitated. "—this episode with Caprice may be over, but I still have the same problem." I smiled, though it wasn't funny. "In case you haven't noticed, I seem to be flypaper for freaks. Particularly dead ones."

Joe sighed, then rolled on his back to stretch. Cool air touched my skin where his had been, but only for a moment. He pulled me close again, guiding my head to his shoulder.

"So you think I should cut my losses, *hm*? Take my stethoscope and go back to the nice sane world of science and medicine . . . forget I ever met a strange girl named Nicki Styx, who died and came back to life with the amazing ability to see the dead. Is that it?"

Hearing it put so bluntly was an eye-opener. The guy would have to be crazy to get involved with me. I wasn't "flypaper for freaks"—I *was* the freak.

Unexpected tears pricked my lids, and I was glad he couldn't see them. Sounding like a total wimp, I said, "That's pretty much it."

Joe gave a rude snort, his hand sliding down to give me a sharp smack on the ass.

"Hey!" I tried to rear up, but he wouldn't let me, pulling me back down with an arm around my shoulder.

"That's what you get for being stupid," he said, definite satisfaction in his tone. "And if you don't shut up I'll do it again."

I could've gotten mad—even smacked him back—but I didn't do either. My butt was stinging and so was my pride, but not enough to make me prefer a cold bed to the warm spot beneath his arm.

Besides, if the guy was determined to stick it out, who was I to argue?

"Do it again," I teased, "I kinda liked it."

Not surprisingly, he did. I squealed and thrashed as he went straight to tickling my ribs, then I defended myself as best I could by gaining control where Joe was most vulnerable. Thirty naughty and playful minutes later I kissed him good-bye at the door, exhausted again, only this time pleasantly so.

Since my house smelled like cold garlic bread and I was starving, I went straight to the kitchen. And there, on the counter, was the envelope of photographs Joe had brought over the night before.

There weren't very many . . . five or six, only one of Kelly in a formal pose. A high school picture, probably her senior year—she looked about seventeen.

There was definitely a resemblance, but almost everything about her was different from me. Where I'd worn my hair short and spiky, she'd worn hers long and straight. At sixteen, I'd dyed my hair black in true goth style, while Kelly's was still the ordinary brown I used to see in the mirror. Not a touch of makeup, not even lip gloss, but smiling. She looked plain and wholesome—very "girl next door."

Nothing like me.

I loved being bold with my hair and clothes, always had. I tried to imagine what I would look like if I'd chosen a more subdued look for myself, but I couldn't. For one thing, I simply couldn't imagine myself wearing sand-washed denim with blue and brown plaid.

With a sigh, I slid the pictures back into the envelope and pushed up the sleeves of my robe. The kitchen was a mess, and those dirty pots didn't care how fashionable I was.

Granny Julep looked beautiful in sapphire blue. Even Audrey Hepburn couldn't have worn the dress as elegantly as Granny did now, lying pillowed in organdy and flowers. I was glad I'd found a netted blue hat to match—pure forties, Granny would've loved it—and white gloves with pearl buttons.

Organ music swelled, rising into the rafters of Trinity Baptist Church. It was the first time I'd been inside. In fact, I hadn't been inside a church in years. The wooden pew was hard, the hymnals dog-eared and worn.

Caprice's cousin Jimmy had come into the store the day after our midnight visit to the graveyard and told me that Granny Julep had "passed." I'd been more struck by his choice of words than by the news itself. It didn't surprise me that Granny left the night Caprice was put to rest. She had fought to the bitter end for Caprice's soul; maybe they were together now.

I hoped so.

Jimmy also told me that Felicia had been arrested for Caprice's murder. It made me feel better to know that while Mojo was a low-down dirty dog for cheating on Caprice, he wasn't a murderer—Felicia had confessed that the fatal shove down the stairs was her doing, not his.

I'd asked Jimmy to wait while I carried the Audrey Hepburn mannequin to the back room and stripped her of her finery. I hardly even cried when I layered the dress into a box with some tissue and added the hat and gloves. I was dry-eyed by the time I gave the box to Jimmy and asked him to give it to Albert. And I was still dry-eyed now, as Granny Julep was put to rest.

Albert sat in the front row, narrow shoulders as straight as age allowed. That grizzled head was all too familiar. I had an unwelcome flash of being in the backseat of the Lincoln, cradling Granny's head in my lap, and then the image of a dour-faced skeleton, grim and silent. I pushed those thoughts away.

"Thou knowest, O Lord, the secrets of our hearts." The elderly black preacher began speaking as soon as the organ music rolled to a stop. He'd already given the eulogy; the service was almost over. "You knew the heart of Julep Joan Johnson. We rest easy in the knowledge that she's home with You now."

I was glad *somebody* was resting easy.

"Julep was a good woman—a loving mother and grandmother, a faithful helpmate to her husband, Albert. We honor her wishes now by gathering to sing some of her favorite hymns, and to rejoice in her everlasting life with Jesus, our Lord and Savior. Please turn to page 319 in your hymnals for 'Nearer My God to Thee.'"

The small church was filled with people, thick with tears and the cloying scent of lilies. The sudden shuffle of hymnals and another swell of organ music was enough to cover me as I slipped from my seat near the back and went outside. I stood in the shade near the parking lot, breathing easier and listening to the hymn while I stared out over the sea of headstones.

I'm not sure what I was waiting for.

For Granny Julep to sit up and say, "*I need your help again, girl?*"

For Caprice to whisper thoughts in my ear?

For Joe's BMW to pull into the parking lot?

I wandered up the hill into the cemetery, letting my feet lead the way. Here was where we'd left the chains and shovels when the cops showed up. Up there was the double headstone. I wound my way toward it, remembering that mad scramble in the darkness.

And there it was, a double stone, shaped like an open book. It was very old. The chiseled inscription was hard to read.

"In memory of Jacob Cross, who departed this world November 18, 1897. In memory of Nancy Cross, who departed this world June 3, 1919." Below that, it said, "Together Forever," and an inscription: THE TRAGEDY OF LIFE IS NOT THAT IT ENDS SO SOON, BUT THAT WE WAIT SO LONG TO BEGIN IT.

Nancy Cross had lived twenty-two years without her husband, yet lay down quietly with him in the end. And someone, probably Nancy, had left a warning about wasted time.

Well, if they'd loved each other and wanted people to enjoy life to the fullest, then maybe they'd forgive us for what we'd done on top of their grave.

"Jacob and Nancy," I said aloud. *Joe and Nicki.* There was that chill down the spine Evan never wanted me to mention. Only no one had walked over my grave; I was the trespasser here.

I turned away and started down the hill just as the double doors of the church opened. Granny's casket appeared, borne on the shoulders of six men. The procession toward the grave site had begun, the mourners following the casket in silence. The afternoon sun was bright, the sky a cloudless blue.

I looked up at the triple crosses on the church steeple and smiled, remembering what she'd called it. "Rest in peace, Granny Julep," I murmured, "here in the shadow of the name of the Lord."

CHAPTER 22

Ivy was wearing Chanel today, a gorgeous hot pink suit with black piping and jet buttons. The vivid color complimented her pale skin tones, bringing out the blue in her eyes and the silver in her hair.

"Aren't you going to ask me how I feel?" I asked her.

I'd just finished telling Ivy about Granny Julep's funeral. After a lot of thought, I'd decided not to tell her about the midnight trip to the graveyard. Not only was digging up a corpse too bizarre to admit to, it was illegal, and I wasn't interested in getting Joe in any trouble.

"I'm sure you'll tell me when you're ready."

Patience must be a virtue they teach in shrink school.

I'd never learned it.

"I feel like I lost a friend." There it was. "She was a cranky old woman with a dark side, scary in a way but sweet in another. I hardly knew her . . . I couldn't trust her. I'm not sure I really even *liked* her. But she's gone and that makes me sad. Kinda. And kinda not." I looked at Ivy. "What I don't understand is why I care."

"You did lose a friend," Ivy said.

"I knew her less than two weeks." I shook my head. "She tricked me, tried to use me . . ." I trailed off, preferring to forget the voodoo drums, the scattered cornmeal. "She was *not* my friend."

"You say the other woman's spirit, the—" Ivy consulted her notes. "—duppy that's been tormenting you, is gone."

"Yes. I think so."

"You feel this happened at the same time your friend Granny Julep passed away, is that right?"

I saw where this was going. "Yes. It's complicated, but Granny and Caprice were linked in a fight to save Caprice's soul." Man, that sounded so lame. Like something I'd read on the back of a video rental. I couldn't even begin to explain Albert's role in all this—in assuming the loa of Baron Samedi, he'd done for Granny the one thing she couldn't.

By worshiping evil, Felicia made herself vulnerable to the consequences of its power; by becoming the Baron, Albert had used that vulnerability against her, letting evil aid him in bringing a murderer to justice.

Ivy rested her elbow on the arm of the couch and regarded me quizzically.

"Do you think Granny's death rid you of the spirit?"

I thought about that. Granny Julep had done her best, but I was the one who'd gotten down and dirty with Caprice, so to speak. Those chains might've been symbolic, but I'd felt the weight of them in my hands and on my heart. Caprice wasn't rising again.

Maybe that had been enough reason to give an old woman her dying wish.

"Has it occurred to you that this woman could've been the source of this all along?"

My mouth dropped open. "Of course not! Granny Julep wasn't like that! She didn't even know me until I went looking for her."

Ivy smiled at me, tipping her head to rest her chin on a finger. "You defend her like she's a friend."

"Oh, all right, dammit." Ivy didn't bat an eye. "She was a friend."

"Here's another theory for you: What if there never was any evil spirit? What if Caprice never really existed? What if it was all a wild suggestion implanted in your brain . . . one that died when the source of the suggestion died?"

One of us was crazy here, and it wasn't me.

"What are you talking about? I tell you everything, and instead of answers, all I get is more questions! Are you saying that you don't believe I've been talking to spirits? You think I made this up?" I felt like sinking into the leather of the chair. I'd thought this was the one place I could be completely honest.

Ivy sat up straight, looking mildly alarmed.

"No, no." She started to say something, then paused. "Let me tell you something about me, Nicki."

I tried to care, but I was ready to walk out. Therapy sessions were bullshit.

"My mother saw spirits sometimes," Ivy said.

Now you're talking.

"Not often. Usually right after someone died— my grandfather, an old woman who went to our church. Mother said she felt they were just saying good-bye." Ivy's face softened. "I've personally never experienced any type of paranormal phenomena, but that hasn't dimmed my fascination with the topic. I assure you I'm being as open-minded as possible here, and so should you. But it's my job to help you think of all the possibilities, including the logical ones."

I was quiet for a time. The trickle of the Zen fountain was starting to get on my nerves, so I watched the second hand on the clock that sat discreetly nearby. The clock was heavy crystal, Waterford maybe, and faced whoever sat in the chair, a tactful reminder that "time's a-wastin'."

"Evan says I'm different."

"Do *you* think you're different?"

I flashed Ivy a look that let her know what I thought of her reversion to technique. She had the grace to smile slightly.

"I guess I'm looking at things a little differently these days," I admitted.

"Since the NDE?" Ivy prompted.

"Since the near death experience, yes." I wasn't comfortable reducing the event to an acronym yet. "I think a lot more about the future, and I worry that I'm wasting the *now*." It was hard to express. "And I wonder about God a lot. I mean, was that who I met when I died? Was it Buddha, or Allah or Krishna?" These were the thoughts that had begun to keep me up at night. "How are we supposed to know which religion to follow? How do we know which one is the right one? How are we supposed to know what to do?"

Ivy looked thoughtful. "Good questions, for which I may have at least one answer."

I'd believe that when I heard it.

"Religion itself is a universal concept. People gravitate toward whatever they feel brings them closer to that concept. But most major religions *do* share a common thread, that of holding ourselves to higher principles in our dealings with our fellow man. Even voodoo."

"Huh?" She'd finally given me an answer, but I'd lost it in the translation.

"Treating others as we would treat ourselves, Nicki," she said gently. "The word 'voodoo' is from the French, *vous*, meaning you, and *deux*, meaning two. 'You, too.' Based on my research, voodoo at its very heart is based on the belief that what you do is what you become."

"As in 'Do unto others as you would have them do unto you,'" I said slowly. "So I'm just back where I started, and I still don't know who or what's behind the Light."

Ivy gave me an elegant shrug, not even trying to argue the point.

"Do we have to know? Are we meant to know?" she asked.

What a rip. My only answer hadn't been an answer after all.

Now all I had were more questions.

* * *

"Hey, babe." I had to smile when I heard Joe's voice on the other end of my cell phone. He'd never called me "babe" before, and I liked it. "I have to be at work by midnight, but I was hoping to see you. How about I come over and grill us some steaks around seven? You can invite Evan if you want . . . tell him to bring his friend Butch." Joe's voice lowered, turning playful. "Unless you want me all to yourself, in which case I've been a *very* bad boy."

As tempting as that thought was, I got a clear mental picture of the four of us out on my back deck, a family, drinking wine and having dinner.

"Sounds great. I'll give Evan a call, and spank you later."

"Promises, promises," Joe teased. "Steaks for four, then. I'll bring the wine."

"No need . . . I'm sure I have some."

"I'll bring more." The way Joe said it raised my radar. "Listen, did you ever get a chance to look at those pictures I left you? The pictures of Kelly?"

"Sure did," I said, waiting for the other shoe to drop. "Do you want them back?"

"No. I got a phone call a few minutes ago from the private investigator I hired to find her. Looks like her Peace Corps records have been updated—she's in Santo Domingo."

"Santa Domingo?" I had no idea where that was.

"Maybe Evan and Butch will have some advice on what to do next, *hm*?"

"Do next?" I didn't seem to be able to put more than two words together.

"I'm assuming that once all the divorce stuff is out of the way, you want me to tell Kelly you two might be sisters, right?"

There was a pause.

"Yeah. Of course I want you to tell her."

Joe waited for a couple of heartbeats. "You wanna talk about it?"

"Not right now. I just came from Ivy's and I'm all talked out."

"I'll see you at seven, then." Another hesitation. "I miss you." Then he hung up.

I thought again of the four of us on my back deck, drinking wine and having dinner—one big, happy family. The gay couple, the straight guy, and the girl who saw dead people.

Kelly's wholesome image intruded, and I sighed. What if she still loved him? What if she wanted him back?

I could only hope Joe would prefer leather and lace to denim and plaid.

Oh well. Who said life had to be easy?